More

By Tempie W. Wade

More
By Tempie W. Wade

Printed in the United States of America.

First Edition Print - ISBN: 978-0-9600257-2-5

Digital Edition - ISBN: 978-0-9600257-3-2

For more information, please visit
www.TempieWade.com

More

By Tempie W. Wade

Book Two

The Timely Revolution Book Series

ACKNOWLEDGMENTS

To Jen…
Thank you for being my partner-in-crime. Your
enthusiasm, encouragement, and support are what keep
me moving forward on the days I need it the most.

To All the Readers...
Thank you for being a part of this journey!

1 CHAPTER ONE

July 5, 1778

As soon as Gabe had read the letter from his brother, informing him of his mother's illness, they had finished their hasty goodbyes in Philadelphia and sailed to Virginia for supplies. Maggie had relayed her instructions to everyone at the estate for an extended, indefinite amount of time, while Captain Russell made his own personal arrangements and stocked the ship. The trip had taken several weeks but went smoothly for the most part. Maggie knew the real meaning of the term 'cabin fever' after the lengthy voyage, her longest ever, just water and horizon for days upon days.

Over the years, the ship had morphed from a cargo vessel, once used to smuggle humans and other illegal goods, into more of a passenger ship. Maggie had the inside completely rebuilt, with plenty of room for Onyx to spread out, knowing full well that, had he wanted, he could have busted a hole clean through the ship's hull. There were still hidden compartments available for valuables and necessities, but the ship and its crew were almost exclusively now for Maggie's personal travel.

Maggie had spent most of the trip trying to keep Gabe's spirits up. He was terribly worried about his mother, who was 73 now. Gabe's father, a very prominent attorney, had passed 19 years earlier, leaving behind his wife and four sons, all whom were still in London, except Gabe, who had joined the military after the death of his wife and child. He had not been back to visit for a very long time, mainly out of concern that his true nature might somehow be revealed, bringing shame and trouble upon his family.

Maggie hated seeing him so distraught, so she had done her best to keep his mind busy, mostly by lying in bed next to him at night, telling him stories about the future.

"Tell me again how long this trip would take in your time."

Maggie was laying with her head at the foot of the bed, legs stretched out, arms folded behind her head on a pillow, with Gabe laying the opposite direction, but the same, so they could see each other's faces. "Hours.... we would have been there in a matter of hours."

Gabe was fascinated, "So, these airplanes, how do they fly through the air? How do they stay up there?"

Maggie tried to figure out how best to explain, "They have a body, kind of like the belly of this ship, and wings, like birds, off to the sides, and the wings have things called fans that turn really fast, keeping it in the air."

"How high do they go?"

"Above the clouds in the sky."

Gabe sat up. "THAT far up? Can you see Heaven from there?"

Maggie laughed. "Not exactly."

That led to the next discussion about sending men to the moon.

Gabe soaked it all in, like a kid sitting cross-legged on the floor at story time, too absorbed in the details to move, for fear of missing any miniscule detail. "Maggie?"

"Yes, Gabe?" He rolled to his side toward her, "I really wish we had an airplane right now."

Maggie crawled up next to him to lay by his side, propped up on her elbow. "You and me both. I had no idea our quick trip to Philadelphia would end up with us on our way to 'merry old London'."

Gabe rubbed her shoulder. "Thank you for coming with me—and handling all the arrangements."

"You don't have to thank me, Gabe; what else would I do?" She rolled out of bed to pour them some drinks. Coming back, she sat next to him, handing him a glass. "I am just very glad that you got the letter before we left. It's no telling how long it would have taken to get to you otherwise."

Gabe smacked his head. "Damn it! In all the confusion, I never told John a proper goodbye."

Maggie gave him a sympathetic look. "Gabe, I'm sure that John understood. You were very upset, and besides, John is an extremely understanding man."

Something about the tone of her voice, and the look in her eye, made a sudden realization fill Gabe's brain and he sat straight up. "Maggie! You didn't!"

Still lost in her own thoughts of John, Maggie did not immediately take his meaning. "I didn't what?"

Gabe shook his head in disbelief. "You bedded him! You slept with John!"

Maggie buried her face in her glass, looked to the side, and mumbled, "I wouldn't exactly call it 'sleeping'."

Staring at her, his mouth completely open, having no ability to form words, Gabe turned his head to the side and finally muttered, "When...why...how?"

Maggie shrugged. "The last three nights we were there... because, we wanted to... and... I can explain how if you really want me to, but I think you still remember how those things work after all this time...or...I mean... I could draw you a picture on some paper if you need a refresher course...."

Gabe held his hand up. "I know HOW! I haven't been alone THAT long, I mean HOW did this all come about?"

Maggie lowered her drink into her lap, looking down. "I don't know Gabe, we were having drinks and talking. He said how sorry he was about the baby, the way things turned out, and he asked me if he could... comfort me."

"Comfort you? Yes, well, John is well-known for his 'comforting' abilities among the ladies."

Maggie shot him a look, "I am well aware of John's...reputation. But, when we...when he... well, let me just say that he took care of me. He made me feel better."

Gabe raised one eyebrow. "I'm sure he made himself feel better as well."

Maggie swatted at him. "I am being serious here. I needed that time with John, and he knew that I needed it.

I care for John a great deal, and it was nice to be with someone, physically, that I care about, without having to deal with the 'inconvenience' of being in love. It was...therapeutic, to say the least."

Gabe looked down at his glass. "Sounds a little like you have given up on love."

Maggie lifted her chin. "I'm just not sure it's worth all the trouble."

Her response greatly concerned Gabe.

2 CHAPTER TWO

It was early evening, just about to get dark, when they arrived in London.

Maggie wasn't able to get a very good look at the city, but what she did see was very busy, crowded, loud, and filthy. London was unlike any of the sleepy little towns in the colonies.

Gabe managed to secure a carriage for hire. He didn't want to waste another moment getting to his mother's home, fearing he may already be too late. It had been pointless to send word they were coming; the message wouldn't have reached the house before them.

Captain Russell agreed to stay with the ship for the night and to bring Onyx over in the morning.

The carriage rolled through the streets of London. Maggie lifted the curtain to look out. The streets were full of people; beggars, drunks, and ladies of the night, spilling out of seedy establishments before gathering on the corners. Maggie actually saw a man 'receiving his goods' from one of the prostitutes as they passed by.

"Classy little town you have here." Maggie proclaimed, sarcastically, leaning back in.

Gabe frowned. "It has become worse since I last visited. This was never the best part of town, but it seems to have gone downhill tremendously in the past few years. The neighborhoods will get better in a bit. My mother's home is in a very affluent part of town."

They moved along, and it did indeed get better, the carriage moving into a middle-class area with lots of shops and nicely maintained homes, and then into a beautiful area with very high-end businesses, expensive mansions, and a wonderful park area.

The carriage stopped in front of a very fine-looking, expensive home. At their sharp knock, a young servant girl opened the front door and identified herself as Lucy, after Gabe informed her who he was.

Gabe was anxious, holding his breath, as he escorted Maggie inside and inquired as to where his mother was.

"She's upstairs, sir."

Gabe let out the breath he had been holding, relieved they had made it in time. He dashed up the stairs.

Lucy called out, "But, she does not want to be disturbed, sir." Seeing that Gabe had ignored her warning, she turned and looked at Maggie with trepidation and fear in her eyes, just before trotting away.

That was strange.

Gabe's very loud exclamation of "Mother!" sent Maggie racing up the stairs to the doorway where he stood, fearing the worst had come to pass.

Gabe stood motionless, pale; he had turned away from the room, one hand covering his eyes, one hand on the wall, in a tremendous amount of distress, the scene before him obviously being very traumatic.

Maggie put her hands on his back and slipped around him to see what kind of horrifying condition he had found his mother in. The situation was one that no child should ever have to endure seeing of their parent.

Gabe had found his mother, completely naked, in the throes of passion, straddled atop a much younger man.

Standing there for a few seconds, Maggie wasn't sure how to react. She finally came to her senses enough to pull the door closed, trying to figure out how to process the scene. She looked over at Gabe, who had not moved, a petrified look on his face, obviously in shock from an image that would never leave his mind.

They both turned as the bedroom door flew open.

Gabe's mother came out tying a robe, exclaiming, "Gabe, darling, what on Earth are you doing here?"

He managed to utter, "I thought I was coming to see my dying mother, but you seem to have made a miraculous recovery." Gabe pointed to her room and demanded, "Mother, WHO IS THAT MAN?"

Gabe's mother sighed. "THAT MAN happens to be my physician."

Maggie pursed her lips and mumbled, "He must be one hell of a doctor, for his house call services alone."

Gabe slowly turned his head towards Maggie to glare at her in disgust.

Downstairs, a few minutes later, Maggie went to pour Gabe, who had collapsed on the couch, a glass of whisky, but after comparing the glass and the decanter, she just handed him the whole container.

He nodded and drank half of it down in one gulp.

Maggie sipped on the glass she kept for herself while Gabe's mother and the 'physician' remained upstairs, getting dressed.

"Are you going to be okay, Gabe?" Maggie asked gingerly, rubbing his tense neck, standing behind him.

"My dear Maggie, I will never be okay again." He took another swig.

Once the unusual couple had made their way downstairs, Gabe's mother spoke, "I suppose introductions are in order. This is my physician, Dr. Martin Barnes. Martin, this is my son, Gabe."

Gabe rolled his eyes up in acknowledgment, lifting the decanter up in a toast.

"…and his friend…I'm sorry, Dear, what's your name?"

Gabe answered. "Maggie Bishop. Maggie, meet my 'on the verge of death' mother, Georgianna Asheton."

Maggie nodded. "I am pleased to meet you and very happy that you are still among the living."

Georgianna smiled, took a seat, then turned to face Gabe. "What made you think I was dying?"

Gabe straightened up. "I don't know. Maybe the frantically worded letter I received from Robert saying that if I wanted to say goodbye that I should get here as soon as possible?"

Georgianna shook her head. "I *was* very ill, but thanks to Martin, I made a full recovery."

"Obviously!" Gabe snarked.

She ignored him, and smiled at the young doctor, who finally spoke, "She had a very high fever from an infection. It was touch and go for a while, but my lovely patient was, thankfully, too stubborn to let her illness win out."

Maggie took a good look at the people in the room.

Georgianna Asheton was still a strikingly beautiful woman for her age: tall, very slim, with snow-white hair down to her waist. She and Gabe shared many of the same facial features. There was no doubt that Gabe got his good looks from her.

Dr. Barnes could not be more than 35, very young, boyishly handsome, with dark brown hair and green eyes that stared adoringly at Gabe's mother.

Georgianna reached over and placed her hand on Gabe's knee, patting it with a gentle touch. "I am sorry, Gabe, that Robert's overreaction caused you such distress. I am, however, very happy that you are here. You have been gone far too long and I have missed you very much."

Gabe reached over and laid his hand over on hers, indicating he was happy to see her as well.

Dr. Barnes cleared his throat. "Perhaps it's best if I leave for the evening."

Gabe looked at him, a sneer on his face.

Georgianna stood up. "I will see you out, Martin."

He nodded. "It was very nice meeting both of you, good evening."

Maggie bid him goodnight, as Gabe just shooed him away with the wave of a hand.

After a few minutes, Georgianna returned to the room. "When did you arrive?"

Maggie answered since Gabe still looked a little shell-shocked. "We just docked about an hour ago. We came straight here, because, well, we wanted to be here in time."

Georgianna nodded an acknowledgment. "The two of you must be starving. Let me get Lucy to get something together for you. I am a little hungry myself. Pardon me for a moment."

Gabe took another long drink. "She must have worked up quite an appetite with the good doctor."

Maggie took a seat next to him, taking his hand, squeezing. "Gabe, I know tonight has been...disturbing, to say the least, but your mother is not sick. She is very much alive and well. You should consider yourself very fortunate. Not everyone is lucky enough to have their mom around. Personally, I would give anything..." Maggie trailed off, a tinge of sadness in her voice.

Gabe returned the squeeze. He knew how much Maggie missed her parents, and he also knew that she was right.

Lucy brought out a tray of food.

Maggie and Georgianna snacked, while Gabe mostly drank.

"Maggie, I am so pleased to finally meet you. Gabe has written me about you so much, that I feel as if I already know you."

Maggie smiled. "Yes, I suppose Gabe and I have been friends for a very long time now."

Georgianna sipped her drink, as she looked at Gabe. "I am rather surprised that the army let you have leave to come home for a visit."

Gabe answered matter-of-factly. "They have no say any longer. I resigned my commission."

"You did what? Gabe, you love the army... why would you leave?"

He shrugged. "Maggie needed me."

Georgianna looked to Maggie for clarification.

"I was injured in Philadelphia. Gabe resigned to care for me and to see me safely home to Virginia. I would not have gotten through without him."

"I see. The two of you are very close, aren't you?"

"But not nearly as close as you and the doctor." Gabe cut in, the alcohol starting to really kick in.

Maggie could sense what was coming next, as he tried to stand but fell back. She stood up. "It's getting late. Perhaps I should help you to bed, Gabe."

He shook his head. "I am perfectly fine," he replied, slurring his words.

"I am certain you are, but I am just going to make sure. Mrs. Asheton, can you point me in the right direction?"

"Of course; his room is the second room on the left, and you may have the next one down."

"Thank you." Maggie helped Gabe up the stairs and down the hall.

He was far more drunk than she'd thought, more than she had ever seen. He drank, but never to excess, always staying in complete control.

She reached the door, pushed it open, and guided him inside. He fell back on the bed, and while Maggie was attempting to remove one of his boots, he broke into a bout of laughter.

Maggie managed to eventually get his legs up, and the rest of him righted on the center of the bed. It was the best she could do for the night. She located a blanket, spread it across him, tucking him in, and as she did, he placed his hand on her back, and whispered, "Maggie, I should have never come back to London."

She looked at him compassionately, pushing his loose hair back from his forehead, then kissed his head. "Go to sleep, Gabe."

Maggie went back downstairs; she needed a drink herself.

Gabe's mother was still there, her legs tucked beneath her in a chair, nursing a glass of port. She looked up as Maggie came in.

"I'm sorry Mrs. Asheton, I didn't mean to disturb you."

"Nonsense, please join me and please, call me Georgie, all of my friends do."

Maggie motioned towards the port bottle, "May I?"

"Help yourself."

Maggie poured a glass, took a long sip, and sat in the chair opposite Georgie.

"Did you manage to get Gabe settled?"

She nodded. "I did. I have to say, I have never seen him this drunk before. He is usually always so in control of himself."

Georgie lowered her gaze. "The army did that to him...hardened him. Gabe was a happy, carefree child that was always into some sort of mischief or another. I never knew what to expect from him, but he was always the sweetest, kindest child you would ever want to meet. He has a heart of gold. He joined the army after...."

"...Penny and the baby," Maggie finished. "He told me about them."

Georgie tilted her head. "I'm surprised. He never talked about them after it happened, but I think when they died, something in him...broke. I had hoped he would marry again and try to move on, but he never did."

"Gabe and I tell each other everything. I think he felt responsible for their deaths."

His mother looked stunned. "Their deaths were not his fault. There was nothing that could have been done. It was just an unfortunate circumstance."

Looking down, Maggie swirled the port in her glass. "He knows that now, but sometimes, it is very hard to see the truth of things in the moment."

Georgie looked at Maggie a slow minute. "The two of you have a very special relationship, don't you?"

Maggie smiled. "He is my best friend in this world. I would do anything for him, and he for me."

"Then why haven't the two of you married?"

Maggie almost choked on her port. "Our relationship is not like that. Gabe and I are more like brother and sister than...that."

Georgie lifted her chin. "I see, and he is not interested in any particular woman?"

Maggie shook her head, "No. He hasn't been seeing anyone, much to the disappointment of the ladies of the colonies."

Georgie lowered her voice, something else on her mind. "I know Gabe is upset, but I hope you will not think badly of me for what happened tonight, Maggie. Martin has been…. a great comfort to me since he came into my life. Gabe's father has been gone for 19 years, and I found myself very lonely when we met."

In complete understanding, Maggie nodded. "You will hear no judgment from me. I have no stones to throw because I know that feeling all too well."

Georgie snapped her fingers. "That's right! Gabe wrote me that you were a widow."

Something like that.

Maggie shrugged. "Women have physical needs just like men do. Women just tend to be more... discreet about them."

Georgie nodded in agreement, as Maggie continued, "I think the most shocking part for Gabe, other than, of course, finding his own mother...in the act... was the age difference."

"Believe me, I never had any intentions of getting involved with a man that young, or any man for that matter, it just... happened, and we have done our best to keep things private. No one was more surprised than I by Martin's interest in me, and mine in him. Although, being with a younger man does have its advantages." Georgie refilled their glasses, a soft, secret smile tracing over her lips.

They both giggled like school girls; they were starting to feel the effects of the port.

"I am amazed that you have not remarried, Maggie. You are still young, beautiful, and wealthy. Surely, you have had plenty of proposals."

Maggie took a sip. "Oh, I get them daily. The proposers leave a great deal to be desired. All they see is the land and money that I have. Love would be the only reason I would ever have to marry...and love, well it is...too complicated for me."

They spent the next couple of hours sharing girl talk and finishing off the bottle of port, before deciding to turn in for the night.

Later on, Maggie lay in bed thinking about the past few hours. She loved Gabe's mom. She was just like him, easy to talk to and very understanding.

3 CHAPTER THREE

The following morning, Maggie came down and had a lovely breakfast with Georgie. Gabe still had not come down, so when they were done, Georgie looked towards the upstairs.

"I should go check on Gabe."

Maggie shook her head with a devilish grin on her face. "Oh no, please, allow me." She scooped as much food on a plate, as high as she could, and the greasier it smelled, the better.

"Oh, you are so bad," laughed Georgie.

Shrugging, Maggie made her way to the door. "Serves him right. Believe me, he would not think twice about doing it to me." She also poured him a cup of tea, as Georgie gave her a questioning look.

"Well, I'm not totally heartless. He is my best friend, after all."

Georgie smiled as she watched her leave the room.

Maggie knocked on Gabe's door. "Gabe, It's Maggie... I'm coming in."

Gabe was still exactly on the bed the way she left him the night before, only now he was slightly groaning. "You didn't come down for breakfast, so I brought some food up for you."

She set the plate next to his bed.

Gabe cracked one eye open as he caught a whiff of the food. "Oh...God...you are a horrible woman!"

Maggie pretended her feelings were hurt. "I just wanted to bring you breakfast in bed, and this is the thanks that I get?"

Groaning, Gabe turned away from the plate, covering his face with his arm.

Maggie picked it up and set it on the floor, before she grabbed the teacup and offered it to him. "Here, sit up and drink this."

"What is it?" He looked at it suspiciously.

"It's tea. It will help settle your stomach."

He pushed himself up against the back of the bed before forcing himself to take a sip. "Thanks, Mags." He leaned his head back. "Please tell me last night was a horrible nightmare, and that I did not see my mother, in bed, doing... those things."

Maggie looked at the ceiling. "I wish I could."

Gabe groaned again.

"Gabe, we need to talk."

He reluctantly straightened up. "So, talk...about anything, except my mother and her lover."

She gave him a stern look. "That's exactly what we need to talk about. Gabe, I spent the better part of the night speaking with her."

Gabe cut her a look. "God help me if you tell me that he is about to become my new stepfather. I have bunions on my feet older than that boy."

Maggie frowned. "At 35, he is hardly a 'boy', especially after last night..."

Gabe scowled.

"...and, I don't think you have to worry about that. Gabe, I hate to break this to you, but your mother is a woman, and women have needs."

He held his hand up. "We are NOT having this conversation."

Maggie sighed. "Gabe, just listen and hear me out. Your father has been gone for 19 years. That's a long time to be alone, especially when you have had someone by your side, and in your bed, every day, for 35 years every day before that." Maggie looked down. "Your mom was lonely. You and I both know how that feels, and how, sometimes, you will do anything just to fill that emptiness, even if it is for just a little while."

Gabe knew she was right on some level.

"But, Mags, this man, he is half her age. She has children older than him."

"I know, Gabe, but they are both consenting adults. It's not like this will lead to anything serious like marriage. They have been very discreet. What harm is there in letting it play out? Your mother seems very happy, and you, yourself, have said that we have to take those good moments when we can."

He lowered his gaze, processing what she had said. "I suppose you are right, to a certain extent. I am just having a very hard time accepting the fact that my mother, has ... those kinds of needs, and that she is meeting those needs with someone that young. I know that I, personally, have no room to judge anyone for who they take to bed, but you have to admit, this is a bit much to swallow."

Maggie took his hand. "Gabe, you are home with your mother, whom you thought was on the verge of death. She is here, healthy and happy. You have been given a special gift, so spend some time with her, get to know her again. We can stay as long as you want." She grinned. "Besides, it's not like you have to worry about him getting her pregnant... he is a doctor, after all. He's probably got that whole rhythm method of birth control down perfectly." Gabe slowly turned his head toward her, a disgusted look on his face. "I hate you so much right now."

Leaning in, Maggie kissed him on the cheek, and whispered, "I know."

Captain Russell and the crew brought over the rest of their things and Onyx later that afternoon. Onyx seemed very intrigued by his new surroundings, and he had apparently taken London by storm. Captain Russell said that on the way over, people stopped to look, admire him, and one man even offered to buy him on the spot. Strangely enough, he was being on his best behavior.

Maggie eyed Onyx curiously, wondering just what he was up to.

Captain Russell left the address of where he would be staying when they were ready for the ship. It turned out that he had a brother, along with several nieces and nephews that lived close by, and he was looking forward to catching up with them.

By the time Maggie came back inside from getting Onyx settled in the stable, Gabe had made his way downstairs and was in the parlor catching up with his mother. She tried to slip by unnoticed, wanting to give them some privacy, but Gabe saw her and called her in.

"I'm sorry, I don't want to interrupt the two of you. I should go unpack." Maggie stayed at the door.

Gabe looked up. "Have our things arrived?"

"Yes," Maggie answered, "and Onyx is all settled in the stable."

"I'll warn the staff," said Gabe dryly.

She could tell he was still not feeling well from the night before.

Georgie turned to Maggie. "I was just about to tell Gabe that I wanted to plan a little get together for family and a few friends to celebrate his return home."

Maggie looked at Gabe, who was looking less than thrilled. "I think that is a wonderful idea."

Gabe cocked an eye up at her. "You hate parties."

Maggie patted him on the shoulder. "I will make an exception for this one."

Georgie clapped her hands together. "Wonderful! I will start making all the arrangements for, let's say, in three days. I need to get busy. Can the two of you entertain yourselves for the afternoon?"

"Yes Mother, we will be fine. I know how you love organizing these things, so go, enjoy yourself."

She started out of the room but stopped to turn back to say to her son, "Gabe, I really am very happy that you are home."

Maggie sat down next to Gabe. "Well, things seem to be going well."

Gabe rested his head back, placing his hand on Maggie's knee. "My mother is in her element. Nothing like a party to draw attention away from any issues that may be going on in the family."

She took his hand. "Regardless, I am proud of you for retaining your composure after everything that has happened."

He squeezed her hand. "You were right, Maggie. She is alive, and I am grateful for the time that I am getting to spend with her. But, for the moment, I think some fresh air might help the enormous headache that I seem to have developed. Are you up for a stroll?"

Gabe escorted Maggie up the street, showing her the area, telling her stories from his childhood about each place as they passed. He turned to escort her into a little garden area, very nicely landscaped with English boxwoods and flowering plants.

Maggie was pleasantly surprised to find that it was an outdoor tea room.

They found a little table in a shady spot to enjoy the beautiful weather.

"Gabe, this is so nice. I had no idea tea rooms were like this." Maggie took a sip of the tea, then scrunched up her face as she looked down at the cup. "That's a little different."

"Here, let me help." Gabe slipped out his flask, adding the brown liquor to both their cups, before she tasted it again.

"Oh, that's much better," she said, cradling the cup.

Gabe smiled, his hangover waning.

"So, tell me again about your brothers."

"I have a better idea. How about we finish our tea and I will introduce you?"

Maggie looked at him quizzically.

Gabe tilted his head, toward the law office across the street.

She could see a little of it from where they sat. "You mean, they all work together in the same building?"

Gabe nodded. "Robert, Edward, and I all worked there with my father before he passed. Alex was only 16 when it happened, so he came into the firm later."

Maggie shook her head. "I can't believe all of your brothers are attorneys, and that you were one as well."

Gabe shrugged. "Our father made a very good living at it, so it only made sense to follow in his footsteps."

"I am sure he was very proud of all of you."

Gabe had a faraway look. "I hope that he was."

Maggie downed her tea. "Well, come on. I can't wait to meet your brothers."

After settling the check, they made their way across the street and into the law office. A young man greeted them from his small desk. "May I help you?"

Gabe stepped forward. "Yes, we are here to see Mr. Asheton."

"Which one, sir?"

Gabe grinned. "All of them."

Just then, a head popped out of the office. "Allen, I need that file…" The man stopped speaking when he saw Gabe, as a wide smile spread across his face. "Gabe? Gabe!" He rushed to him, slinging his arms around him.

Gabe patted him on the back. "Hello, Robert!"

Robert was the oldest brother. He looked a great deal like Gabe, only shorter, with darker blond hair. He had a little weight around his midsection from spending too much time behind the desk.

"Gabe, what are you doing here?"

Gabe looked at him strangely. "What do you mean? I came because of your letter."

Robert cocked his head. "What letter?"

Gabe's eyes narrowed. "The one about Mother's illness."

Robert shook his head. "I never sent any letter."

They exchanged puzzled looks.

Maggie cleared her throat, and Gabe remembered her.

"Maggie, I'm sorry. Maggie, meet my oldest brother Robert. Robert, meet Maggie Bishop."

"A pleasure," he said, bowing slightly. He escorted them into a cozy little law library with several armchairs and a large round table. He poured three glasses, as Gabe pulled the letter out of his coat pocket and handed it to Robert. Robert read it and handed it back.

"Gabe, I did not send that. Mother was ill, and I was about to write to you, but she made a full recovery. I thought it best not to worry you. I have no idea who sent this."

Gabe pulled up a chair. "That's very strange. It arrived in Philadelphia moments before we were to depart."

Robert sat down. "You are not in Philadelphia anymore?"

"Not in the military anymore. I resigned."

Robert was astonished. "I never thought I would see the day. Why did you leave?"

Maggie waved her hand. "He did it to take care of me."

Robert smiled. "I see. Is there another engagement announcement that needs to be made?"

Maggie and Gabe both answered an emphatic, "NO!" at the same time.

Gabe looked up and asked, "Another engagement? Who else is engaged?"

Another Asheton man appeared at the doorway. "That would be me."

Gabe stood to embrace and introduce his baby brother, Alexander—Alex for short. He looked exactly like Gabe, just several years younger.

"Congratulations! Who is the lucky lady?"

Alex poured himself a drink. "Miss Josephine Williams. We are to be married in three weeks. I sent a letter, but you must have missed it in passing. I am happy to have you here for the wedding."

As toasts were being made, the final brother appeared at the door. "What? A family reunion without me?"

Gabe introduced his brother, Edward. He was a tad shorter than Gabe, with the same facial features and light brown hair, a note of sleeplessness in his eyes.

"Edward, how is Annabelle?"

He sat down. "Tired. The new baby is keeping us both up."

"The baby's here?"

Edward nodded. "A bouncing baby boy. Charles, Charlie for short. And his two sisters are making all over him." Edward turned to Maggie, "We already have two girls, Olivia is 5 and Izzy is 2."

Maggie laughed. "That is quite a full house."

Edward laughed back. "Yes, it is. Especially for a man my age. I am getting too old to chase little ones."

They all happily chatted, and the conversation came back around to the letter. None of the brothers had sent it, which made the whole situation even more odd.

The afternoon passed by, and all the brothers had work to do, as much as they hated to break up the celebration. They promised to be at their mother's party with the rest of the family members.

Gabe had a great smile on his face as they left, delighting Maggie. He had been so troubled and gloomy on the ship ride over, that he had just not been himself.

"It's good to see a smile on your face again."

He looked over at her. "I didn't realize how much I had missed my family. It's wonderful to see them all." He grabbed her hand. "Come on, we have one more stop to make."

They walked until they came upon a store with a shingle reading, 'The Tree of Knowledge.' Gabe helped her inside, Maggie giving him a curious look.

A voice from the back sounded, "Good afternoon. Welcome to The Tree of Knowledge. How may I help you?"

Gabe answered for them. "Well, you can come out here and show your Uncle Gabe how big you have gotten."

The young man appeared from the back. "Uncle Gabe? Is that really you?"

A handsome slim fellow of medium height with dark hair came over to greet him.

Gabe hugged him, then stepped back to get a better luck. "My goodness, Henry, you have really grown into a fine young man. Your father wrote me that you had opened this shop, and it looks like you are doing very well. Henry, meet my dear friend, Maggie Bishop. Maggie, this is my nephew, Robert's son and bookshop owner, Henry."

Henry had the warmest feeling about his person.

"It's nice to meet you, Henry. I love your shop."

Henry blushed. "Thank you, ma'am. I am very proud of it."

Gabe turned back to him. "Where is your brother?"

"Scotland. I sent him up for a load of books. I handle the day to day here, and he travels to pick up new stock."

Gabe explained to Maggie, "Wyatt is his brother, who is 18 now. They opened this up together last year and now they are shipping all over, even to other countries."

Maggie looked around. "This is very impressive. I am a book lover myself, Henry. I could get lost in here for days."

And she could; there were thousands of books, from floor to ceiling, stacked in every nook and cranny, with the building being two story. Hooked ladders that slid, hung from the ceiling, and moved from one side to the other for access to the top shelves. Maggie looked through a line of book titles as she called out, "Henry, I have several books that I am always on the lookout for. May I put together a list for you to keep an eye out?"

Henry readily answered, "Oh yes, I would be pleased to help you."

They made it back to the house shortly before suppertime.

During the meal, Georgie chatted away about her plans for the party, while she and Gabe caught up on the latest in town.

After supper, Maggie remembered that she had yet to unpack, so she excused herself to give them even more time to catch up. After she put everything away and changed for the night, she lay in bed with the book John had given her. He had marked the page with a note that read, 'Until we meet again.' She looked down at the bracelet he had given her, sorrowful in the knowledge of his fate yet to come, wondering why she had been the one who had been cursed to know the future of the people she cared for. The old saying 'everything happens for a reason,' echoed in her head.

Sometimes the reason is that you are in the wrong place at the wrong time and you have shitty luck.

Maggie opened it to the page. The crest belonged to a family by the name of 'GREGOR.' The crest did indeed have a lion head with a crown upon it, just like on her sword and just like in the Faerie Tale book. The clan motto translated as 'Royal is my Race,' for a clan that was based in the Highlands. There was also a vague reference to the clan being descended from the ancient Celts, calling them 'children of the mist'. That was the extent of it. Not much information, but there was a name.

That was something, and it was just another small piece to the puzzle that may mean nothing or may mean everything. *Who knew?*

Maggie put that book to the side and picked up the Faerie Tale book. She flipped back through the stories, nothing standing out. It was just a collection of old Celtic lore. She set that one aside on the bed, as well.

It was one of those nights when she was restless, and her mind had more questions than answers. She had those nights occasionally, and they usually lasted until she gave up from sheer exhaustion as the sun rose. Her mind was in overdrive and sometimes the only thing she could do was dull it. She had packed a few bottles of rum in her trunk. Hopping off the bed, she rambled through her trunk until she found them. She pulled one out, popped the cork, and drank straight from the bottle.

Maggie heard Gabe say, "Good night, Mother. Sleep well."

She rushed over and cracked the door.

He was already standing in front of it, arms folded, waiting.

Pulling him inside, she closed the door and handed him the bottle, which he immediately took a large swig from. They crawled on the bed, lying propped up side by side, feet crossed, looking up at the ceiling.

That was the great thing about their relationship. They could read each other without saying a word.

Maggie spoke first. "How did it go?"

Gabe handed her the bottle back. "As one would expect. She thinks it is time for me to marry a woman, settle down, and give her lots of grandkids and I think she should stop doing 'things' with her young doctor friend. We agreed to disagree."

Maggie took a drink. "Sounds about right. Relationships with parents can be difficult, to say the least." She handed him back the bottle.

"And what about the relationship with your parents?"

Maggie closed her eyes, suddenly serious and silent.

Gabe turned on his side towards her. "Mags, you never speak of them, except to say that you miss them terribly. You have never told me anything about them, not even their names."

She opened her eyes. "I haven't?" Maggie hadn't even realized. She thought about them all the time, but she hadn't told anyone about them, not even Gabe, for fear of revealing too much about who she actually was. She rolled over to face him.

"My mother and father are...will be...were, the best parents ever created. My dad, Steven Bishop, is a professor of history. In my time, he teaches at the College of William and Mary, in Williamsburg."

Gabe looked at her oddly. "You lived in Williamsburg before?"

Maggie nodded. "Yes, for several years. In my time, Colonial Williamsburg is a living history museum. The original buildings were gone, for the most part, but were rebuilt to look much like they are now."

"How incredible it must be to see the old after seeing the new."

"It is something to behold." She continued. "My mother's name is Ana. She was visiting from Scotland when she somehow ended up on the campus of the college my father was giving a lecture at. She slipped into his class, became so fascinated with hearing him speak, that she came back every day for a week before he approached her, knowing she wasn't a student. They both said that they fell instantly in love... and that love never waned, only grew stronger with each passing day. I would slip out of bed sometimes at night, hear music playing softly downstairs, and find them embraced in a slow dance, gazing into each other's eyes like they had just met. Mom stayed home to raise me. She was always in her garden, growing things, talking to her flowers as if they understood every word. Everyone said that her flowers were among the most beautiful they had ever seen. I would even see them from my window at night sometimes, lying in the garden, covered with a blanket, candles romantically lit all around them, just happy to be together. Dad was always leaving single roses around for her to find in the most unusual places, and she was always leaving little love notes in his books and at the office for him to find in the middle of lectures. Their love, it was...is...magical, the kind that only comes around once in a very long while. Those two were the ones that fairy tales were written about, not for, like the rest of us." Maggie smiled. "And I was the wonderful product of their epic love, a fact they constantly reminded me of on a daily basis."

Gabe whispered. "They sound wonderful."

Maggie choked up. "They were the best of the best! And their only daughter, whom they loved more than anything, disappeared without a clue. They have spent all these years not knowing if I were dead or alive. That's what hurts more than anything about me ending up here, is knowing how much agony that I have caused them."

Gabe saw the unmistakable pain in her eyes. The knowledge of the future was a big enough weight to bear alone, but he realized that all this time, the biggest burden on Maggie had been the guilt she felt for leaving her parents without the benefit of a goodbye. No wonder she never spoke of them. She had pushed the pain down so deep, that even mentioning their names would have caused it to furiously erupt, a grief she could not allow herself the luxury of having in her unique and unusual position. Gabe looked deeply into her teary eyes, that, at that instant, looked much like the eyes of a heartbroken, lost and lonely little girl, and his heart ached for her. He pulled her into a tight embrace. "Maggie, what happened was not your fault. There was no way anyone could have possibly foreseen what would happen to you, and you cannot continue to blame yourself for it. If your parents love each other as much as you say, they have had each other to lean on, to take comfort in. They have not had to go through it alone the way you have."

She shook her head. "I haven't been alone; I have had you, Gabe."

After she was all cried out, he sat her up and wiped the tears away from her face. He handed her the bottle of rum. "Drink!"

She took a big swallow and Gabe moved his fingers in a circular movement, motioning for her to continue. He took the bottle back, then finished off the rest. By then, they were both well past the numb point.

Maggie patted Gabe on the face and giggled. "Gabe, if you preferred women, I might just marry you and make your mother a very happy woman."

Gabe snorted back, patting her face in return. "Maggie, if I preferred women, I might just let you."

They both fell back on the bed laughing and ended up falling asleep, with their arms wrapped around each other.

4 CHAPTER FOUR

The next afternoon, Edward brought his
wife, Annabelle, and all their children, over to meet their
Uncle Gabe for the first time. Gabe had been gone from
England so long, he hadn't officially met any of them,
only getting to know them through letters.

Annabelle was a delightful young woman, tiny and
petite, with very high cheekbones accented by big,
beautiful eyes. She was younger than Edward by 15
years. Olivia and Izzy were tiny versions of their mother,
both having adorable brown curly hair and gorgeous
eyes. They were also, very much a handful,
being fuller of energy than their mother and father
combined. No wonder Edward looked tired.

The very precocious Olivia had about a million
questions for her Uncle Gabe, leading him all over the
house, and showing him around, Izzy close on their
heels.

Gabe was very happy to play the doting 'Uncle Gabe',
even sitting down to have 'proper' tea time with the
girls.

Maggie enjoyed seeing this relaxed, carefree side of him. She wasn't the only one who had isolated themselves for too long, but she was thrilled to see Gabe making a change, embracing his family, and his newfound nieces who were rapidly wrapping him around their little fingers.

He collapsed on the couch next to Maggie, the girls having completely worn him out. His mother had been gracious enough to take pity on him to take the children outside for a bit.

"Marching drills have nothing on those two girls," he joked. "No wonder you look so old, Edward."

Edward laughed. "Oh Brother, you have no idea."

Maggie had been chatting with Annabelle, who was holding Charlie. The baby was fast asleep, having gotten used to the constant ruckus around him enough to sleep right through it.

Edward turned to Gabe. "So, now that you have left the military life, are you hanging out your old shingle?"

Gabe shook his head. "No, I don't think I can go back to being an attorney."

Annabelle spoke, "Then, what will you do?"

Before Gabe could answer, Olivia and Izzy flew through the house, covered in mud from head to toe, laughing and tracking up the floors that had just been cleaned.

Annabelle was horrified. "Girls, STOP!"

They didn't.

Standing, Annabelle looked around. "Edward, help me stop them before they dirty the entire house!" She turned to Maggie. "Can you please take Charlie?"

Before Maggie could protest, Annabelle pushed him into her arms, and was off with Edward to locate their girls.

Maggie looked down at the sleeping little blond-haired angel. She settled herself, cradling him carefully in the crook of her left arm, while using her right hand to touch his tiny fingers. She just stared at his precious face, imagining that this is what it would have felt like to hold her own baby in her arms.

Gabe put his arm around the back of the couch, putting his hand on her shoulder, seeming to know exactly what she was thinking.

Maggie whispered. "He's perfect, Gabe."

Gabe squeezed her shoulder. "You will make a great mother, Maggie."

Maggie laughed with a tear in her eye. "I am afraid my chance for motherhood has passed."

He looked at her with a perplexed expression on his face. "Maggie, why would you say something like that?"

She shrugged with a sniffle. "I am not as young as I used to be, and women.... we run out of time long before men do. Besides, it's not like I have a husband, and I haven't seen any sperm banks on any corners here."

Gabe leaned over, whispering, "What's a 'sperm bank'?"

Maggie whispered back, "It's a place where men deposit...their seed...in little jars and they use that to make women pregnant without going through the whole act of sex. You never even have to meet the 'father' or...you know, be with him to get pregnant. It's more of a medical procedure."

Gabe looked flabbergasted. "That happens?"

Maggie nodded, amused by the look on his face.

"That sounds horrendous, and like a terrible way for a child to be brought into existence."

Maggie bobbed her head. "Life in the 21st century."

Gabe couldn't decide what concerned him more, these 'sperm banks', or the fact that Maggie seemed to have given up on being happy and having children of her own.

5 CHAPTER FIVE

The night of the party arrived.

Georgie had planned a formal affair, much more than Gabe was comfortable with. He was expecting just family; however, she had invited over a hundred people.

Maggie didn't mind. It had given her a chance to go shopping and shopping in London was much more fun than it was in Virginia. The London shops contained lots of lacy, beautiful things that you would never have expected in the 18th century.

When Gabe had gone out to take care of some business, Maggie slipped out, coming back with boxes upon boxes of pretty, new items. She was never a frilly girl, but for some reason, she just couldn't help herself.

For the party, she dressed in a green velvet gown with an ivory lace underlay. It was tight around the waist and low cut. Maggie didn't wear any of the underdress devices that most of the ladies wore, thinking they looked ridiculous, so she went with a slim fit that clung to her natural curves. She wore her hair up, a few strands pulled down, and even put on a little face powder just to accent her natural look.

Darn it!

Maggie could hear the party downstairs; she was running a few minutes late. She gave herself one final look in the mirror and went to join the festivities. Hoping to go down the back stairs, just to slip in unseen, Maggie was blocked by supplies for the gathering; she had to use the main stairs.

Reaching the balcony, she peeked over the railing. Gabe was at the bottom, probably waiting for her. She started down as Gabe glanced up.

Before he turned his full attention to watching her descend, a surprised grin split across his face. He wasn't the only one to smile; several people had turned to see who he was staring at.

Reaching the bottom, he took her hands, kissing her cheek. "Maggie, you look absolutely stunning tonight."

She leaned over. "Are you sure it's not too much? I'm not up on the London fashion scene."

He shook his head slowly. "Not at all. You are the most beautiful creature here tonight. I don't think I have ever quite seen you like this."

Maggie blushed. "You look pretty handsome yourself, mister. I am going to have to beat the women off you tonight."

He laughed. "Promise?" She took his offered arm as he escorted her into the party, stopping to introduce her to a few different people.

"Let's go find some drinks, shall we?" he said as he led her outside.

Maggie stopped as they soon as they reached the terrace, taking in the scene before her.

Gabe noticed her wonderment. "My mother knows how to throw a party."

The entire backyard had been turned into a romantic wonderland. Tables filled with food and beautiful rose flower arrangements flanked the sides. Lanterns and candelabras, draped with ivy and other greenery, were lit everywhere. Several loveseats had been brought in, strategically placed in little corners and hideaway places throughout the garden for couples to sneak off to. The garden itself was in full bloom. It reminded Maggie a great deal of her parent's special nights in the backyard.

Georgie, dressed in a stunning crimson gown, saw them and came over. "Maggie, you look lovely tonight."

"Thank you, Georgie, as do you. Red is definitely your color."

Maggie looked around, gesturing with one hand. "You have done an amazing job. This is beyond beautiful. How did you do this in such a short amount of time?"

"It's what I do, Dear."

"And you do it very well."

Georgie looked at Gabe. "I have some people I would like you to meet. I'm sure Maggie can find the refreshment table."

Gabe looked back at his mother, a little irritated. "Mother, I am not leaving Maggie. That would be rude. She doesn't know anyone here."

Maggie was still staring at the garden. "It's fine. I am just going to grab a drink and enjoy the view. I'll be here when you get back."

Gabe turned to Maggie. "Are you sure?"

Maggie nodded. "I am. Go, have some fun; this party is for you. I am sure you have a lot of people that you have not seen in a long time to catch up with."

He sighed and went with his mother, who was smiling like the cat that ate the cream.

Grabbing a glass of punch, Maggie wandered around the garden, still amazed by the beauty of the whole scene. She was lost in identifying flowers when she heard a voice behind her say, "You must be Maggie."

Maggie turned to see a middle-aged woman in a lovely silk pastel gown. "I am."

The lady smiled warmly. "Maggie, I am Edwina Asheton, Robert's wife."

Maggie stepped closer. "Oh yes, it's very nice to meet you. I had the pleasure of meeting Robert the other day, and one of your sons, Henry. Gabe took me to his store. I was very impressed."

Edwina motioned to a seat for them. "Yes, Henry is a wonderful boy. We are very proud of him."

"I haven't met Wyatt yet."

Edwina sipped her drink. "He is in Scotland. He has been spending a lot of time there lately. Between you and me, I think he may have a sweetheart."

Maggie raised her glass. "Well, that will do it."

They both laughed.

"We are very happy to have Gabe back. The family has missed him so much."

Maggie looked towards the house. "It has been good for him to be back. He was very anxious the whole way here, afraid that we would be too late according to the mysterious letter he received, but once we found out his mother was well, he relaxed quite a bit."

"Yes, Robert told me about that. We have questioned the entire family, but no one has claimed to be the one to send it."

"It is very odd."

Edwina smoothed her gown. "At any rate, we are very glad to have him back, and since he has resigned from the army, the timing was perfect. Now, he can take a wife and settle down here with the rest of the family."

Maggie stopped mid-sip. "Excuse me?"

"Well, since the two of you are only friends, naturally he will need a wife. That's the whole point of this party." Edwina smiled.

Maggie narrowed her eyes. "I'm sorry, did I miss something? What do you mean 'the point of this party'?"

Edwina looked confused. "You didn't know? Georgie invited the most eligible ladies in town here to meet him tonight, to help find a suitable match for him."

Maggie took a good look around, and while there were a few men, mostly family, the majority of the people here were women, all dressed to the hilt and staring in Gabe's direction...and the garden had the most romantic setting she had ever seen. How had she not seen this sooner?

"OOHHH! Gabe is not going to be happy about this."

Edwina went pale. "You mean, Gabe does not know?"

Maggie shook her head.

"Well, it looks like Georgie is up to her old tricks again."

"Again?"

Edwina nodded. "Yes, she is always trying to make matches, but never more than when one of her sons needs a wife. Maggie, I am so sorry. I thought you and Gabe knew."

Maggie eyed her warily. "No, and given what happened when we got here, Gabe is going to be furious. I need to warn him."

Maggie went to stand up, when Edwina grabbed her arm. "What happened when you got here?"

Maggie looked down. "It's a long story, but I have a feeling you will find out soon enough and, hopefully, for your sake, not the way we did." She quickly related the scene of their arrival, Edwina's eyes growing larger with each bit of tale.

"Oh."

Nodding her goodbye, Maggie made her way into the house, through the sea of women. Good Lord, how many eligible women were husband-hunting in London? Of course, Gabe's unusually handsome looks didn't help the matter, either.

Gabe stood by the fireplace, playing the perfect gentleman—as he always did, just like the night they first met.

Georgie kept a hard look-out from the other corner of the room.

"Excuse me, ladies, I need to steal Gabe for a moment."

They looked very disappointed.

She tapped his shoulder. "Gabe, I need a word in private."

Georgie headed their way, so Maggie grabbed his arm and pulled him out of sight, whispering in his ear.

The angry, stunned look on Gabe's face spoke volumes as he turned to catch sight of his mother. He stormed towards her, taking her around the waist. "Come with me Mother, we need to talk."

A few moments later, Georgie made her way to the stairs to make an announcement.

Gabe stood a few feet away, his arms folded across his chest, clearly still infuriated.

His mother glanced back before she announced that she wanted to thank everyone for coming, but something had come up and the party was now over. People made their hasty goodbyes, eyes darting from Georgie to Gabe and back again.

Gabe whispered to Robert.

Robert nodded and disappeared.

A half an hour later, Maggie, Gabe, Georgie, and the rest of the family were in the parlor, Maggie in the far corner, sipping on a drink, trying to stay unnoticed.

Alex, who had escorted his fiancé home, came through the door. "What the bloody hell is going on?"

Gabe was sucking down a whisky, pacing the floor, very little of the anger gone. "I will tell you what's going on. Mother, unbeknownst to me, had this little party to invite all the eligible women in London over to find me a wife...a wife that I do not want, nor need."

The rest of the family turned to look at her, Edward speaking first, "Mother, please tell me you didn't."

Georgie raised her chin. "I most certainly did." She turned to Gabe. "You have left the military. Now that you are back in London to stay, there is no reason you shouldn't take a wife and start a family."

Gabe looked at her incredulously. "Mother, what gave you that idea? I am NOT coming back to London. I only came to visit because I thought you were ill. We are returning to Virginia, where I intend to stay, permanently."

It was Georgie's turn to look stunned.

"Why wouldn't you come back here? Your family is here, the law office is here...this is your home."

"Not anymore. It hasn't been for a long time."

Georgie didn't understand. "But, what will you do? How will you live in that God-forsaken land?"

Gabe wiped the perspiration from his forehead with his hand. "I am going in with Maggie on her shipping business."

They all turned to look at Maggie, and she sighed. "Virginia really isn't as bad as you think. I have made a good life for myself—and Gabe will, too. He is having a house built, as we speak, that should be completed by the time we return home."

Georgie turned to plead with Gabe. "But I need you here. I have been in this big old house all alone since your father died, and YOU have not been here at all."

And, THAT is where Georgie made her mistake.

Maggie and Gabe both became painfully aware of what she was doing. She was trying to guilt Gabe into staying, and it just might have worked, if they hadn't walked in on her that first night.

Gabe was so angered by her attempt to manipulate him, he slowly, deliberately spat, "Do NOT try to play upon my sympathy, Mother. We both know you weren't very lonely in your bed the other night when you were straddled atop your lover, Dr. Barnes."

The entire room went dead silent. Maggie winced, looking around at the others.

Georgie stared straight ahead, defiant.

Gabe was breathing hard, still furious over his mother's attempt to play the victim, when everyone in that room knew that Georgie Asheton always played the cards to her own advantage.

Everyone else just looked back and forth between Gabe and Georgie, waiting to see what came next.

Georgie slowly got up, without saying a word, and went straight upstairs to her room, closing the door.

Maggie got up and started pouring glasses of whisky, handing them out.

They all took them gratefully.

Robert was the first to speak, "How did you find out about them?"

"I was in such a rush to get to my dying mother's bedside, that I walked in on them...in the act."

Edwina looked at Maggie. "The doctor that took care of her? But he is so...young."

Alex spoke up, disbelief in his voice, "He and I are the same age."

Edward said what everyone else was thinking. "Dear God, you saw our mother...on top...of Barnes? Why have you not burned your eyes out with a hot poker?"

Gabe turned toward Edward. "Because burning out my eyes would never be enough to erase THAT image."

Maggie covered her mouth to cover the smile from Gabe's remark, stifling a laugh. She caught Gabe's narrowed eye.

The sight of her trying to conceal a laugh, caused him to cover his own eyes and chuckle. "This whole situation is ridiculous."

Robert stood up. "I think it's been a long night and we should all get some sleep."

Edward agreed. "We can talk about this tomorrow, when we all have clearer heads."

They all left for the night, leaving Maggie and Gabe alone on the couch.

Maggie put her hand on Gabe's knee, rubbing it. "I'm sorry Gabe, that all of this happened."

Gabe covered her hand with his. "I can't believe she set up this whole party just to get me married off to force me to stay in London. That's true Georgie Asheton style."

"You mean, this is not unusual for her?"

"Oh no. Mother is one of those women that can stir a pot of shite all day and still come home smelling like a rose. It's a very useful skill."

"Gabe, what are you going to do about your mother? You can't leave things like this. The next letter you get, she may not make that miraculous recovery and you may not get here in time."

"Mags, I have no idea."

The next morning, Maggie came down for breakfast, hoping to get a few minutes alone with Georgie. She wasn't there, and Lucy said she had not seen her all morning.

Maggie went back upstairs and knocked on her door. "Georgie, it's Maggie."

No answer.

She knocked louder.

Still, no answer.

Gabe came out in the hall. "What's going on?"

"Your mother hasn't been down this morning, and she isn't answering her door."

Concerned, Gabe pushed opened her door.

She wasn't there, and her bed had not been slept in. She was gone.

Maggie and Gabe dressed quickly. They were on their way out the front door to go search for her when they were met by Robert and Edwina.

"Gabe, what is happening?"

"Mother is missing."

Robert held up a note. "This was waiting for us this morning.

Gabe opened it and it simply read...

'Be at the house at 9 o'clock in the morning. Mother.'

The rest of the family arrived, as well, having all received the same note. They were all waiting in the parlor when Georgie and Dr. Martin Barnes arrived, hand in hand, Georgie looking very pleased with herself.

Uh oh.

The vein in Gabe's head throbbed, his elbow propped up on his knee, his hand holding his head. They all waited for Georgie to speak.

"Martin and I have an announcement to make. Early this morning, we were married."

Dead silence.

Martin glanced at Georgie, his voice quivering when he spoke, "I know that you are all concerned about your mother's welfare and about our age difference, but I want you to know that I love your mother very much and I will devote my life to making her happy."

Maggie looked closer at Martin Barnes.

He had the look; it was unmistakable. He was totally, head over heels in love with his new wife.

She looked at Georgie, and the older woman had it as well. She was in love with him. There was no denying it, so what was the point of it fighting it?

Maggie was the first to speak, "Allow me to be the first to congratulate you."

Georgie looked at her with a grateful look in her eye, a silent message. "Thank you, Maggie. I knew you would understand."

No one else spoke, so Maggie broke the silence and the tension—again, "Georgie, why don't you and Martin go find something for a toast?" giving Georgie her own silent message, asking for a few minutes of privacy.

Georgie nodded, "That's a wonderful idea." She pulled Martin away.

After they left, Maggie closed the door.

Gabe gave her a disgusted look. "Maggie, how can you wish them well?"

Maggie looked around the room at all of them. "Because, it is what it is. That man is your mother's new husband. Yes, he is half her age and, I know, none of you are happy about this, but it is her life and her decision. And I am not sure if any of you took a good look, but I did, and those two are undeniably in love with each other."

Annabelle spoke up, "But, what will people say?"

Maggie sighed. "Well, that will depend on all of you. If the family makes a big deal about being happy for them, so will everyone else. If this family shuns and shames them, the rest of London will do the same."

Edwina agreed. "She's absolutely right."

Maggie continued. "Look at it this way. Your mother now has someone to take care of her. The rest of you don't have to rush over to check on her or feel bad about her being in this house alone—no more guilt-tripping any of you. The best part is, she has a live-in physician that will most likely outlive her. Besides, it's done. You can either make peace with it and your mother, who may or may not have a lot of time left in this world, or you can spend the rest of your life letting the anger eat you alive, depriving yourselves of your own peace of mind. It's your choice."

Robert looked at Gabe. "What do you think, Gabe?"

Gabe closed his eyes. "I think…. Maggie just made some really good points."

Edward spoke, "Well, at the very least, he is making an honest woman out of our mother."

Alex agreed. "And he is a good, respectable man. I know that for a fact."

After some lively debate, they all agreed to do their best to be accepting of the marriage, even allowing Georgie to plan a celebratory dinner for the family for that afternoon. The dinner went very well, and at the end of it, they were all more comfortable with Dr. Martin Barnes being their mother's new husband.

Georgie pulled Maggie to the side, thanking her because she knew that Maggie was the one who had brought them around. Hugging Maggie, Georgie whispered, "I consider you my daughter, even if you never marry my son, but I would be very happy if you did."

Later that night, after Georgie and Martin had retired, and everyone else had left, Gabe and Maggie sprawled out on the couch. Gabe was completely worn out by his new best friend—Olivia—who had not left his side the entire night.

Maggie kicked off her new shoes, throwing her feet into Gabe's lap. "Gabe, the women just can't get enough of you."

He cocked his head in a questioning manner.

"Olivia." Maggie clarified.

"Ah," he acknowledged, "she is something else, isn't she?"

Maggie stretched her back. "She is very taken with her newly found Uncle Gabe."

He smiled. "I am quite fond of her, too. She makes me wish…"

Looking over, Maggie saw a thoughtful look in his eye. "She makes you wish what?"

He shook his head slightly. "Oh nothing, I was just thinking how it would have been if Samuel had lived… or if I had another child… maybe even a little girl."

Maggie felt his melancholy. She put her feet down and moved to lay against his chest. "I'm sorry, Gabe. You would make a perfect father."

He wrapped his arm around her. "Yes, well, we both know, given my lifestyle, that would be rather difficult. It does make me wonder, though, about something you said. You told me about these 'sperm banks' where women could have children without husbands. Does it ever happen the other way? I mean, I know that women are required to be part of the process, obviously, but are there cases of men having children without the mother involved?"

Maggie raised up. "Well, yes. There are women called surrogates, who are implanted with a man's seed, in a medical procedure instead of the regular way, that are paid to only carry the baby, and after he or she is born, she signs over all her rights to the child, completely leaving the scene. Couples, who are unable to conceive themselves, sometimes use them. Especially if the man wants a child that carries his bloodline. The process is also used by same-sex couples who want to have a family."

Gabe frowned. "But something like that would be impossible now. If a man were to offer a woman money for a child, he would probably, promptly, be thrown in the nearest gaol."

Maggie agreed. "No doubt. But there are other ways."

Gabe was suddenly very interested. "What do you mean?"

Maggie straightened up beside him. "Adoption?" Maggie thought for a second, "But that may not be a big thing yet." She continued, "The world is full of children who find themselves with no parents, of no fault of their own. They end up in orphanages, being treated very badly or on the streets. I am sure, any one of them would consider one parent better than none, especially if that parent loves them and treats them well. Besides Gabe, you and I both know that family doesn't have to be blood. Look at the two of us."

Gabe spoke softly, "I have never even considered taking in a child. The military life, and being the way that I am, made me push the thought of fatherhood completely out of my mind. But, now...well…." he trailed off.

Maggie snuggled against his chest, suddenly exhausted, and as she started to drift off, she dreamily said, "Any child would be lucky to have you as a father, Gabe."

He looked down at her, seeing that she was fast asleep. He kissed the top of her head, before carefully carrying her upstairs, and tucking her into her own bed as he thought about what she had said.

There were only a few days until Alex's wedding, so Gabe spent that time showing Maggie around London, taking her to places and regaling her with stories of his childhood. They would take horseback rides to the country to let Onyx out, who was enjoying his new-found fame as London's newest celebrity. Everywhere he went, people would comment on his beauty and how unique he was. After one of those trips, Maggie asked Gabe, "Is Onyx really that unusual?"

Gabe snarked, "Unusual is not the word I would use."

Maggie gave him a look.

"I don't know, I suppose, maybe a little. He is a magnificent horse, although a little shorter and stouter than most. But in all honesty, his size is a perfect fit for you, as if he were bred just to be your horse. His personality leaves a great deal to be desired. He seems to understand humans much more than any horse I have ever met, and I have never seen a horse as loyal to anyone as that one is to you."

Maggie shrugged. "Unusual seems to be my forte; just makes sense my horse would be that way as well."

"Indeed."

Georgie and Martin enjoyed their newfound newlywed status. After talking with Alex and Josephine, it was decided that three days after their wedding ceremony, the family would throw a huge party to celebrate both of their nuptials together. It would be a grand affair that London would not soon forget.

Gabe was not thrilled with the idea after Georgie's last party disaster, but Maggie convinced him that they were due for at least one party to go well, because, how bad could their luck be?

Maggie found herself shopping again, dragging Gabe along this time.

Gabe was amazed at how much fun she was having, buying things for herself and for him, and he was happy to see her so carefree for a change. "Mags, you seem so different here in London than in Virginia. What's wrong with you?" he asked sarcastically, eyeing her up and down.

Maggie shrugged. "I don't know, Gabe. At home, everything is so serious with what's going on there, and I know what's to come there. English history never was my strong suit, meaning, I have no idea what will happen here today or tomorrow. I don't know when or how anyone will die, or when the next disaster will strike and truthfully, being away from Virginia has taken my mind off…. well...you know. If I am being completely honest, spending time with your family has been a good distraction for me." She furrowed her brow. "I know we have to go back to...all of that soon enough, and I guess I have just enjoyed the break from the stress, even if it is for just a little while."

She seemed a little sad as she finished her last sentence, so Gabe pulled her into a tight hug. Sometimes, that was all he could do.

6 CHAPTER SIX

Alex and Josephine's wedding was a magnificent affair.

Georgie had seen to all the decorations in the church, the entire place covered from top to bottom with flowers and candles. Producing romantic ambiance was rapidly becoming her specialty. Becoming the new Mrs. Barnes had done wonders for her, as well; her face radiated a glow of happiness.

Maggie had a chance to spend some time with Josephine, who was a lovely young lady, hopelessly in love with her groom, looking forward to their future together.

After the wedding, there was a small, intimate reception back at the house for family and a few friends, since the bigger party would be later. The Asheton brothers enjoyed drinks and cigars, giving their little brother a hard time about his upcoming wedding night.

Some of the ladies had entrapped Josephine, giving her horrifying wedding night advice, while Maggie managed to slip outside to the garden for some air before they dragged her into their conversation. She noticed Henry, sitting on a bench, with his nose in a book.

"May I sit?"

Henry looked up and smiled. "Of course, please."

Maggie sat down. "You do love your books, don't you?"

"I do. I always have. They are my constant companions."

Maggie remembered something. "Oh, I still need to get you my list of books that I am on the lookout for. Your Uncle Gabe will also want to talk business with you, as well. We can start shipping some of the books from your shop to the colonies through our company if you are interested in doing so. It could prove to be very profitable for you since books are in short supply there."

Henry was excited by the prospect. "Yes! Thank you! That would be wonderful."

A sudden thought came to Maggie. "Henry, you know a great deal about books. I have one that might interest you. It is a bit unusual."

Henry looked intrigued. "Unusual? In what way?"

"It's hard to explain," Maggie replied. "I have it here. Would you like to see it?"

He grinned. "Very much so."

Maggie slipped inside the house and returned with the book. She handed it to Henry. "It is a book of Celtic Faerie Tales, but the binding is unlike anything I have ever seen."

Holding it with care, Henry looked over the book, running a finger down the spine. "It is indeed unusual. The intricacies of the cover alone are amazing, and these symbols... Maggie, this book is very old and very rare.

Workmanship like this simply doesn't exist anymore. Wherever did you get it?"

Maggie shook her head. "I have no idea. It showed up on my doorstep a year or so ago; no note, just my name on the packaging. I thought it was a gift from Gabe, but he didn't send it."

"When did you say you received it?"

She thought back. "It was January of '77. I remember thinking it had to be a late Christmas gift from Gabe. Why do you ask?"

He looked a little perplexed back down at the book. "I had a man in the shop last summer, looking for a book exactly like this. He said that one had been stolen from his family home and he was desperate to get it back, searching every bookstore he could find. He even left his name and an address, asking me to send word if I were to ever acquire it. He offered an enormous amount of money as a finder's fee."

"Do you by chance remember his name?"

Henry tapped a finger to his forehead. "It was a Scottish fellow. I have his information back at the shop, but I believe his name was...MacGregor?"

Maggie was beyond shocked. "Henry, would you mind terribly giving me that information? I would be very grateful, and if this is indeed a book that was stolen from his home, I would like to return it."

"Of course. I will get it for you tomorrow." He looked back at the book again, perplexed by something.

"What is it?" Maggie asked.

He opened and closed the cover. "There is something odd about this." He held it up closer to her. "Do you see the thickness of the front cover?"

"Yes."

He flipped it over. "Now, look at the thickness of the back cover. The front is twice as thick as the back."

Maggie looked at him. "And that's not normal?"

Henry shook his head. "It may or may not be, depending on the one who does the binding, but in a book this old, there can be another reason for it. I wonder…" He peeled a tiny part of the corner of the inside cover up. "Yes, I believe it is. Look here," he pointed, "sometimes, the inside front covers were used to conceal things, like documents. May I have your permission to check? I can repair it afterward."

"Please!" demanded Maggie. "I am dying to know."

He peeled it up, and sure enough, there was a folded parchment paper beneath it. He pulled it free, damaging as little of the cover as possible, and handed it to Maggie.

Maggie looked closer. It was the same type of paper that the note in the bottle was written on. She unfolded it.

It appeared to be a map.

Henry looked over at it. "It looks like a very old map of Scotland; the land shape is unmistakable."

There was only one thing marked, a small symbol at the edge of a Loch. Nothing else was labeled.

But the strangest thing was the symbol: it matched one of the ones on the bottle that Maggie had when she came back and the same one on the spine of this book.

"What do you make of that?" Maggie asked aloud, pointing.

"I have no idea," answered Henry, "but it should be simple enough to compare it to a current map of Scotland and see what lines up. I have some maps back at the shop if you would like to bring it by."

"Yes, Henry, I will most certainly bring it by. Thank you."

They chatted for a while before Maggie slipped back into the house to return the book and map to her room. When she passed by an open bedroom door, she saw Josephine sitting on the bed, alone and looking very distressed.

Don't get involved, Maggie, don't get involved, Maggie.

She sighed and stepped in. "Are you alright, Josephine?"

Josephine wiped a tear from her face. "Yes. I am just overwhelmed.... with joy, of course."

Maggie sat down beside her. "Oh, I thought you may have been overwhelmed with all of that information you were getting from the ladies downstairs."

Josephine whispered, "That too."

Maggie stood up and closed the door for privacy. "Why don't you tell me what is bothering you the most? Some of the advice you were being given from the older wives was, well... maybe a little inaccurate, depending on your perspective."

The younger woman lowered her eyes and her voice, "They said that the first time was painful and horrible, that I wouldn't enjoy it, only that I should... endure it."

"Stay right here, I need to get something from my room. I will be right back." Maggie needed alcohol for this, and Josephine would, too. Returning with a bottle of rum and two glasses, she poured, handing one to the new bride.

"What's this?"

Maggie poured her own. "It's called rum, and it is a girl's best friend."

Josephine took a tiny sip and smiled. "It's good."

Maggie raised her glass. "Yes, it is. Some days, it is the best part of my day." She looked over at Josephine. "Josephine, you are in love with Alex, are you not?"

"Oh, yes; more than anything. He is very sweet to me."

Sitting down, Maggie was determined to provide the poor girl some peace of mind. "When he firsts...enters you, it will sting, but only for a moment, and, if he does his husbandly duty the correct way, you won't even notice it. Trust Alex. Let him take the lead, and if he does something you don't like, tell him. But, don't get offended too quickly, sometimes the things that seem the strangest, lead to the best...feelings in the end."

Josephine looked up at her with wide eyes, "Really?"

Maggie smiled, hoping against hope, for Josephine's sake, that Alex knew what he was doing. "Really! Drink! The rum will help your nerves and make it more enjoyable."

Josephine drank a little more of the rum. "And, do you enjoy it?"

Geez, Maggie, how do you get yourself in these conversations?

"Yes, I do. On the extremely rare occasions that I get to experience it." Maggie topped off their glasses.

"But Maggie, what am I supposed to do, while he is doing...that."

Maggie drained her glass and encouraged the girl to do the same. "Just do what feels good. The two of you will figure out your own way. If he loves you as much as I think he does, both of you will be just fine in the bedroom."

Josephine was smiling and in a much better mood when Maggie heard Gabe and Alex in the hall.

Alex was speaking, "Someone said they saw Josephine head upstairs."

Maggie stood up and pulled open the door, almost tripping. "We are in here."

Alex and Gabe appeared at the door.

Gabe knew Maggie's look. He leaned against the doorway with his arms folded and asked, "And what pray tell is going on in here?"

Maggie tried to look innocent. "We were just having a little girl talk."

Alex looked at Josephine. "And a few drinks?"

Josephine nodded. "Maggie introduced me to the best part of her day...it's called rum...and I very much like it."

Alex looked at Maggie, and Maggie winced, trying to explain, "Josephine was a little nervous about her wedding night, so we had a drink to help take the edge off."

Alex acknowledged Maggie, understanding completely. "I see. Darling, we should be getting home."

Josephine smiled confidently, stood up, and took her husband's hand, while gazing at him adoringly. "Yes. I am ready for our first night as husband and wife."

Alex seemed very pleased.

As they headed off, Josephine turned to Maggie. "Thank you, Maggie, for the girl talk. I shall heed your advice."

Maggie nodded. "Congratulations again. I hope you will be very happy together."

After they departed, Gabe went over and sat by Maggie, picking up the rum bottle to see how much was gone. "How much did you give her?"

Maggie sipped her glass. "She only had a few sips, just enough to 'warm' her up, literally."

Gabe raised an eyebrow. "And you had the rest?"

"You try talking a virgin through her wedding night, especially after that bunch of old biddies downstairs had scared the poor girl to death. She was terrified and in tears when I found her up here."

Taking Maggie's glass, Gabe sipped from it himself, grinning a little behind the glass. "Well, you are the expert on deflowering virgins, aren't you?"

Maggie scowled at him.

"What did you tell her?"

"I told her to let Alex take the lead and she would be fine. Please, tell me Robert took Alex to the whorehouse for his first time, too, otherwise, that girl is going to be seriously disappointed tonight."

Gabe handed her back the glass. "Oh, he did indeed. He felt it was his 'duty' as the older brother to have us all educated, a rite of passage if you will...and it gave him an excuse for his own time with Monique."

They both chuckled.

Maggie's laughter faded, remembering the book. "Oh Gabe, I almost forgot! Come to my room."

She led him by the hand to her bed, closing the door behind them. She sat him down and grabbed the book, hopping over beside him. "You, my dear Gabe, have the most wonderful nephew ever. I showed him the book because I thought maybe he could shed some light on it."

Gabe took the glass back from her, sipping again. "And did he?"

Maggie nodded, her head feeling a little spacey from the rum. "He did indeed. He said the book was very old and rare, and that these types of books had hidden things. He found this in the cover."

Setting the glass down, Gabe opened the page. "It's a map."

Maggie pointed to it. "He thinks it's an old map of Scotland. In addition to that, he said that a while back, a man came looking for that same book, claiming it was stolen from his home. He left his name and contact information, desperate to reclaim it."

Gabe was astonished by all this new information.

"Gabe, he thinks the man's name was MacGregor."

Gabe's eyes widened. "The name on the crest?"

"All of these pieces are connected. Henry also has some good maps of Scotland. We can take this over to compare and see what lines up."

Folding the map, Gabe lay it to the side as he looked directly at Maggie. "Mags, where do you think all of this is leading? Is this something that you should be pursuing? We have no idea what, if any, connection this even has to you personally."

She sighed. "Gabe, I really don't know, but my gut feeling is telling me that I need to follow through. Maybe there are some answers for me, about why I am here, why I was the one thrown back in time and not someone else. If everything happens for a reason, then I need to know what that reason is. The universe owes me an explanation, and I intend to collect on it."

The next day, Maggie and Gabe went by the bookshop. Henry gave Maggie the information on the man looking for the book. His name was Quinn MacGregor and he had instructed Henry that he could leave word at a certain tavern in Edinburgh if he came across it. Henry pulled out several maps and they compared them to the one in the book. All the maps showed the same thing...there was nothing at the spot marked. No castles, no claimed lands, the current maps didn't even show the place existed.

The frustration was evident in her voice. "How does a place just disappear?"

Gabe answered, "Time. You know that, Maggie. Over time, things just go away. This map is very old. There may have been something there once, but there's nothing there now."

Maggie didn't believe that for one second.

7 CHAPTER SEVEN

The day of the grand celebration arrived. The house was abuzz with a flurry of activity, Georgie attending to every detail. The Asheton matriarch was expecting over a hundred people and she wanted to make sure everything went smoothly. The house looked much as it did for the party she had thrown for Gabe, but on a much larger scale.

The family arrived first.

Josephine immediately pulled Maggie to the side to thank her for all her advice on her wedding day. She was right; Alex had done everything perfectly and she was a very happy woman. She also asked Maggie to send her a few cases of rum.

A little later, Alex also pulled her to the side to thank her for her kindness to his bride that day. Her advice—and rum—had made things go much smoother than he had anticipated.

The party was in full swing and things were going well. Gabe was still the center of attention to all the single ladies in attendance, being the only available Asheton son left. A few were trying to corner him, but Gabe had become a master at dodging and ducking husband-seekers, and he was still the perfect gentleman, as always. He hung close by Maggie, not wanting her to feel alone in a sea of people she didn't know. He had introduced her to so many people, that there was no way she could keep up with any of their names.

Gabe and Maggie were standing in the garden chatting, when a voice called out, "Colonel Asheton, as I leave and breathe."

Gabe turned. "General Howe! What a pleasant surprise."

It was the former commander-in-chief of the British army under whom Gabe had served in Philadelphia. They shook hands as they greeted each other.

"Mistress Bishop, how good to see you again, or surely, it is Mrs. Asheton by now?"

Gabe and Maggie looked at each other, coming to the same horrific realization at the same time. They had screwed up. In their haste to get Maggie back to Virginia, they had never 'officially' called off their engagement. Gabe silently asked the question with his eyes, "what do we do?" as Maggie responded with a shrug of the shoulder and a tilt of the head, indicating to "just go with it, it's easier."

Maggie smiled at General Howe. "No, we have not married yet."

Gabe took over, slipping his arm around Maggie's waist. "Time has not allowed, and my lovely fiancé believes in long engagements."

Howe patted him on the shoulder. "Gabe, you are a fool. If you had any sense, you would have married this beautiful creature on the spot."

Unbeknownst to Maggie and Gabe, Georgie was standing right behind them and heard the entire conversation, her face lighting up with so much excitement and joy, that she could hardly contain herself.

They finally got away from General Howe, finding a quiet seat in the garden, drinks in hand.

"Gabe, how could we have forgotten to call that engagement off?"

Gabe answer was arid. "We were a little busy departing Philadelphia."

Maggie sighed. "Yes, and I completely forgot about it when we went back to visit."

Gabe gave her a sly look. "Yes, it must have been all of that 'comfort' you were receiving from John that made you forgetful."

Maggie covered the smile on her face with her hand. "Well, I suppose that would have been a good reason for you to use to call off our engagement. I am sure the eligible ladies of Philadelphia would have rushed to your side to offer up their shoulders and bosoms to comfort you in your time of need."

Gabe rolled his eyes. "I'm sure." He lifted his glass. "Anyway, I wouldn't worry too much about it. He is the only one who thinks we are engaged. We will be on our way back to Virginia soon and this will all be a moot point."

Georgie spotted the two of them sitting in the garden and made her way over to them. "Gabe, Maggie! I cannot tell you how thrilled I am. Come with me!" she exclaimed, taking them each by the hand, pulling them off their seat to the middle of the backyard. "I cannot wait to make the announcement."

Maggie and Gabe shot each other quizzical looks. Before either could ask to what she was referring, Georgie had grabbed a glass, clinking the side of it with a spoon.

Martin made his way to her side, all smiles.

"Excuse me, everyone. May I have your attention, please? I want to thank everyone for coming this evening to join us in our celebration of not one, but two happy occasions that have recently occurred. Not only were our dear Alex and Josephine married in a lovely ceremony at the church a few days ago, but Dr. Martin Barnes and I were also wed shortly before that in a very small, and private ceremony. I cannot tell you how full my heart is at these two new additions, and I hope you will all join me in welcoming them to our ever-growing family."

Everyone stopped to clap and raise a glass.

"And just when I thought I could not possibly be any happier, I have learned additional news that I am overjoyed to share with each of you here tonight."

Maggie leaned over to Gabe. "What's she talking about?"

Gabe shrugged, "I haven't the foggiest."

She nudged his shoulder. "Maybe you are getting that baby sister you always wanted."

Gabe snorted. "Don't even joke about that."

Georgie was all smiles as she raised her glass. "Please, allow me the pleasure of announcing the engagement of my son Gabriel and his beautiful bride-to-be Maggie Bishop."

Maggie and Gabe froze.

"Oh dear God in Heaven," Gabe closed his eyes.

Maggie downed the drink in her hand while looking at Gabe. "So, we're back to this again?"

Gabe nodded his head. "So, it would seem."

People gathered around to offer their congratulations.

Georgie made her way through the crowd, pulling Gabe and Maggie into a group hug, pleased as could be. "I can't believe the two of you kept this from us. I can't tell you how much this means to me."

"Mother, we really need to talk."

"Of course, Gabe, we have so many plans to make. This changes everything."

As Georgie turned to speak to someone, Gabe managed to grab Maggie and slip out of the crowd to a dark corner of the garden where there was a little loveseat. Before they sat down, Maggie started patting at Gabe's coat.

"What are you doing?"

Maggie continued her search. "You know what I'm doing. Where is it?"

He rolled his eyes upward, reached in his coat and pulled out his flask, handing it to her.

Spinning off the top, Maggie drank half of it down in one gulp, before handing it back to him to finish the other half. "You really need to start packing two of those things for these parties."

Gabe collapsed to the loveseat. "Duly noted."

Maggie sat next to him, rubbing his back. "Gabe, what just happened back there? Why would your mother announce that?"

Gabe leaned over with his head in his hands. "I have no idea, but I intend to find out."

They hid out in the same spot until the crowd had thinned down to just the family before making their way back inside. Georgie and Martin had said 'good night' to the last of the guests and joined the rest of the family in the parlor before Maggie and Gabe came in.

Georgie looked up. "There's the happy couple."

Everyone offered their congratulations at once.

Gabe moved to the front of the fireplace, a solemn look on his face. "Mother, why, in God's name, did you make that announcement? Maggie and I are NOT engaged."

Everyone looked up at him, questions evident on their faces.

Georgie stood up. "What do you mean 'you are not engaged' when I clearly heard the two of you talking to General Howe and you told him that you hadn't had time to get married yet, wanting a long engagement instead."

Gabe and Maggie looked at each other, understanding now where the information had come from.

Gabe looked back at his mother. "Mother, General Howe was under the mistaken assumption in Philadelphia that we were engaged. We just never corrected him."

Georgie looked back and forth between Gabe and Maggie. "Why on Earth would you do that?"

Maggie knew they couldn't tell her the real reason, so she stepped in, telling Gabe the story as much as everyone else. "You see Georgie, I had a man in Philadelphia who pursued me well past the point of propriety, and Gabe, being concerned about my safety, suggested that we pretend to be engaged to deter this man's dangerous advances. We kept up the ruse until we left, and never let anyone there know any different for fear that this man may come to Virginia and start to harass me again." She came over and took Gabe's hand, who was giving her a grateful look for her quick thinking. "Gabe was only protecting me, as he always does."

Gabe squeezed her hand.

Georgie looked at Gabe, collecting her thoughts. "I see. I am not sure what to say. While I am truly disappointed that you two are not engaged...I am proud of the fact that I have a son who would go to such extremes to see to the protection of a lady in need. Given the extreme circumstances, perhaps it is best if we just let everyone, aside from the family, of course, continue to believe that you are indeed engaged...for Maggie's safety."

Gabe leaned towards his mother, kissing her cheek. "Thank you, Mother, for being so understanding."

Later that night, Gabe knocked on Maggie's door, holding up a bottle and two glasses when she opened it. "Want to have a nightcap with your fiancé?"

Maggie feigned modesty, clutching her hand to her chest. "I am not sure it is proper for you to be in my bedroom before we are married, sir."

Gabe leaned forward and kissed her forehead. "It's a good thing you aren't a 'proper' woman," he whispered with a grin on his face, stepping inside.

They sat on the bed while Gabe poured the drinks. "The explanation for our engagement, that was pretty quick thinking on your part."

Maggie looked at her glass. "It was fairly close to the truth, just a little role reversal."

"At any rate, it was a very good story. My mother thinks highly of her son, I don't have any more women in search of a husband throwing themselves at me, and my mother gets to save face by not having to tell people we aren't really engaged. It's a win-win situation all the way around."

Maggie held up her glass. "I will drink to that."
Gabe laughed. "You will drink to anything."
"No argument there.

8 CHAPTER EIGHT

Early in the morning a few days later, Gabe tapped on Maggie's door again. "Care to take a ride with me?"
"I would be delighted."
They saddled Onyx, along with a horse for Gabe, and headed out. Gabe led them through town, out into a more rural area dotted with an occasional building here and there. Onyx was ecstatic to be out of the stables, enjoying the freedom to run after being cooped up for so long.
Gabe had been quiet most of the trip, which concerned Maggie. She was just about to ask what was troubling him when they came upon a small church in a little grove of trees.
Stopping the horses, Gabe helped Maggie down, taking her by the hand and leading her forward, not saying a word.
The quaint, stone building, with its beautiful stained-glass windows, rustic cross in the front, and stone wall surrounding it, was quiet, peaceful, and picture perfect. It was the warmest and most inviting place Maggie had ever seen.

Gabe noticed the wonderment in Maggie's eyes, happy to see her so pleased.

"Gabe, this place is enchanting."

He smiled, sadness in his eyes; still not saying a word, he led her inside. The interior was just as wonderful as the exterior. The pews and the pulpit were made of a fine, dark wood—obviously well cared for, shiny and clean. Candles lit the windows and the front, giving off an exquisite, ethereal glow. Gabe picked a pew and motioned for Maggie to sit down, then slid into the seat next to her.

She waited for him to speak.

He stared ahead, lost in a memory, the words coming out softly. "This is the church where Penny and I were married."

Maggie took his hand, as he looked down and continued.

"We met when I was taking care of some legal matters for her father. Her mother had recently passed, and he wanted to ensure that his two daughters were cared for if something were to happen to him. There was no other family; he had been an only child and their mother was raised in an orphanage. What little family they did have, had passed on years before. He was setting up trusts for the girls.

"Penny accompanied him on one of those trips. My parents had been encouraging me to seek out a wife, so, out of respect for them, I asked her father for permission to visit with her. We got along very well. She was a gentle, kind soul, very easy to talk to and I grew fond of her. I proposed not long after. We married here, in this church, a short time later. She became with child a few months in, and... well, the rest you know. They are both buried here in the church cemetery."

Maggie's heart ached for his pain, her eyes watering.

"Sometimes, I think their deaths were God's way of punishing me for being the way I am, for not loving her the way a man is supposed to truly love a woman."

She turned to him. "Gabe, look at me."

He looked up with guilt in his eyes.

"God was not punishing you. You are not responsible for what happened to them. Sometimes, bad things happen to good people, and you are the best person that I know. And even if that were true, you had not acted on your feelings with another at that point. You did everything that was expected of you, and it still happened. Let me ask you this question: If they were still alive today, would you still be married to her and raising your son?"

Gabe answered without hesitation. "Of course! Without a doubt!"

Maggie squeezed his hand tight. "Then tell me how your theory makes any sense. If they were still alive, you would have never been with anyone else and no so-called 'sin' would have ever been committed. People aren't punished for sins they might commit."

She wiped a small tear from the corner of his eye.

"Maybe this had to happen to put you on the path you truly needed to be on."

Gabe nodded.

A voice from the front spoke. "You should listen to your friend." It was a man dressed in long robes and a hood. He stepped into sight. "Forgive me, I was here when you came in. I should have made myself known, but I did not want to disturb you."

Maggie and Gabe looked at each, in fear they may have said something that would have exposed Gabe.

The man approached with a smile on his face, lowering his hood. "Hello, Gabe. It has been a long time."

"Father Tucker?" Astonished, Gabe stood to shake his hand. "I had no idea you were still here."

Father Tucker smiled. "The Lord's work has no end."

Gabe suddenly remembered Maggie. "Father Tucker, allow me to introduce my dear friend, Maggie Bishop. Maggie, this is Father Tucker, the priest of this church. He is the one who married us and..." Gabe trailed off.

The priest finished his sentence. "...and who laid his wife and child to rest." The Father laid his hand on Gabe's shoulder. "Gabe, forgive me, but I overheard part of your conversation. Please, tell me you have not blamed yourself all these years for what happened to them."

Gabe lowered his eyes, not responding.

Father Tucker sighed, debating something in his mind, looking at the man before him that needed absolution more than he needed to keep his promise to someone who was no longer in this world. "Gabe, would you and your friend please join me in the garden?"

They followed him through the church, outside, to a small flower garden off to one side, connected to the small rectory. It was in full bloom, with the most beautiful red roses Maggie had ever seen. She stopped to admire them, even sticking her nose close to one bloom, while closing her eyes to fully enjoy the sweet fragrance.

Father Tucker noticed her admiring them.

"They are exquisite, Father."

"They are my guilty pleasure. There is an enormous amount of peace in watching things grow from a tiny little cutting into something so strong and beautiful. It is amazing what a little care and nurturing can do. Of course, that can be said for many things." Father Tucker looked back at Gabe, who was very morose. They reached a half-circle bench under a shady tree. He motioned for them to sit and he sat on the end, facing them.

Father Tucker looked at Gabe thoughtfully. "Gabe, there is something you need to know. "

Gabe looked at the Father, puzzled as the priest continued.

"I knew Penny and her sister from the day they came into this world. They were two of the sweetest, most caring children I have ever had the pleasure of meeting. They got that from their mother. She was always helping here at the church, doing what she could to help those less fortunate, the girls taking right after her. Penny was about 11 when she knocked on my door one day, in absolute tears. She had found a bird with a broken wing, and she wanted to help it. I brought her in, looked at the bird and didn't see much hope for it. I gently suggested that maybe we should relieve it of its suffering.

"Penny would not hear of it. She demanded that we figure out a way to help that poor creature. We patched it up the best we could, said a prayer over it, and waited to see. We put it in a little cage that I had, and she kept watch over that bird, night and day.

"Miraculously, that little bird healed and was able to fly back into the world as if nothing had ever happened to it. No one was more surprised than I was. When I said to her that she was the reason that little bird was alive, she corrected me. She told me that she didn't save that bird, that God did because only God decided when it was someone's time to be called back to His side, it was just her job to care for His creatures while she was here."

Father Tucker took in a deep breath, "Gabe, Penny came to me a few weeks before the baby came. She told me something in confidence that she did not want you to know. After she and the baby passed, there seemed no need to add to your suffering, so I said nothing. I see now, that was a mistake. Knowing her as I did, she would not have wanted you to blame yourself all these years. Please forgive me for not telling you sooner."

Gabe went pale, and Maggie took his hand. "What didn't I know, Father?"

Father frowned. "Gabe, Penny was unwell. Her illness is what caused her death, not the childbirth."

Gabe's entire body went numb listening to Father Tucker recount his memories.

"I came into the sanctuary that day, and I noticed Penny on the back pew, her head bowed as if in prayer. I was going to quietly leave when she lifted her head and I saw that she had been crying. I sat down beside her and asked if I could do anything to help her.

"She told me that she had just visited her doctor. She had been feeling unwell, thinking it was from carrying the child, but soon realized that it was not. I don't know the details of the illness; she didn't tell me, only that the physician had told she had only a few months to live. Penny was in the church praying to God, not to cure her, but only asking Him to let her live until the baby was born. She loved you, Gabe and didn't want to leave you alone. Her sincerest hope was that the baby would provide comfort to you when she was no longer in this world. Penny asked me not to tell you. She said that she would, but only as the end neared, and after the baby was born, so the two of you would be able to enjoy what time you had left together.

"The doctor's time frame was inaccurate. A few short weeks later, her labor pains started far too soon, most likely brought on by the illness, and her body was just not strong enough." Father Tucker leaned forward. "Gabe, nothing you thought or did caused this. Only God decides when He is ready to call someone home, and He wanted Penny and Samuel home."

Years of guilt and pain released in the stream of tears running down Gabe's cheeks.

Maggie stood in front of him, pulling his head to her chest, as he wrapped his arms around her waist and broke into a mournful sob. Maggie held him, stroking his back, trying to soothe him, as a few tears escaped her own eyes, as well.

Father Tucker slipped away to give them some privacy.

Gabe was exhausted and drained by the time he raised his head.

Maggie reached inside his coat pocket to pull out the handkerchief she knew he kept there. She wiped his face for him and kissed the top of his head.

His whisper was soft, "Thanks, Mags."

She sat down next to him, rubbing his back as he composed himself.

"How could I not know?"

Maggie laid her head on his shoulder. "You didn't know because she didn't want you to know. She couldn't bear to see you in pain. Gabe, Penny loved you and you made her very happy for the short time you were together. Maybe that's the reason you came into her life, and maybe she came into your life to help you realize who you really are and put you on the path...to me...and for that, I am beyond grateful."

Gabe took her hand and kissed it. "Mags, make sure you are in my life for the long run."

"Gabe, you couldn't chase me away if you tried."

Gabe and Maggie strolled, hand in hand, to the cemetery.

Father Tucker had left two cut roses on the gate for Gabe to take in for his visit.

Maggie stood next to him for a little while as he lay the two roses on the grave. She leaned over, touching his back. "I will wait in the garden for you. Take your time."

When she reached the gate, she looked back him.

Gabe stood there, somberly saying his final goodbyes.

Maggie went back to the bench and Father Tucker came to join her. He handed her a cut rose. "I thought you might like this."

She took the rose, smelling it. "Thank you...for everything. Gabe needed to hear what you had to say."

The Father sat down. "I had no idea he blamed himself for what happened. If I had, I would have sought him out sooner."

Maggie looked down at the rose. "He knows the truth now. I think he will find the closure that he needs now to move on."

Father Tucker took a good look at Maggie. "Gabe may not be the only one who needs to find some closure. You seem quite burdened by something yourself."

Maggie raised her head. "Oh Father, I'm afraid the answers that I search for are not so easy to find."

He patted her hand. "I will pray that you find the answers you seek. You and Gabe come to see me before you leave. I want to do something for you both."

A half an hour later, Gabe found her in the garden. He had composed himself and seemed much better. He took her by the hand. "I wish to light some candles before we leave."

He lit one for Penny, one for Samuel, and one for Jonathan.

Maggie lit one for her unborn child.

Father Tucker found them as they were finishing up. He asked them to both sit. He dipped his finger in Holy Oil and made the sign of the cross on each of their foreheads. "I absolve you both of any of your sins, real or perceived. May you both go with God."

They thanked him for his blessing and started back to town.

Maggie could tell Gabe was exhausted, mentally and physically, but when he started to make little jokes, she knew he would be fine.

"I'm surprised Onyx didn't burst into flames when his hooves touched holy ground."

Onyx rammed his head into Gabe's leg.

"Hey, watch it you beast. That actually hurt."

Onyx seemed to laugh as Gabe rubbed his leg.

Well, it's good to know that some things never change.

Maggie's stomach started to rumble, and Gabe heard it. "Oh, my goodness, Maggie, I am sorry. I did not realize it was so late. There is a tavern up the road a bit, we will stop and get you something to eat."

A few minutes later, there were sitting at a table and had ordered food and drink. Gabe reached across the table and took Maggie's hand. "Thank you for coming with me today. I had no idea things would take the turn they did, but I am grateful you were there for me."

Maggie squeezed his hand. "Gabe, I wouldn't have wanted to be anywhere else. And I hope now you will release some of this unnecessary baggage you have been carrying around for so long."

"Maggie, I think I am well on my way."

They were enjoying their food when Maggie noticed a woman that kept looking over at Gabe. Maggie was used to women staring at Gabe, it was hard not to. He was just too handsome for his own good, and age just increased his appeal, but there was something different about this one.

For one thing, she was very pregnant and with another man.

They finished their food and were enjoying some drinks when Maggie noticed the lady get up and move towards the table.

In a shy voice, she said, "Please forgive my intrusion, but are you, Gabe Asheton?"

Gabe turned to the lady, not recognizing her. "Yes, I am Gabe Asheton. Do I know you?"

The lady's eyes lit up. "Well, I was 10 the last time you saw me, so I am not surprised you do not know my face. It's me, Hannah."

A look of awareness came to Gabe's face. "Oh my God... Hannah!" He stood up and hugged her. "Look at you, all grown up...and with child." Gabe laughed.

The man came over to join them.

Gabe looked at Maggie. "Maggie meet Hannah. This is Penny's sister. Hannah, this is Maggie Bishop."

Maggie was stunned. "Oh, it's very nice to meet you."

Hannah turned to her. "It's so nice to meet you. I just heard this morning that Gabe was back in town for a visit and engaged. You must be the lucky lady. Congratulations. I am very happy for you both."

Maggie tilted her head. "Thank you."

Hannah turned to introduce the man, pulling him closer. "This is my husband, Derek Spencer."

Gabe invited them to sit down and join them.

They spent the next hour catching up. Hannah and Derek had been married for a few years and she was now pregnant with their first child, due in two weeks. Derek was the proud owner of an apothecary shop in the middle-class district of town. They lived in Hannah's family home, not far from Gabe's mother's home, being the sole heiress to her family's money when her father passed a few years prior. They spoke of Penny, and Gabe told them that they had just returned from a visit to the church.

Hannah spoke of the joy that Gabe brought to Penny and how happy she would be that he was taking another wife.

Hannah and Derek were enthralled by stories from the colonies, expecting it to be completely wild wilderness, like everyone else in London who had never been there. Hannah and Derek were a lovely couple that Gabe and Maggie liked very much. They promised to make plans to catch up before they went back to Virginia as they each headed their own ways.

On the way back to the house, Maggie asked Gabe, "Was Penny much like Hannah?"

"Yes, in many ways," Gabe replied. "They have much the same personality. Hannah was still a child when

Penny passed, so I really didn't know her very well, but she reminds me of her in many ways now."

Maggie smiled. "Well, I think I would have liked Penny very much."

"She would have liked you too, Mags."

9 CHAPTER NINE

Gabe was very different the next few days. Finding out that he was in no way responsible for Penny and Samuel's death made his heart much lighter. He smiled more, he joked more, and he seemed to enjoy life so much more.

Even Olivia and Izzy couldn't wear him down.

He had offered to take them and Charlie for the day, so Annabelle could take a nap and have some time for herself. Annabelle had a new favorite brother-in-law.

Maggie mainly looked after Charlie while Gabe did everything the girls wanted. He was having the time of his life and Maggie was ecstatic to see it.

The day after, Maggie and Gabe decided to pay a visit to Derek's apothecary shop.

Derek was glad to see them, proud to show them around his store.

Maggie bought a few things, including some candy for the girls.

It was later in the afternoon when they were ready to leave. Derek had a delivery for Martin, so they offered to take it back with them to save him a trip. Derek had another delivery to make closer, to the poorer side of town, that being a big part of his business. He bid them 'good afternoon' and said he hoped to see them soon.

During supper that evening, a frantic pounding was heard at the door. Gabe and Martin rushed from the table.

A man, that neither of them recognized, was frantic. "I am looking for the doctor."

Martin stepped forward. "I am Dr. Barnes."

The man pointed. "You are needed up the street at the old Johnson house. Derek Spencer has been shot."

Martin grabbed his bag and followed the man, Gabe behind him, Maggie right on their heels.

Hannah met them at the door, hysterical.

Gabe pulled her into an embrace taking her to the couch, trying to calm her down.

Maggie nodded at Gabe and went to the bedroom with Martin.

Derek was in bad shape. He was barely breathing and there was blood everywhere.

"What happened?" demanded Martin.

Another man, who had had been one of the ones to bring him home, judging by the amount of blood all over him, answered, "He was robbed. They shot him when he didn't have enough money to suit them."

Maggie went to the other side of the bed to help Martin. The shot had hit him directly in the chest and the slug had broken apart.

"Damn," said Martin.

Maggie took some rags and started cleaning him up, so Martin could see what he was doing. She ordered one of the men to bring over some more light. Maggie looked over at Derek's face, his lips turning blue. She checked his chest, to see that it had stopped moving.

"Martin, he's not breathing."

Martin stepped back. "He's gone."

Maggie shook her head. "Not yet." She started CPR.

Martin looked at her in horror. "Maggie, what are you doing?"

Pushing up and down on his chest, she counted. "Three...It's called CPR...four... I am trying to get his heart started back up." She blew into his mouth and went back to working on his chest.

Derek coughed slightly.

Realizing the young man was now breathing, Martin wiped the astonishment off his face and went back to work as soon as Maggie moved her hands back.

Martin looked up. "Maggie, you and I need to sit down and have a serious talk after this."

Maggie went back to wiping the blood away, Martin working to pull out fragments. They spent the next hour, repeating the process.

When they were done, Derek was alive, barely, the room looked like something from a horror movie, and Maggie and Martin were completely covered in blood.

Martin handed Maggie a towel for her hands, shaking his head, and whispered, "I don't have high hopes, but he may live long enough for his wife to say goodbye. I will go tell her."

Maggie agreed. The man's color was bad, and he had lost way more blood than any one person should. She grabbed a blanket from the corner to cover him, and as much of the carnage as she could before Hannah came in.

Hannah entered, terrified by what she saw.

Maggie moved to her.

"Hold his hand, talk to him, while you still can."

Hannah indicated that she understood.

Martin pulled up a chair for her, as Maggie stepped out in the hall with Gabe.

The amount of blood on Maggie frightened Gabe for a moment, until he reminded himself that it wasn't actually hers. He asked the question with his eyes, and she responded with a shake of the head.

Gabe rubbed his jawline with his hand. "Poor Hannah, and with a child on the way."

Maggie looked down at the red stains covering her hands.

Gabe put his hand on her back and led her to the parlor. He poured a large glass and made her sit to drink it.

They sat in silence until Martin came down.

Gabe poured him a drink too.

"I don't think he will make it through the night, but thanks to you, Maggie, he was able to open his eyes briefly to tell his wife that he loved her."

Gabe looked at Maggie, then back at Martin. "What do you mean?"

Martin downed half the glass. "He had stopped breathing and Maggie did something to make him start again. What did you call it?"

Maggie didn't even look up. "It's called CPR. It stands for cardiopulmonary resuscitation. It's a technique to keep the blood pumping to the brain and the heart... for all the good that it did."

Gabe placed his hand on her shoulder. "He was able to speak to his wife one last time. That made it worth it."

Martin set his glass down. "Still, it was very impressive. I would be very interested in knowing how to do it."

Maggie nodded.

"Where in the world did you learn it?"

Shit.

"An army doctor in the colonies developed it..." Maggie lied, "...for use in the combat field."

Martin looked at Maggie, then turned to Gabe. "Why don't you take Maggie home to get cleaned up and some rest? I'll stay the rest of the night."

Gabe stood, holding out his hand. "I think that's a good idea." They walked home in silence.

Georgie met them at the door, and after seeing Maggie, she sent Lucy to prepare a bath.

Gabe filled her in.

"Oh, that poor girl. She doesn't have another soul left in this world. She is all alone with a baby on the way."

Maggie bathed and changed into some clean clothes, then crawled into bed.

Gabe brought her up another drink. "Are you alright, Maggie?"

"I'll be fine, Gabe. It's just that what happened was so senseless."

Gabe sat down on the edge of the bed. "No crime in the future?"

"Oh, there is plenty. With six billion people on the planet, it's a given, but we do have hospitals that can handle wounds like Derek's. Modern medicine is a wondrous thing, especially after you see how much it lacks in the 18th century." Maggie turned to Gabe. "You should go check on Hannah. She will need someone to lean on."

"I don't think I should leave you, Maggie. You have had a rough night."

Maggie touched his hand. "Not nearly as rough as Hannah. Go, check on her."

Gabe kissed her head. "Get some rest."

Gabe and Martin didn't return until the next morning. Derek had passed in the middle of the night. They had finally gotten Hannah settled down and the servants were cleaning up the house. Gabe was exhausted.

"Gabe, go get some sleep. I'll go stay with Hannah."

He didn't argue.

Hannah was still resting when Maggie arrived. She jumped right in, instructing the servants on what to do and getting the house back in order. Maggie handled everything, so Hannah wouldn't have to. When she came downstairs, Maggie comforted her, took care of her, and made sure that she ate.

Gabe came over later in the day to help, as well.

In the days following, the local community jumped into action to rally around Hannah. Each family took a different day to bring over food, visit and to help care for her.

The ones who shot Derek were taken into custody. Turned out, they were part of a roving gang who had been robbing businesses and unsuspecting people. Derek was the first and only one that they had done any harm to before they were caught.

Gabe would go over every couple of days just to check in on Hannah. She thought of him as her only remaining family and took comfort in him being there, handling things that she was unable to, physically and mentally.

About a week later, Maggie and Gabe were having breakfast when Gabe suggested they take the day to ride out into the country for a picnic. "I haven't seen much of you in the recent days with everything going on. I think it will be nice to just spend some time together."

Maggie agreed.

Soon, they were out enjoying themselves. They had a wonderful day and arrived back well after dinner. Maggie sensed something was wrong as soon as they came through the door.

Lucy informed them that Hannah had gone into labor that morning and that Georgie and Martin had been gone all day. They rushed over to the house.

When they went into the house, Martin met them at the door, wiping the blood from his hands while shaking his head.

"She didn't make it. The stress from Derek's death, combined with some complications...it was just too much for her body.

Gabe sat down in the nearest chair in shock, his head in his hands closing his eyes. "Not again."

Maggie reached around him, pulling him into a hug, laying her face against his back. Robert and Alex sat in a couple of chairs watching while exchanging worried looks. Gabe never saw his mother and Edwina come down the stairs.

Georgie silently moved to stand in front of Gabe, holding a tiny, precious package wrapped in a towel.

His head was still down when he heard his mother say, "Congratulations, Gabe, it's a girl. You have a daughter."

Gabe's head snapped up, the blood draining from his face. Standing before him was his mother, smiling down at him, rocking a tiny newborn in her arms.

"What do you mean, Mother, 'I have a daughter'?"

Alex stood and came to stand next to his mother to explain. "Gabe, Hannah called me to the house a few days ago. She wanted to make sure, since she had no other family left, that if something were to happen to her, that the child would be cared for. She felt that you were the closest thing that she had left to family, and she named you as the child's guardian in that event. Hannah had me draw up all the paperwork and she signed it. Robert and Edwina witnessed it. It's all legal. The child belongs to you."

Maggie stood next to Gabe in utter astonishment, looking at the sleeping baby, a broad smile spreading across her face, whispering, "Gabe, you're a father."

Gabe looked between her and Alex. "I can't be a father. I know nothing about children. There has to be someone else who can take her."

Maggie touched his shoulder lovingly. "Of course, you can. You are wonderful with children. You are no longer in the military, you have a home, and a stable income.... you have me. Gabe, this is what you have wanted and needed for a very long time."

Robert came to stand behind Alex. "Gabe, if you don't take her, she will end up in an orphanage and, as we all well know, that never goes well for the child."

Maggie took the baby from Georgie, looking at her sweet, little angelic face. She kneeled in front of Gabe, tears in her eyes. "Look at her, Gabe. She doesn't have another soul in this world to care for her. She needs you... and you need her, whether you know it or not."

Gabe stared at Maggie for a moment before dropping his gaze to the baby. He looked down at the innocent, motherless little baby...and instantly fell completely and utterly in love.

He held out his arms as Maggie gingerly placed her there.

"Hello, beautiful girl."

The baby fluttered open her eyes and offered a tiny grin up to her new 'father,' before going back to sleep. She had just hooked her very first man's heart.

That night, Maggie and Gabe lay in his bed, with the baby between them. Gabe couldn't stop looking at his new daughter, wonder in his eyes. Maggie couldn't stop looking at the joy in Gabe's eyes.

She had never seen him so happy. "How does it feel to be a dad?"

Gabe never broke his gaze from the baby. "Strange and wonderful at the same time. It pains me greatly that Hannah did not survive...after all that she lost, and to look so forward to the birth of her child for comfort, only to never get the chance to meet her...it's so unfair...and too much like history repeating itself. But then, I look at this amazing little gift she entrusted me with, and I can't help but be overjoyed...and grateful. Is that wrong of me?"

Maggie shook her head. "Of course not. Look at it this way, all of this would have happened anyway. If you had not been here for her, her baby would have ended up an orphan with no one to care for her and how fair would that have been?" She touched his shoulder. "And Gabe, do you think it was a coincidence that we learned what we did at the church that day, and just happened to stop at the same tavern that Hannah was at that exact moment, only for her to recognize you after all these years? Especially after we were just talking about how much you had wanted to be a father. Sounds a little like divine intervention, if you ask me. Maybe, just maybe, this is God's way of giving you back a little of what you lost all those years ago."

When she put it that way, it seemed to comfort Gabe. "I just hope I can do this. I don't want to let this little one down."

Maggie squeezed his shoulder. "You won't. You are going to be the best father in the world."

Gabe gave her an appreciative look.

"So, DAD, have you thought of a name?"

Gabe looked at her questioningly.

"Well, you can't call her 'the baby' for the rest of her life."

Gabe grinned. "No, I suppose I can't."

Maggie looked at Gabe, as he looked down. "I have always been rather fond of the name Katherine, and it was Hannah and Penny's mother's name."

"I rather like it, Gabe."

He took the baby by the finger. "What do you think, little one?"

The baby smiled.

"Katherine it is. Katherine Hannah Spencer Asheton.... Kat for short."

Maggie laughed looking at the baby. "It's very nice to meet you, Kat Asheton."

The entire family rallied around Gabe to help him adjust to his new-found role as 'father'. Annabelle, who was still nursing Charlie, took over feeding duties until Martin located a wet nurse, a patient of his who had recently lost a baby. The woman was unmarried and had lost her job as a nanny when her employer discovered her pregnant with his child, that had passed away a few days after being born. The lady's name was Cora Rogers, and she was more than agreeable with the idea of a job, especially one caring for a newborn, that would soon take her out of London permanently.

Georgie taught Gabe everything she knew about taking care of babies.

Gabe took to it like a duck to water. After a week, he was an old pro.

Olivia and Izzy were thrilled about their new cousin, showering Kat will all sorts of attention. She had managed to wrap the entire family around her little pinky finger at just one week old.

Gabe made the arrangements for Hannah's funeral. She was buried next to her husband and near her sister in the same church cemetery. Father Tucker performed the funeral. Later that day, he baptized little Kat into the church, officially making Maggie her godmother. He said a prayer over Kat, and then one over Gabe and Maggie for the future.

After another week, everyone had settled into a nice little routine. Maggie had given Gabe a fine baby carriage as one of many gifts. They used it to take little Kat out on daily walks to take in the fresh air. On one particular morning, Maggie was so lost in thought that she didn't realize they had stopped in front of the family law office.

"Are we visiting your brothers today?"

Gabe checked the baby. "I just need to sign a few papers. Hannah left the house and a good deal of money. I want to make sure that it is all held in trust until Kat is old enough for it."

Robert was the only one there when they arrived, and he looked deeply troubled.

"What's on your mind, Robert?" asked Gabe.

Robert looked up. "I have just received a letter from Wyatt. It seems the boy has gotten himself into some trouble in Edinburgh. He is being detained until he makes restitution for some sort of damages he has caused. I am trying to figure out how to handle it. I can't break away to go get him myself, and while it won't take long, truthfully, I would rather his mother and the rest of the family not know about this."

"I can go and get the boy for you," offered Gabe, rocking the carriage.

Robert sighed, looking down at Kat. "Gabe, you have your own responsibilities to handle now, and yours are much more pressing than mine."

Gabe looked down at Kat knowing he was right. He couldn't just up and leave on a moment's notice anymore, he had the baby to think about.

"I can go," offered Maggie.

Gabe and Robert both looked at her.

"I appreciate the offer Maggie, but I cannot ask you to do that."

"It is far too dangerous. Scotland is not like London," added Gabe.

Maggie rolled her eyes. "And London is nothing compared to the colonies in the middle of a war. Gabe, you and I both know that I can take care of myself."

Gabe raised his eyebrow. "I know all too well how you 'take care of yourself'."

Maggie cut him a sideways look. "At any rate, I have my own ship at my disposal. I can sail on a few hours' notice and be there in no time. You just said it wouldn't take long, and if it is a matter of restitution, it should be a simple trip. Besides, you can tell the family I am just going to check on some things for the shipping company. I will back before they know I am even gone."

Robert rubbed his chin in thought. "It would be a quick, easy trip."

Folding his arms, Gabe shook his head. "Maggie, we both know that nothing is ever simple where you are concerned."

Maggie patted him on the back. "And we both know that you worry too much. Gabe, I will be fine."

10 CHAPTER TEN

The next day, at breakfast, Gabe tried to convince Maggie not to go.

Maggie was resolute. She kissed Kat and Gabe each on the top of the head. "Spend this time enjoying your daughter. She will be grown before you know it. I will be back soon."

He walked her to the door, pulling her into an embrace, whispering in her ear, "Please be careful, and if you are not back in a timely manner, I will be coming to get you."

With that, Maggie and Onyx were on their way to Edinburgh. They enjoyed the trip, not having much time alone together of late.

Clear sailing and three days later, they stepped off the boat in Edinburgh.

Maggie instructed Captain Russell to stay close to the ship as she wasn't expecting this to take very long. She mounted Onyx and headed off into town. She didn't wear a gown today, only her leather trousers and peasant top covered by a long duster-like coat, sword at her back and daggers in her boots in case of trouble.

The letter that Robert received from Wyatt gave an address where to send the money for the damages. Maggie had read over the letter a few times on the trip over, and something seemed odd about it. Reading between the lines, it basically said, 'Dad, send money' with an address, not 'Dad, come save me, I am in terrible trouble.'

Edinburgh was a very unusual little town. One side was older, darker, and much more ancient with lots of beautiful, gothic stonework, while the other side was on a definitive upswing with new construction going up all around.

Maggie preferred the older side. There was something a little more magical—primordial—about it that seemed to call out to something deep inside of her. This town made her feel very connected to it for some reason.

The streets were crowded; the town appeared to be bursting at the seams. Maggie and Onyx made their way through the streets, most people giving Onyx a wide berth once they caught sight of him, seemingly out of fear of him. Maggie even saw a few people cross themselves as he passed. He asserted his domain over the very ground they stood on, and he dared anyone to question his authority.

Maggie managed to locate the address on the letter; it was in the older part of town. She dismounted and looked for somewhere to leave Onyx. There was a hitching post close by that mysteriously cleared when Maggie approached it. She knew there was no point tying him up, so she just told him to wait there. She knew he was safe, no one even coming close to him; rather going out of their way to get *away* from him.

That's weird.

She shook her head, locating the address on the letter that Wyatt had sent. When she opened the door, she knew why he only asked for money, not help. Maggie was standing in the doorway of...a whorehouse.

Maggie mumbled to herself. "Like father, like son."

Women were in various stages of undress, from mostly covered to full-on, 'the carpet matches the drapes,' completely naked. Maggie looked around for someone who might be able to help her.

The 'madam' of the establishment made her way over to Maggie, looking her up and down. "If yer looking for work, yer a little older than I care to hire."

Maggie put her hands on her hips. "I am NOT looking for work. Why do people always assume that?"

The lady shrugged. "I do have a couple of men available if yer willing to wait until they've finished up with their current clients...if ye have the money, that is."

Rolling her eyes, Maggie mumbled, "No penicillin yet, no thank you."

"What did ye say?"

Maggie cleared her voice. "I am looking for a man by the name of Wyatt Asheton. I was told I could find him here."

The lady folded her arms and stared at Maggie. "And, what would ye be wanting with him?"

Folding her own arms to mimic the other woman's stance, Maggie leaned in. "I understand he has run up a bill that needs settling, and I am here to pay it."

A sly smile grew across the lady's mouth. "Well, why didn't ye say so? Come with me, lass."

The madam led Maggie through the sea of bodies—
Maggie trying her best to avoid touching anyone—to the
back of the building and into a small office.

"Please sit," she said, flipping through a book. "Mr.
Asheton is one of my best customers, but he seems to be
a little cash-strapped lately, letting his bill run up. He
takes a room here with some of my best girls when he
comes to town and that can get.... expensive."

She began writing down his charges and the
numbers were adding up by the minute. The madam laid
out a rather lengthy bill in front of Maggie. "This is the
boy's total."

Maggie looked at the lady in astonishment. "How many
women does he keep in that room?"

The madam raised an eyebrow. "The boy has a very...
healthy...appetite. Sometimes three, four at a time.
He is a very popular client."

Maggie rubbed her forehead. "Is Romeo here now?"

"Oh aye, today's charges are at the bottom," she
pointed.

Maggie leaned forward. "I will pay his bill, but I want
something in return."

The madam opened the bedroom door of the room
Wyatt was in and told all the girls inside to leave.
Three half-dressed girls came out into the hall,
scattering.

Three? Really? Ew!

"Mr. Asheton, I have a very special surprise for you."

The madam backed out of the room, motioning to
Maggie that he was all hers.

Maggie walked into the room to find Wyatt Asheton
lying on in his back, propped against the back of the bed,

a sheet draped strategically over his private
parts, and smiling a dreamy smile.

*Damn! Another Asheton man that looked just like Gabe.
Where did these people get these genes from? No wonder
he was a 'favorite' client.*

"So, you are my special surprise?"

Maggie simply nodded and smiled.

He rubbed his hands together eagerly in anticipation. "I
can't wait!"

She strolled over to the foot of the bed, dragging her
fingers along the wall in a sensual way. With a devilish
smile, she let her index finger glide up the front of his
leg, all the way up to his chest, and underneath his chin.
She leaned close and let out a low, sultry, guttural
growl, then laughed softly.

Wyatt Asheton licked his lips, his mind filled
with lustful expectations.

"You're new around here, because I wouldn't
forget someone like you."

As he leaned over to kiss her, she stepped back,
just shy of his reach, and winked at him.

"You're going to tease me like that?" he asked,
playfully.

She shrugged innocently in response as she bit her lip.

Maggie moved forward and planted her hands on the
bed, her face close to his. She breathed in deeply, moved
to brush her lips to his, and as he closed his
eyes, she slid her fingers lightly up the length of his
spine, then used her hand...to abruptly smack him on
the back of his head.

Wyatt's eyes flew open wide as he reached to cover the
spot with both his hands, looking offended and
hurt; not comprehending what had just transpired.

A thought suddenly occurred to him as a wicked smile appeared on his face.

"Oh! You are one of 'those' girls that I have heard about. I have never been spanked before, but, if you do it, I think I just might like it."

Maggie rolled her eyes. "If your parents had spanked you, maybe you wouldn't be running up bills in whorehouses that you can't pay, begging your father to come bail you out."

Wyatt gave her a puzzled look.

"Your father sent me," she clarified.

He looked even more confused, "My father sent me a whore?"

Reaching over, Maggie grabbed him by the ear, pulling him out of bed and making him yelp.

"I am NOT a whore, you nitwit." She picked up his clothes and smacked them into his chest. "You can call me Aunt Maggie. Now get dressed! You are going back to London."

Wyatt's face went pale, as he stuttered, "AUNT Maggie?"

She nodded.

He pulled on his trousers as fast as he could, trying to cover his nakedness. "My father sent you? Does he know..."

Maggie finished for him. "That you are holing up in a whorehouse running up a bill you can't pay? No! And if you want to keep it that way, you will pull yourself together and be ready to leave this place in the next five minutes."

Wyatt started gathering his things. "But my bill..."

She picked up one of his shirts with her two fingers, smelling the sweat and sex on it, flinging it in his direction, a disgusted look on her face. "I paid your bill and so help me, if you come back here and run up another one, I will tell your mother and your grandmother what you have been doing."

"Please don't!" Wyatt's eyes grew wide as he grabbed the last of his things. "I'm ready to go."

There was tavern nearby and it was after dinnertime. Maggie dragged him in and found a table, ordering for them.

Wyatt took a sip of his ale and asked, "So, how are you my Aunt Maggie?"

"I am not technically your aunt, but your Uncle Gabe and I are the best of friends. We were in London visiting when your letter came. We were under the impression that you were picking up a shipment of books for your brother."

He blew out a breath. "I was, but I got… 'distracted'."

She shot him a look of disdain. "I have a feeling you get 'distracted' a great deal."

He attempted to hide his smirk as he looked down into his tankard of ale. "Well, I do love women."

Maggie leaned over. "I wouldn't call what you were doing 'love'."

Their food came, and Wyatt ate like he had not eaten in days. Maggie filled him in on his grandmother's marriage, his Uncle Alex's wedding, and on his Uncle Gabe's new state of fatherhood.

Wyatt looked overwhelmed. "I guess I have missed a great deal."

Maggie finished her food, and asked, "Do you actually have a shipment of books to take back or was that just an excuse?"

He drank down his ale. "Oh, I do indeed have the books. I have someone keeping them safe for me. I would not let Henry down like that."

Maggie softened a little. "You love your brother, don't you?"

"He has always taken care of me, and when I didn't want to become a lawyer like everyone else in the family, he let me come to work with him."

She started to warm up to the kid, and he was still, very much, a kid... that needed to get home.

They collected the book shipment from the person holding it. They had to rent a horse and wagon to get them since there were so many. Maggie followed him on Onyx back to the ship. After everything was loaded up, Maggie looked at Wyatt and Captain Russell. "Captain, I want you to take young Wyatt and his shipment back to London."

The Captain eyed her suspiciously. "You are not coming back with us?"

Maggie's answer was firm, "No! I have some business to attend to here." She pulled a letter out of her bag. "I want you to return in two weeks. Take this letter to Gabe. He is not going to be happy, but whatever you do, do not let him convince you to come back sooner. That is an ORDER! I promised to get his nephew home safely and that is what I need you to do. I will be fine."

She turned to Wyatt. "You have three days to come up with a good story for why you were detained here. Make it a good one for your parents, and remember, I had better never catch you in a whorehouse again."

He grinned and nodded. "Yes, Aunt Maggie."

They went to board the ship.

"One more thing, Wyatt," she called, and he turned, "Get your new step-grandfather to check you over for...anything you may have picked up on your little adventure."

He gave her a confused look, waved, and boarded the ship.

11 CHAPTER ELEVEN

Maggie went back into town and, using the information from Henry's letter, left word for Quinn MacGregor at the tavern, but no one seemed to know who he was. She took a room for the night.

She felt bad about deceiving Gabe, but she knew he would find a way to stop her if she told him ahead of time what her plans were. As soon as she'd found out she was coming to Scotland, she'd made up her mind to get some answers. She'd brought the bottle, the book, her sword, and the map. She might never get back to Scotland again, so it was now or never.

The next morning, Maggie bought some provisions. She had the map from the book and a current one of Scotland. If she read it right, her destination was only two long days' ride out. There was nothing suggesting anything was in that spot except a very old map and Maggie's gut feeling. She would not rest until she found out for certain.

The first day passed uneventfully on a well-traveled road. Onyx seemed very happy to be out to run as fast as he cared to. She really needed to take him out more often. They managed to find a very small tavern for the night and Maggie talked with the tavern owner.

He was unaware of anything in that area, but Maggie had to find out for herself.

After a night's rest, the pair got an early start the next morning

The second day's ride was tougher. The road was nothing more than partial, narrow paths
through woods, followed by stretches of open, rocky areas with nothing to see. Maggie could only hope she was headed in the right direction; there were no markers or people to ask.

Late that afternoon, Maggie came upon another stretch of woods. Passing through, something felt off, like she was being watched.

Onyx must have felt it as well, snorting and pawing at the ground, alerting her to the danger around them.

Maggie readied herself.

As she left the woods into the next open area, three highwaymen attacked.

Maggie whipped out her sword, striking the first man across the chest from atop Onyx, causing a superficial wound. She kicked another in the face with her boot, sending him flying backward.

The third man pulled her off the horse.

She rolled onto her feet. The man rushed her, but she dodged, twisting as he ran by, swinging her sword to slice him across the back. The sword sliced deep, blood spewing, and he fell to the ground, unmoving.

The man she had kicked came after her with his own sword overhanded, screaming.

Stopping his swing with her own sword, she held him in place long enough to knee him in the groin. He loosened his grip, and Maggie took the opportunity to swing down and slice open his leg. As he went down, she plucked a dagger from her boot and sunk it into his chest.

He fell forward, dead.

The first man came at Maggie from behind; she felt him before she saw him. She tossed her sword up in the air, catching and flipping it as it came back down, sinking the sword backward and into the chest of the man directly behind her.

All three men lay dead around her.

Maggie walked over to calm Onyx, stroking his mane, leading him to a large boulder. The adrenaline was wearing off and she leaned back against it, attempting to calm her heartbeat before she passed out. She closed her eyes, opening them only when she felt a single cold, blade against her throat, an arm around her chest and heard a voice say, "Where did ye get that sword?"

Another man came around in front of Maggie, taking the sword from her hand.

He nodded back at the man holding Maggie. "It's one of ours."

The man holding Maggie tightened his grip. "I won't ask again, lass, where did you get the sword?"

Maggie let out the breath she was holding. "I have had that sword for many years. I am rather fond of it and I would appreciate it if you gave it back."

The man in front of her leaned close to look at her. "Ye are not Scottish nor English. Where are ye from?"

Maggie debated answering until the arm around her tightened. "I am from the colonies; Virginia. That is where I acquired the sword."

He stepped closer. "There are no MacGregors of our clan in the colonies."

Maggie narrowed her eyes. "Are you MacGregors?"

They didn't answer.

"I am searching for a man by the name of Quinn MacGregor."

The man holding the knife demanded, "And, why are ye looking for him?"

A feeling urged Maggie to tell them the truth. "I have acquired a book that I think he was looking for. It may have been stolen from his family, and I wanted to see about returning it."

The two men looked at each other and the one in front asked, "What book?"

Maggie felt a few drops of blood trickle from the blade at her throat. "I will be happy to tell you if you lower that dagger. It will be hard to talk if you get too excited and slit my throat by accident."

The man in front nodded.

The one holding the knife lowered it and moved beside her, his blade still aimed in her direction.

"Thank you," Maggie said as she wiped her neck. "It is a book of Celtic Faerie Tales; very old and unique. Quinn MacGregor came into a bookstore in London last year looking for one just like it. I received the information from the shopkeeper and was on my way to try and locate him. I desperately need to speak with him. Do you know where I can find him?"

The man with the knife lowered it a bit. "Why would ye so desperately need to talk to me?"

Maggie pointed at him. "YOU are Quinn MacGregor?"

He folded his arms, planting his feet. "I am!"

Leaning back against the rock, she looked over at the dead men. "Is this how you roll out the welcome wagon around here, by attacking poor, helpless women traveling alone?"

The other man spoke up, "Those men are nay MacGregor; they're filthy MacLarens and aye, they would attack a helpless woman. But, then again... ye do not look very helpless to me."

Quinn took a step closer to Maggie. "The book. Where is it?"

Maggie folded her arms in response. "I will give it to you, but I will be needing some answers in return."

Quinn leaned in close. "Or, we could just take it."

Maggie moved even closer to his face, her smile mischievous. "You could try."

Quinn called back to the other man, "Check her horse."

Maggie shook her head. "I wouldn't do that if I were you."

The man started towards Onyx and tried to take his reins.

Onyx reared up on his hind legs, knocked the man on his backside and used his front hooves to hit the man square in the chest, sending him sliding across the ground.

Quinn turned to look. "Are ye alright, Evan?"

Evan got up while brushing himself off. "Aye... I'll live."

Maggie watched as the man climbed to his feet, confounded. "Huh! Onyx must be losing his touch. I have never seen anyone actually get back up after he does that."

"Does that a lot, does he?" Quinn looked back at Maggie.

She bobbed her head. "More than you would think."

Quinn looked back at Onyx, eyeing him up and down with a pensive look, stroking his chin.

Maggie noticed Quinn looking him over. She flipped her hand towards Onyx. "Care to give him a go yourself?"

The man called Evan grinned. "Yes Brother, why don't ye give him a go?"

Maggie looked between them and asked, "You two are brothers?"

Quinn sighed, realizing this was not going the way he wanted and decided a change of tactics was in order. "Aye, we are Quinn and Evan MacGregor. And who might ye be?"

Maggie decided she could get more flies with honey. "My name is Maggie Bishop."

Quinn nodded his head. "Pleased to meet ye, Maggie Bishop. Now, why don't we have that talk?"

Maggie walked over to Onyx, stroking his mane while taking the book out of his saddlebag. She held it up. "First of all. Is this the book you have been looking for?"

Quinn looked shocked, stepping forward to take it from her. "Aye, it is indeed." He flipped through it, then looked up at Maggie. "Where did you get it?"

Maggie shrugged. "I found it on the doorstep of my home in Virginia. It was wrapped in brown paper with my name on it and nothing else. I thought a friend had sent it to me, but I found out it did not come from him."

Evan came to stand next to his brother. "How the devil did it end up that far away?"

Quinn shook his head in disbelief, flipping the book over in his hands, before looking up again. "And the sword? Did that just appear as well?"

Maggie frowned. "No. That I bought off of a very strange peddler about 13 years ago."

Quinn and Evan exchanged looks, both thoroughly confused.

Evan spoke, "That's just not possible."

"I am afraid it is." Maggie tilted her head. "I only recently was able to make out the MacGregor crest on it. The same crest on the inside of the front cover of that book."

Quinn looked at Maggie hard. "And what led ye out this way to look for me?"

Maggie turned to pull out the map. She unfolded it and handed it to him. "This. It was hidden in the cover of that book."

Fear settled into his Quinn's face when he took it and saw what it was. He handed it to Evan, who developed the same look on his face.

"I have looked at every current map of Scotland that I can find. Not one of them shows anything being where that old map is marked. I know there's something there that I am supposed to find...I just don't know what or why."

Quinn looked at her harshly. "And what makes ye think that?"

Maggie sighed. "It is a very long story, not that you would believe it."

Evan looked up. "Ye would be surprised by what we would believe."

Quinn looked her over, trying to make an important decision. He finally spoke, "I think ye should come with us back to our home. Our mother will want to meet you."

They rode for two hours, barely speaking. The two brothers were the epitome of every Scottish Highlander romance novel cover ever printed...living, breathing clichés. They were tall with broad shoulders, dressed in tartans that clung to their bodies in all the right the places, accenting their finer features. They both had long dark hair, tied back in long plaits, that displayed their finely chiseled facial features, good teeth, and bluish-green eyes.

She should have immediately recognized them as brothers. Riding their horses—solid white with not a speck of any other color on them—was a sight to behold.

It was getting late and Maggie was tired and hungry after a long day. "Are we there yet?"

Evan looked back at her strangely. "It's not much further, lass."

Maggie was doing her best to keep her bearings, trying to figure out if they were still on the map's path. She thought they were, but she could not tell for sure. She was just about to ask when 'it' came out of nowhere and completely engulfed them.

A thick, heavy fog rolled out, so dark and dense that Maggie could not even see Onyx's head in front of her.

Maggie heard Quinn's voice beside her on her right. "Don't worry lass, ye have nothing to fear."

Evan's voice came from the left. "We can see, even if ye can't."

Onyx was unusually calm; he didn't balk or complain, just stayed the course until they were through it.

Once past it, Maggie looked back. The fog clung to a thick forest of trees that acted as a protective wall. What Maggie saw in front of her was nothing short of astounding.

Stretched out before them was the most gothic, medieval fortress-like structure that Maggie had ever seen. Its slate-gray stone majestically rose up, surrounded by a tall, stone wall that was entered through on a lowered bridge that could be raised to protect the inhabitants inside.

The mysterious power of this place ebbed like a pulsing heartbeat. It was ancient, mysterious, mystifying, and... oddly comforting to Maggie.

They rode into the enclosure, and much to Maggie's surprise, there was an entire little community between the gate entrance and the massive front doors of the castle. The compound was much bigger than it appeared from the outside, containing small homes and businesses. There was a market area in the middle, full of buyers and sellers. Several children were running around, playing. It was its own little village, much like Maggie's home on the estate.

The MacGregor brothers led Maggie inside the main house, both disappearing while giving her a few minutes to look around. The inside was stunning. The front foyer faced a grand, sweeping staircase. To the right was a room that appeared to be a library that doubled as a comfortable family room. Further up, to the left was a long table used for meals that had to be 25 – 30 feet long, flanked with benches.

Looking closer, Maggie could see the staircase was two-sided, forming a long hallway upstairs that overlooked the dining area. Ornately carved fireplaces were all over the place, the biggest one beneath the staircase, forming a type of open-pit area. Tapestries hung on every wall, giving the entire place a warm, inviting feel.

When Quinn reappeared, Maggie turned to him. "Your home is magnificent."

A woman's voice replied, "Thank ye, we are quite fond of it."

The voice came from the staircase. An exquisite woman stood halfway up the staircase; her skin was porcelain-white, her very dark hair wavy, and highlighted by silver streaks, hanging loosely all the way down to her waist. The bluish-green eyes were a dead giveaway that this was 'Mother'. The woman glided down the stairs, never breaking her gaze from Maggie.

"My sons tell me that I have ye to thank for the return of a book that was...misplaced." She moved closer to Maggie to get a better look. "Are ye hurt?"

"No. Why do you ask?"

Quinn walked past his mother and stated, "It's not her blood."

Maggie caught sight of her reflection in the mirror in the foyer. Her leather trousers and duster coat were covered in the blood of the men who attacked her earlier, even her face was covered in a splatter pattern. She looked like someone who had just stepped out of a horror movie. "Forgive me. I ran into some trouble along the way."

The woman turned to her son for an explanation.

Quinn grabbed an apple off the table and bit into it. "It's MacLaren blood. Three of them attacked her on the path. She killed them...all by herself."

Evan appeared from the side hall. "With this sword."

The woman turned, taking the sword from her son, her eyes wide with concern as she examined it.

"I just checked. It did not come from our collection."

The three of them looked at each other with puzzled looks.

The woman turned back to Maggie. "Forgive my rudeness. I did not introduce myself. I am Aurnia MacGregor, the Lady of this house."

"I am Maggie Bishop."

"Well, Maggie Bishop, I am very interested in speaking with ye. Please, stay on as our guest. It will be suppertime soon. Perhaps ye would like to clean up a bit with a bath. It appears ye have had a trying day."

Maggie looked down. "Thank you. I appreciate your invitation and will gladly accept the bath."

Lady Aurnia had a servant girl by the name of Flora show Maggie to a bedroom.

Much to her surprise, it looked a great deal like Maggie's room at home, with a large four poster bed, with red bed drapes and thick, heavy matching curtains. There was a fireplace at the foot of the bed, a hot bath already waiting for her, and windows overlooking the courtyard. Flora had also brought up a clean gown for her to change into.

Maggie stripped down, her clothes so filthy she was afraid they wouldn't come clean. She sank into the tub, dunking herself completely to wash her hair. Flora had left a wonderful lavender soap, and when she was done, Maggie looked and smelled like a different person. She brushed out her hair that was mostly dry now and headed down the stairs towards voices. When she looked down, the two brutally handsome Highlanders had multiplied into four, and all four were staring right at her.

Be still my heart...and other womanly parts. It's going to be a long night.

Lady Aurnia MacGregor stood at the door of the library, sipping from a glass, watching her sons carrying on in the hall. All these boys over the age of 30 and not one of them had taken a wife, nor given her a grandchild. It wasn't just that she wanted grandchildren, she needed them. Her boys were the last of a line that must continue. It could not die out.

The secrets they protected were too important and the line needed to endure to do that. She had secretly hoped that one of them, at least, would show up with a bastard child, but they were all too careful with their activities for that. It wasn't that women didn't want them, they just didn't want wives. It was much too easy for them to relieve their needs with willing women than to bother with the trouble of taking a bride.

Lady Aurnia noticed they had all gone quiet. She looked to see what had caused it—and smiled. Maggie Bishop had cleaned up nicely. She was a beautiful woman when she wasn't covered in blood and there was something different and very special about her. Lady Aurnia felt it as soon as the woman had stepped foot in the house, even before she laid eyes on her.

Maggie Bishop was not here by accident...there were other forces at play.

Lady Aurnia hoped that her desires had been heard and that this young lass was the answer to all her problems. "Maggie, join us, please." Lady Aurnia moved around the boys in the hall, taking Maggie's hand once she reached the bottom of the stairs.

"Ye look very lovely this evening. That gown looks as if it was made for ye."

"Thank you, Lady Aurnia. I am grateful for your hospitality."

Lady Aurnia smiled. "Come, meet my other boys. Quinn and Evan, you know; this is Reade and Logan. Boys, this is Maggie Bishop."

They all nodded in acknowledgment.

"Come, supper is ready."

Maggie had not realized how hungry she was until the aroma of the food hit her nose, and she devoured her supper. Sated, she studied her host. Something told Maggie that this woman had the answers she was looking for. "Lady Aurnia, please tell me about this lovely place of yours. I have never seen anything quite like it before."

"This place has been in the MacGregor family for well over a thousand years. It was built as a fortress to protect... all that is within its walls. My family has always been here."

Maggie looked at her confused. "MacGregor isn't your married name?"

"Nay, I did not take my husband's name. He took mine to protect my family lineage and maintain the MacGregor name. It is very important that this particular line of the MacGregor family carries on." She shot a shaming look around the table at her sons.

They all looked down pretending not to hear her.

"Forgive my ignorance, I am not familiar with the ways of Scotland," said Maggie, "Aren't all of the families part of the same clan?"

Lady Aurnia set down her glass. "That is the usual way of all the other clans and the main MacGregor clan, as well, but we are members of a different... branch if ye will. We maintain the MacGregor name, but we live aside from the main clan's rules. We make our own."

Maggie nodded. "I am very familiar with having to make your own rules. I have had to make a few myself."

Logan looked at Maggie. "Quinn said ye were from the colonies. Were ye born there?"

Maggie hesitated to answer.

Lady Aurnia noticed.

Finally, Maggie spoke, "I have lived in the Virginia colony nearly all my life. I have an estate there now."

"Is it your family's estate or husband's estate? Do they always let ye travel alone in dangerous places?"

Maggie wiped her mouth with her napkin. "It is MY estate. I purchased it, I built it up, made it profitable, and I alone run it. I have no husband and... I have no family here. My only family is a close friend and the people that I support."

"What are the colonies like?" asked Quinn, "We do not get much news out here."

"The colonies are at war with the British, fighting for their independence. It is dangerous in places. The colonies have experienced some losses, but they will prevail in the end."

Lady Aurnia looked at her oddly. "Ye say that as if ye know it for sure."

"Did I? I meant that I hoped they would."

Careful Maggie.

"Where did ye learn to fight like that?" Evan asked, making an abrupt change of subject.

Maggie took a sip of her wine, trying to figure out how to word it. "My friend Gabe taught me. He is an excellent swordsman. I was attacked many years ago by two men and vowed to never let myself be vulnerable again. That was when I acquired the sword from an old man who said that he felt like it was meant for me."

They all looked up at her, curious.

"I hope you don't mind me asking, but you said that my sword was not one of yours. What did you mean by that?"

No one answered.

"I came here looking for some answers, and I am happy to answer any of your questions, but, please, I am begging you...I have had things happen to me that I cannot explain, and I find myself unable to rest at night because of them."

Lady Aurnia finally spoke, "Our family was gifted with a set of those very specially made swords many generations ago to use in defense of our home, if it were ever necessary. Those swords are kept in a special, hidden location. Evan went to check when you arrived, and all of our swords are accounted for, which begs the question, how did ye end up with one just like it?"

Maggie nodded. "And the book?"

Quinn looked around before he answered, "That did indeed come from our library—a library that is concealed just as the swords are. As soon as I noticed it missing, I left here and traveled for months looking for it, but never found it. And then ye turned up here with it, looking for us, with a map straight to our home."

Maggie sucked in a quick breath. "Which begs another question: Why is the map that I found in that book, the only one that shows this place exists? No other map of

Scotland shows anything here, much less a place this big that contains as many people as this does."

Lady Aurnia laid down her napkin. "It has been a very long day. Let's table this talk until another time. Maggie, please feel free to make yourself at home here. If ye need anything, please do not hesitate to ask. I will bid ye all good night."

All the men stood, each moving in turn to kiss their mother on the cheek.

Maggie smiled at her as she left.

Then, the men excused themselves, leaving Maggie sitting there alone with only her thoughts.

Later that night, Maggie lay in bed wide awake. Every time she closed her eyes, she saw the men who attacked her earlier. She knew she was justified in killing them, but that didn't help to ease her conscience. That, combined with the million other questions running through her head, meant that she needed help getting to sleep. Deciding a drink might do the trick, she slipped downstairs with the bedside candlestick to see what she could find.

The best place to look was probably the library. She tip-toed her way in, looking around. Bingo! Maggie located a buffet table with several decanters.

Well, Lady Aurnia did say to make myself at home.

Maggie sniffed the different ones until she settled on a stronger whisky.

When in Scotland.

She poured a glass and took a sip. *Wow! That was good stuff.*

The fire was out, so the candle was the only source of light. Maggie sat in one of the big easy chairs for a while. After finishing her second glass, the warmth kicked in, making her think she might be able to drift off. She headed back upstairs with the candle to light the way.

At the top of the stairs, a sudden draft of wind blew out the flame.

Damn it! Maggie had nothing to relight it with and the only other light was coming from the moon streaming through the windows. She was going to have to wing it.

Maggie grabbed the stair rail and used it to guide herself. *Now, where was her room?* It was further back, the fourth door to the right. The whisky kicked in and Maggie's head became foggy. How many doors had she passed? She felt along the wall, reaching the third door and starting toward her room when she was grabbed from behind, an arm around her waist and a hand over her mouth.

Maggie froze when a voice whispered, "Let me show ye what we do to thieves in this house."

She couldn't scream; her feet were off the floor, she had no weapons, and she was being dragged down the hall. Maggie did the only thing she could do. She bit as hard as she could into the hand over her mouth.

He yelled "son of a bitch" and loosened his grip.

It was enough for Maggie's feet to hit the floor and for her to get one arm free. She reared back with her elbow as hard as she could, and met solid muscle, sending pain shooting up through her entire arm.

"Fuck!" she shrieked. Maggie stomped her back right foot down on the outside of his right foot. She then threw her weight forward, pulling him down and tripping him over her foot.

He hit the floor with a heavy thud.

Maggie jumped over him and tried to run, but he caught her, pulling her back until he was able to get on top of her, straddling her, pinning her arms back.

Her legs were free, so she pushed up hard against the floor, creating a rocking motion, until she propelled them both over, so she was straddling him, he still holding her arms. They sat there locked in that position for a few seconds, their faces inches from each other before doors started flying open, and the hall became illuminated by candles.

Lady Aurnia came out of her room, shaking her head. "Maggie, I see ye have met my oldest son, Duncan. Duncan, will ye kindly release our house guest, Maggie Bishop."

Duncan looked at his mother. "Our guest? I thought she was a thief."

"She is our guest."

Duncan looked up at Maggie and she down at him. They were still locked in the same position, neither willing to yield.

All of Duncan's brothers came out to watch, arms folded, and grinning from ear to ear.

"Duncan! I SAID release her," his mother demanded again.

"Well, Mother," he said dryly, "as ye can see, I am not holding HER down, so can you kindly tell your guest to get off ME?"

Duncan loosened his hold and Maggie released hers.

She rolled off him, breathing heavy, while holding her elbow and curling on her side.

Duncan jumped to his feet. "Mother, who is this woman?"

Lady Aurnia moved to Maggie's side, looking her over. "This is the woman who ye just badly injured." She turned to Quinn and Evan. "Help her up, gently."

They moved to her side.

Maggie shook her head. "I'm alright. I'll be fine...just give me a minute to catch my breath."

Lady Aurnia kneeled by her side. "Maggie, I must insist upon checking ye over to make sure ye are well. Let the boys help ye to your bed."

Sighing, Maggie nodded; Quinn carefully picked her up, carried her into her room, and laid her on the bed.

"Evan, go downstairs and bring up a bottle of Quinn's 'special' whisky." Lady Aurnia cut Duncan a look.

Duncan turned to Logan. "What is going on around here?"

Logan patted him on the back. "Come downstairs and I will fill ye in. And pay ye the wager ye just won."

"What wager?"

Logan laughed. "The one we all made about who would be the first one to end up in a tumble with her."

Lady Aurnia checked Maggie's elbow. "I do not think it is broken, but it is badly bruised. I am sorry for my son's unacceptable behavior. I will be having a wee chat with him shortly." She handed Maggie a glass. "Drink this. It will help with the pain."

Maggie accepted the drink. "Thank you, but I am really fine. It was my own fault for going downstairs to get a drink when I couldn't sleep. I was too wired up from everything that happened today. I shouldn't have left the room."

"Nonsense. I told ye to make yourself at home and I meant it."

Maggie sipped the drink and suddenly felt woozy. She tried hard to fight the feeling that was rapidly overcoming her.

Quinn leaned over and whispered, "It's alright Maggie. We just gave ye something to help ye sleep through the pain. Don't fight it and ye will feel better in the morning."

Everything went black.

12 CHAPTER TWELVE

Maggie woke up late the next morning. She
groaned, trying to move, sore from head to toe. Sitting up
on the edge of the bed, pain shot through her
arm; looking down, her arm from elbow to wrist was
black and blue, as if she had elbowed a brick wall instead
of a man.

*Talk about abs of steel. Come to think of it, that must be
a family trait.*

Maggie thought about the day before when
Onyx had kicked and trampled Evan... he had gotten
back up and brushed himself off as if it were nothing.

Standing, she looked around. Her own clothes were
washed and folded on a chair nearby and water had been
left in a basin for her to wash up. She dressed in her
trousers and duster to cover her bruises, made sure her

daggers were strapped in her boots, and headed out into the hall.

As soon as she stepped outside of her room…she heard several voices in a heated discussion. She couldn't make out the words, but someone was angry. Taking the first step to descend, she saw Duncan stomp out of the library, looking furious.

He caught sight of her and shot her an irate look, before slamming the front door on his way out.

Lady Aurnia appeared from the same room, smiling at Maggie when she saw her. "Good morning, Maggie. Please come down and let me get ye some breakfast."

A few minutes later, the two women were seated at the long table in the dining area; they were alone.

"How are ye feeling this morning Maggie? How is yer arm?"

"It's perfectly fine," she lied. "Lady Aurnia, I want to apologize if I have caused you trouble with my presence in your home. That certainly was not my intention."

Lady Aurnia tilted her head, confused.

"I overheard the arguing this morning when I came downstairs. I do not want to upset your family."

Lady Aurnia nodded in acknowledgment. "Och! Maggie dinna fash yourself over that. I live in a home with five stubborn, pig-headed Highlander men. If I do not hear arguing daily, I am checking to see how many of them have taken ill."

Maggie laughed. "All sons? No daughters?"

"Oh…I wish. I love my sons more than anything, but all of them are well past marrying age and I have not one grandchild to show for it." She looked at Maggie thoughtfully. "Why are ye not married, Maggie?"

Maggie shrugged. "I have no need of a husband. I don't need the money or the title. I have managed just fine on my own."

"And ye have not found anyone you wanted to be with...for love?"

Maggie set down her glass. "There was someone...but things did not work out. He was meant to take a different path...I needed to make sure that he did."

Lady Aurnia noticed the sadness in Maggie's words and sensed there was a great deal more to the story. She laid her hand over Maggie's, giving her a concerned, motherly look. "Maggie, if there is something ye ever wish to talk about, I am a very good listener, and anything ye say will never leave these walls. Ye have my word upon that."

Maggie nodded as Lady Aurnia patted her hand.

"There is one thing, however, that I must insist that ye tell me about though."

Maggie's eyes widened, waiting for the worst.

"You must tell me about... the trousers."

Looking down, Maggie chuckled, letting out a nervous breath. "Oh, yes, the trousers. I have a rather spirited horse who likes to ride hard. It was impossible to keep up with him side saddle and...sword training was out of the question in a gown...so I came up with this idea. I had my seamstress stitch up several pairs of these trousers out of leather."

Lady Aurnia looked closer. "Fascinating."

"I also had her make a tie-on skirt that I could wear to at least appear somewhat proper, as needed. It is held by one string that I can pull loose and shed in an instant in case I need to move quickly. This coat also helps to cover the trousers." Maggie stood to give her a better look. "I know it must seem like a very strange idea and you must think me terribly unladylike for it…"

Lady Aurnia raised her eyebrow. "Actually, I was thinking it was an ingenious idea and I was wondering where I might get some for myself."

They continued chatting, and Maggie noticed the house was very quiet. "Where is everyone?"

"Oh, the boys are outside getting ready for the men. They train our small castle army every few days, in case we need to defend our home." A sudden, devilish thought came to Lady Aurnia. "Why don't we go watch for a while? Ye might find it...intriguing."

'Intriguing' was not the word Maggie would use to describe the 'training' going on outside.

She got her first good look at Duncan MacGregor...and oh, what a look it was.

He and Reade were involved in a sword fight. Duncan was stripped to his waist, wearing nothing but his tartan and his boots. He stood a foot higher than all his brothers and made the rest of them look like they needed to hit the gym…. hard.

No wonder her arm was so bruised.

His very tanned, muscular body glistened with sweat. He had the same facial features as his brothers, only more defined, a definition that only came with age. His hair hung loose to his waist, wavy and dark like his mother's.

Maggie couldn't help but stare at this man, thinking of a great many things that she could do to him.

Lady Aurnia followed Maggie's gaze, then looked back at her, amused, a wide smile spreading across her face. There may be hope for some grandchildren in her future after all.

Duncan was taking out his anger from his earlier conversation with his mother on his brother Reade, and Reade was taking the opportunity to get in his head to mess with him. When they were close enough for no one else to hear, Reade would say little things to throw off his concentration.

"Seems ye have a little pent-up, aggression ye need to get out brother." "You are not frustrated from last night, are ye?" "How long has it been since ye were that close to a woman anyway?"

Duncan came at him harder; Reade only laughed.

"Maggie looked very comfortable on top." "I am guessing she is no inexperienced virgin." "Maybe she can teach me a few things."

Duncan was so distracted, that Reade got the upper hand and knocked his brother on his backside.

The other three brothers, watching from the side, roared with laughter.

Reade held out his arms and shrugged while laughing. "We all have an off day every now and again, Brother."

Duncan growled at him as he got back on his feet and stomped off to get water from a nearby bucket.

Logan came over laughing, slapping him on the back. "Compose yourself, Brother. The men will be here soon and ye need to be ready to train."

"I am composed!" Duncan shouted, slamming the ladle back into the bucket, sending the bucket of water flying, causing his brothers to laugh even harder.

That made Duncan even angrier and he tromped off toward the side entrance of the house.

"Where are ye going, Brother?" called Evan.

"I need to cool down...and have a drink," Duncan mumbled back.

Lady Aurnia saw the brotherly 'fun', and Duncan trudging off. She shook her head. "Och...these boys. Maggie, will ye excuse me? I need to see to something." She disappeared into the house.

The brother's horseplay seemed to have broken up, so Maggie thought she would head over to check on Onyx in the stables. As she moved that way, she noticed a bunch of men had gathered and were looking very uncomfortable.

A large, burly bearded man was standing over a little boy, no more than ten, holding a sword to his face that had just been used to gash the boy's cheek open. Another sword, way too big for the boy, lay beside him on the ground. The little boy looked terrified.

The man laughed sadistically at him. "Get up, boy. I'll teach ye how to use that sword, right before I bugger you with it."

Maggie couldn't believe her ears.

Rage flew through her as she rushed to the child's side, helping him up and motioning him to go. Maggie picked up the sword, ignoring the pain in her arm, holding it up in front of her as she shed her coat, tossing it aside.

"I have a better idea. Why don't you try that with me?"

The man leaned on his sword, a perverted look in his face as he looked Maggie up and down.

"Why don't ye put that thing down before ye hurt yourself, woman? I have another sword ye can come hold instead."

He turned around to laugh, looking at the other men, and as he turned back, Maggie took the sword in her right hand and sliced the side of his face open in the same place that he had cut the little boy's.

The man looked stunned and confused, his hand slapping to his face. When he saw the blood, he became enraged. "You fecking cunt," he screamed.

Maggie tsked him. "Such language! I don't know one woman that likes to be called that. I guess I am going to have to teach you some manners."

Duncan was downing a glass of whisky, looking out the window, when his mother came in.

"Something troubling ye, Son?"

He turned to face her. "Mother, that woman has got to go. She is causing nothing but trouble here and, as ye well know, we cannot afford trouble here. We have too much to protect."

Lady Aurnia's smile was sly. "Ye seem to be the only one troubled by her."

"Ye KNOW what I mean, Mother. This woman dinna find her way here by accident. She sought us out, and ye said yourself, she is hiding something from us."

Moving to stand beside her son, Lady Aurnia pushed the hair from his eyes. "I am still Lady of this castle, and Maggie Bishop is my guest. She will stay. Besides, it's not like she was the one causing the trouble last night."

Something caught Duncan's eye outside the window. "Bloody fecking hell! Nay, but she is causing it today." Duncan slammed his glass down and stomped outside.

The man had come at Maggie with his sword and she disarmed him in three swift moves. He was so outraged that he rushed at her.

By the time Duncan and his brothers reached them, she had him on the ground, on his back the way he had the boy. She placed the tip of the blade at his throat, leaned over, and whispered, "If you ever go near that boy again, I will slit your throat while you sleep."

Maggie raised the sword and heard someone command, "HALT!" Sparing a second only, she brought the sword down, planting it into the ground, inches from the abuser's head.

Maggie turned away, shooting him a dark look.

Duncan had barked the order.

She moved to the side, grabbing her coat to storm off in the direction the child had gone, but someone grabbed her arm, jerking her around. She was still angry, so she whirled around, ready for another fight.

"What?" she demanded, fire flashing in her eyes.

It was Duncan. "What the hell is wrong with ye? How dare ye come to our home and embarrass one of our soldiers that way?"

Maggie spat back in his face. "How dare YOU defend a man that rapes children?" She jerked her arm free and stomped off.

Duncan was too stunned to speak. He watched her stalk away, his mind trying to process what she had said. He turned to look back at Angus Riley. No, it wasn't possible that one of his men would do something so heinous...to a child no less...was it?

It took Maggie a while to find the boy; he hid in the herb garden adjacent to the kitchen. He was sitting on the ground with his back against the wall, tears mixing with the blood on his face.

All the anger left Maggie as her heart filled with pain for this little boy. She knelt in front of him. "Are you alright?"

The little boy wiped away his tears. "Aye, ma'am."

She sat down beside him, her back against the wall like his, waiting a good ten minutes before softly asking, "Has he.... hurt you before?"

The little boy shook his head. "No, ma'am. He has tried to get me alone in the stables many times, but I always managed to get away from him. I am smaller, and I move faster than him. But this morning, he told me that if he could not have me, he would take my little sister." He looked like he was about to start crying again. "She is only 6. I have to protect her."

Maggie put her arm around the little boy, pulling him to her as he started to sob. "I promise you, he will not hurt you or your sister. I will see him dead before I let that happen to either of you."

He stopped crying and looked up at her.

"Really ma'am?"

Maggie looked him in the eye. "Really! What's your name?"

"Christopher Manus."

Standing, Maggie pulled him up with her. "Well, Christopher, I am Maggie. Let's go see to that cut on your face." She led him into the kitchen to find some hot water and rags to clean him up.

Duncan MacGregor stood in disbelief, outraged by what he had just heard. He had asked some of the other men what had happened, and they quickly filled him in. He had come to seek out the child to see to his welfare when he heard Maggie Bishop talking to the lad.

He stayed out of sight while listening to the entire conversation.

Children under his protection as Laird had been endangered by one of HIS men, the same men who were there to protect them and keep them safe. In his heart, he knew there had to be others that had been victimized by Angus Riley, and he had failed them all. He would have never known if Maggie Bishop had not been there. He would make sure that Angus Riley would harm no other children on his watch.

Duncan was absent from supper that night.

Lady Aurnia looked around at the rest of her sons. "Where is your brother tonight?"

Reade broke into a grin. "I think he is out checking the house for thieves again."

Logan looked at Maggie. "I don't think he will find any that put up the fight that ye did, Maggie. I think ye gave him a tumble he will not soon forget."

Maggie rubbed her aching arm. "I know I won't forget it anytime soon. I am getting too old for this stuff."

Maggie found herself unable to sleep for the second night in a row. Her arm throbbed from the night before and the events of the morning still bothered her. She had gone looking for Angus Riley that afternoon, but he appeared to be gone. The place that she was told he stayed at had been cleared out. She found out that the children's grandmother was Mrs. Manus, the head of the kitchen. Maggie told her what happened, and the woman was not shocked. Her son, the children's father had passed a year ago, and her former daughter-in-law had been entertaining Angus Riley for the past couple of months. She thanked Maggie profusely and agreed to keep the children in the main house with her, just to be on the safe side.

It was no use; it was one of 'those' nights: too much on her mind and not enough hours in the darkness to think about it all. And to top it all off, there was 'that' picture burned in her mind: Duncan MacGregor drenched in sweat, naked from the waist up, looking like something that just stepped off the pages of a magazine.

Great! Now she was horny on top of everything else.
No sleep for you tonight, Maggie.

Maggie slung back the covers and dressed in her trousers and top, slipping on her boots with the daggers secured...she wouldn't get caught unprepared two nights in a row. She peeked into the hall; it was entirely lit. No one wanted a repeat performance of last night.

She slipped down the stairs to the front door, considering sneaking in a late-night visit with Onyx until she looked out the window and realized it was pouring down rain. Maggie made a disappointed face and turned to head into the library. Maybe she could find a good book to occupy her mind.

The room was dimly lit by the fireplace and a couple of candles. She moved over to the shelves and started looking through the titles.

"Do ye ever sleep or do ye just roam the halls every night?"

Maggie jumped. "Geez, you scared me."

Duncan sat, silent, in a large leather chair by the fireplace.

Maggie had not even noticed him there when she came in.

He was sipping a glass of whisky, staring into the fire, never even looking up at her.

She walked over and poured herself a drink. "I have a great many sleepless nights. At home, I usually just drink myself into a stupor in the comfort of my own house. There is no one around for me to disturb there."

She was just about to excuse herself when he spoke softly, "I did not know. I would never have allowed anyone under my protection to be harmed, least of all a child."

Maggie looked at him, feeling the wave of guilt that rolled off him, and moved to the chair angled next to his.

He never looked away from the flame.

She knew without asking that Duncan was the reason she could not find Angus Riley that afternoon. He had 'handled' the situation.

"Why are ye here, Maggie Bishop?"

Maggie whispered, "That's what I need to know."

Duncan leaned in close to Maggie's face, so close that she could smell the alcohol on his breath and the scent of fresh soap on his skin, searching her eyes with his own.

She felt dizzy, weak and intoxicated by his mere presence. Maggie was pretty sure that she was going to burst into flames from just being so close to him. Judging by the look on his face, and the heat from his breath, he was feeling the same way. The only sound that could be heard was the crackling of the fire.

"Go home, Maggie Bishop. There is nothing for ye here." He rose, downed his drink, and left the room.

Except for a whole lot of sexual frustration.

Maggie sat back in the chair, panting from the encounter. She had never felt anything even remotely close to what she had felt in that one moment. Downing her own drink, she prepared for a long night of being awake.

13 CHAPTER THIRTEEN

The next morning, there were more loud voices coming from the library.

Maggie moved closer to the door.

"She is hiding something from us, Mother," Duncan stated from his chair.

Maggie steeled herself and stepped into the room. "You are correct, I have not told you everything. But I am not the only one keeping secrets, am I?" She moved to the group; the entire family was there, and they were all looking at her. "I don't have much time left here in Scotland, and I really would like to get some answers before I go."

Lady Aurnia spoke, "Maggie, what would ye like to know?"

Maggie excused herself for a moment to get something from upstairs. When she returned, Quinn stood and closed the doors behind them. Maggie set the bottle on the table in front of them. They all leaned in for a closer look.

"What is it?" asked Lady Aurnia.

"I was really hoping you could tell me. I think that bottle started everything."

Maggie took a deep breath. "I have only shared this with one other person in the world and he initially thought I was insane, but I swear to you, everything I am about to say is the truth. I have no idea why I am telling you, except that my gut feeling is saying that you are the ones that can help me find some answers." She looked around; their eyes all locked on her.

"I was born in the year 1996. In 2018, I was on a beach in North Carolina when I found that bottle and read the note in it. I passed out and when I woke up, I was in the year 1765."

Maggie told them the entire story about what had happened. When she was done, she looked around, everyone looking silent, pensive...and did not appear to be shocked at all.

Lady Aurnia was the first to break the silence. "Maggie, that is quite a story." She paused a moment, "and, yes.... I think we may be able to help ye."

Maggie was stunned. "You believe me? You really believe me? I don't need to show you proof, tell you the future...anything?"

Lady Aurnia smiled. "We believe ye, Maggie. We have seen more than our fair share of highly.... unusual things, but to help ye, ye need to hear our story."

Duncan stood up. "Mother! No! Ye cannot tell her."

Looking at her oldest son, Lady Aurnia took him by the shoulders. "Duncan, we must. Maggie was put on a path to us for a reason. She is no ordinary person; I think we all felt that the day she stepped foot across that tree line."

The rest of the brothers looked at Duncan, nodding in agreement with their mother.

Duncan shook his head, rubbing his forehead with his hands before taking his seat. He stared at the floor, remaining silent the whole time his mother spoke.

"Maggie, we too have our secrets and I must ask that ye keep ours, just as we will keep yours."

Maggie nodded. "Of course! You have my word."

Lady Aurnia began her story...

"Many years ago, long before the time of Christ, a race of beings existed throughout the Highlands and across much of Europe. They were immortal, always being, always here, never dying. They were worshiped and revered as gods until Christianity came along and forced them out when they retreated to the underground.

"These beings were referred to as the Seelie Court or as we call them now, the Fae. They were very fond of the people of Scotland and the people of Scotland loved them for the kindness and favors they would bestow. The Fae once had wonderous castles spread all around that they resided in before they were destroyed by religious martyrs and forced to relocate to the underworld for their own safety and peace.

"The people of Scotland continued to worship them in secret and the Fae were very grateful to them for that. When the Fae lived in their palaces, they recorded everything in books...their history, the powerful spells they weaved, the great secrets of the world they kept, and their desires for a better way of life.

"Often, if some great wrong needed to be made right, they would step in and lend mankind a helping hand. Afraid that their secrets might fall into the wrong hands, before they went underground, they went to a loyal family who had worshipped and protected them, as no other had. In this family, Fae blood had mingled with theirs, taking the form of half human, half-Fae children for many generations. They asked this family to take in their collection consisting of books, some weapons, and personal items and to keep them safe until such time that they were able to walk among humans freely again.

"In exchange for keeping their secrets safe, the family would be provided a bountiful stronghold and the means to protect it and the people within its walls. The Fae promised to bless them and give them special abilities to aid mankind, abilities that have been somewhat watered down over the years. That family was known by the name of Gregor and the house, where you now stand, is its fortress.

"The MacGregor family has grown and prospered over many generations, but only our single, direct line know and maintain these secrets. One of the gifts given to us was the power to raise a permanent foggy mist to protect and conceal our whereabouts, which is why the MacGregor clan members are referred to as the 'children of the mist', and why we are located on no map of Scotland that ye found. The fact that a map with an exact location of our home came into yer hands is proof that ye were meant to find your way here.

"We have no idea how the book was removed from our library and can only assume it was by non-human hands for it to find its way across the ocean to ye. The book itself was not a book of Faerie Tales, but a book of their actual stories. As far as the sword, it was obviously forged for ye, and ye alone, but for what reason, we are unsure. And as to the bottle, I have no knowledge of it. However, we can go through the books and try to find a reference to it and your reason for being here.

"If I had to venture a guess, I would say it is because a great wrong needs to be righted and that ye are the only person who can do it."

When she finished, Maggie sat, pale, dumbfounded, and on information overload. She was unable to move, unable to speak, was only able to force herself to breathe through the tightness in her chest; anxiety set in. Maggie felt lightheaded, as if she were going to pass out.

Her eyes fluttered and she started to fall. The last thing she saw was Duncan's concerned face as he caught her in his arms.

When Maggie woke up, she was laying on the small couch in the library. Lady Aurnia was at her feet, pouring a glass of whisky and handing it to Quinn who was at her side.

Quinn helped her sit up and made her drink.

Maggie threw her feet over, planting them on the floor, her head down in her hand.

"How are ye feeling, Maggie?" asked Quinn.

"Honestly...overwhelmed. That was a lot," she replied.

Logan stepped forward. "I think that can be said all the way around. Are ye really from the year 2018?"

Maggie nodded and sucked down the amber liquid.

Lady Aurnia looked at Maggie. "Maggie, I think ye could use a little time to come to terms with what ye have learned, as do we, but I think it's best if ye rest and clear your head. It will give some of us the chance to start searching the books to see if anything like this has ever happened before."

Maggie agreed. "I think I am just going to take a walk and get some fresh air."

Outside, she wandered aimlessly until she found a little path off to the side of the house. It led down to a very scenic and peaceful little sandy area by the water. She sat down on the sand, looking out over the water, trying to process everything in her mind.

Faeries? Seriously? How is that even possible? Faeries weren't real. They were only figments of the imagination…characters in bedtime stories for children, mythical being with wings. Tinker Bell came to mind…the cute little creature from Peter Pan that you had to clap to bring back to life.

Maggie thought back to something that her father had once told her: Most crazy stories from history often had some basis in truth. While stories may be exaggerated and expanded, they were usually born from something that, in fact, did occur. A tiny grain of truth that took root and grew, continued to grow, and sometimes even morphed into something totally different over generations of time.

Even if it that was the case, why would Maggie be the one chosen to get thrown back in time? She was an ordinary person, just living her life, minding her own business. It wasn't like she was special in any way, or from a family that had connections to these…Fae. How could she be part of their grand plan when she had no idea they even existed?

An old familiar feeling crept in… the beginnings of a panic attack. She had started to have more of them lately. She had always had minor ones that would pass quickly, ones that she was able to talk herself through, and could conceal from the people around her, but they were steadily getting worse.

The last major one had put her on the floor, curled up in a ball, completely shut down, back in Virginia. Gabe had been the unlucky one who found her, and he had been frightened out of his mind, not knowing what to do. He had gathered her up, taken her to her bed, and held her while speaking softly to her until it had passed. Later, when she explained what had happened to him, he recalled seeing them occur to men in battle, some of them never fully recovering.

Maggie tried to breathe, but the tightness in her chest made it hard. She laid her head down on her knees, wrapping her arms around her legs, willing and pleading with it to go away, but it was unyielding.

Something touched her back: A comforting nudge, soft but demanding, and it brought her around. When she raised her head, horse drool dripped down her shoulder. She laughed and rubbed Onyx's nose, her breathing regulating and the darkness receding.

Onyx, her faithful companion, was doing what he did best, bringing her comfort in her most dire moments.

She looked at him, trying to figure out how it was that he always knew when she needed him the most. Their bond was undeniable. Standing, she sunk her face into his mane, and he wrapped his head back around her in a hug, as he always did when she needed it.

They stood there, unmoving, until Maggie laughed, feeling much better. She caught sight of something out of the corner of her eye and turned to see Duncan and Quinn coming down the path.

Duncan's face was beet red and he looked furious.

Maggie turned to Onyx. "Ohhh...Onyx, what did you do?"

He looked angry enough to wring Onyx's neck. He pointed and raised his voice. "There ye are, ye unholy beast!"

Maggie grimaced, and asked, "What did he do this time?" stepping between Duncan and Onyx.

"Your demon just splintered his stall gate and demolished part of our fence."

Onyx looked at Duncan and whinnied, but it sounded like a snicker.

"Did he just...." Duncan stepped closer and turned his head to examine Onyx closer, "laugh at me?"

Maggie closed her eyes. "Yeah, he does that... and he really doesn't like to be fenced in."

Duncan gave her a look. "He has done this before?"

Maggie nodded. "He has destroyed stalls, gates, 18-inch-thick front doors...my stableman just gave up on replacing them. It's easier and cheaper to just to let him come and go as he pleases."

She looked at Duncan. "I will cover all the costs to rebuild, but please don't be angry with him. He broke out because he sensed that I was in need."

Duncan gave her a questioning look.

Maggie rolled her eyes, not really wanting to explain. "I was upset, and he somehow knew. He came to calm me, as he always does."

Quinn moved to stand in front of Onyx, his arms folded. "He does that a lot, Maggie...senses when ye are in trouble and comes to your aid?"

"Yes, he has since the day we met. He has always protected me and kept me safe." She turned to rub his muzzle, and Onyx nuzzled against her.

"And where did ye say ye found him?"

"More like he found me. When I woke up in 1765, he was there on the beach, and he just...followed me."

Duncan looked at Onyx, the anger gone from his face, replaced with curiosity. "What a strange horse."

Maggie snorted. "Yeah, I have heard that a few times."

Quinn narrowed his eyes at Onyx and whispered, "I am not so sure he is a horse."

Maggie and Duncan looked at Quinn.

"What do ye mean, Brother?"

Quinn looked closer into Onyx's eyes. "I am not positive, but Mother could probably tell. I think he may be a 'puca'."

"What's a 'puca'?" Maggie asked.

Duncan put his hands on his hips and looked closer. "Tis a Fae spirit creature, that can appear in different animal forms. What your witches may call a 'familiar'."

Quinn continued, "They take animal shapes but retain human-like qualities. They are either solid black or solid white, they have incredible strength, and are fiercely loyal. They can be good or evil, helpful or mischievous. They are always sent by the Fae to help humans in their time of need. But...."

Maggie looked at Onyx. "But what?"

Duncan finished Quinn's sentence for him, eyes narrowed, speaking slowly. "But, according to the lore, pucas in the form of horses are exclusively sent from.... the King of the Fae."

They stood silent, looking at Onyx—and he nodded in acknowledgment.

Maggie licked her lips to say something, then closed her mouth. She opened her mouth again. "I think I may need a drink... or twelve."

Duncan nodded slowly. "Aye, I think that may be in order."

Maggie spoke to Onyx, "Um...can you go behave yourself and not destroy anything for a while? I really don't think I can mentally handle much more today?"

Onyx nodded and departed, trotting off up the path as Maggie, Duncan, and Quinn all stood there watching him go.

14 CHAPTER FOURTEEN

Maggie sat in the chair by the fireplace.

Duncan handed her a glass and took the seat next to her.

Quinn had gone to fill in the rest of the family and to start the men on repairing the fence.

"Thank you," Maggie said, taking a sip, as she laid back against the chair, one hand to her head in deep thought.

Duncan looked at Maggie thoughtfully, admiring the strength she must have to endure all the new information placed before her today. He was glad to see her upright anyway; her fainting spell earlier had caused him great concern. He could see now that his mother had been right: Maggie Bishop had been sent to them, but for what reason, he did not know. That information would be revealed in time, he had no doubt.

Something Maggie had said on the beach troubled him.

He looked down at his glass. "Maggie, ye said something about Onyx earlier, that he sensed your need. Did you become ill on the shore?"

Maggie closed her eyes and whispered, "I was having a panic attack."

Duncan looked at her with concern. "What's a... 'panic attack'?"

"It's when fear overcomes your mind and body to the point that you are rendered completely helpless. It affects people in many different ways. For me, the minor attacks disrupt my breathing and speed my heartbeat. The major attacks are far worse. They leave me unable to move or speak... until my mind calms. They are horrible and debilitating...and they are getting worse. The knowledge I have of the things that will happen in the war at home has caused them to progress. Knowing when and how people you care about are going to die...or the life choices the ones that live need to make and knowing that you cannot interfere without risking changing the course of history...it is almost unbearable at times." Maggie sipped her drink. "I do my best to keep anyone from knowing that I have them. I have so many people at home that look to me and depend on me...I cannot fail them. Onyx has a special way of comforting me during them...and my friend Gabe, he knows how to handle me when they strike, as well, but I live in fear of when the next one will come...and I never know which one will be the one that my mind doesn't return from."

Duncan leaned over, compassion filling him for the woman that sat in front of him. "Given all that ye have had upon ye, Maggie, it is...understandable. It is your body's way of calming your mind when your mind cannot calm itself."

Maggie looked down. "I don't know what these...Fae were thinking by picking me, but I am pretty sure they picked the wrong girl."

He sat back. "Given all that I have seen, I highly doubt that."

By suppertime, Maggie was in a better mood. She had—or rather the whisky had—forced her to take a nap that afternoon, dulling the rawness of the new information a bit.

Talk at the table was livelier than the past two nights, all the secrets between them now out in the open.

Lady Aurnia, Reade, and Evan had started going through their library looking for any references that might be of use. They had also taken a closer look at the bottle, determining that, it was indeed, of the Fae.

Quinn, Logan, and Duncan had gotten the repairs made to the stable and fence, Maggie profusely apologizing for the trouble Onyx caused. Duncan was no longer angry now that he understood what Onyx truly was. They all had many questions about the future, that Maggie happily answered, amused by the looks on their faces from her answers.

It was a good night.

Maggie's insomnia had not been helped by the day's events, so this time, she just remained in the library after everyone else had retired, not even attempting to go to bed. She was on her third glass of whisky and feeling more than a little tipsy, when Duncan came in to pour himself one.

"Did ye even try to go to sleep tonight?"

"No, I just saved myself the extra trip up and down the stairs this time. It's probably for the best. I'm pretty sure

I would have fallen flat on my face anyway," she said, holding up her glass and shaking it.

He brought the bottle over to top off Maggie's glass and took the chair beside her, giving her a good once over. "How are ye feeling?"

Good Lord, he smells like whisky and Heaven. I wonder what he tastes like?

Maggie could tell by his light-hearted mood that he was well on his way to being inebriated. She smiled. "I'm better. I got some rest this afternoon and it helped a great deal."

He stared into the fire. "Ye said your friend...Gabe, was it...knew how to handle these...panic attacks. What does he do to comfort you?"

"Oh, for the little attacks, he usually just pours rum and makes me drink it until I calm down. The last big one that he found me in was bad. He took me to my bed and stayed with me until it passed."

Duncan whispered, obvious disappointment in his voice, "He took ye to bed then?"

"Yes." Maggie then realized what he was really asking, the alcohol slowing her mind. "Wait...what? NO! NO! NO!"

Duncan slyly smiled. "Well lass, if ye are unsure IF he took ye to bed, then he must not be much of a man."

Maggie rolled her eyes. "Gabe and I do not have that kind of relationship. He is more like a brother to me." She sipped her drink and leaned towards Duncan in a flirtatious way. "Besides, IF I were to let a man take me to bed, he'd better make damn sure that I know it."

Duncan tilted his head, stroking his chin with his thumb, a mischievous smile on his face. He leaned forward, close to her face, and whispered in her ear in a low, sultry growl, "IF I were to take ye to bed, I would make damn sure that ye knew it until ye were too weak to move your lips to tell me that ye wanted... MORE."

He brushed his cheek lightly against hers on the word 'more' and slowly pulled back until his lips were barely touching hers.

An electrical jolt shot between them and they froze, looking deeply into each other's eyes.

Duncan was silently asking for permission and Maggie was silently inviting him in.

In one swift move, his tongue broke through the barrier of her lips and invaded her mouth, claiming her as his own and demanding her unconditional surrender in return. He dropped his glass, taking her head in both of his hands.

She did the same, greedily accepting his invasion and launching one of her own. A primal passion took over as they stood up together, kissing hard and deep, wrapping their arms around each other, exploring each other with their hands.

Maggie ran her hands down his back, bringing them back up under his shirt. She went to take it off when he pushed her hands down. She stopped, her lips swollen and her eyes dreamy, giving him a confused look.

He pulled back from the kiss, breathing hard. "Nay, I will not take ye here on the floor. I want ye in my bed." He pulled her back into a deep kiss, lifted her off the floor and carried her upstairs. At the foot of his bed, he stood her in front of the fireplace, kissing her neck while he ran one hand down her back, wrapping one arm around her waist.

Maggie felt like she was on fire. She closed her eyes as he kissed her neck, feeling as if she were in some rhythmic trance, unable to do anything but accept the waves from his body's movement. She was drenched in sweat, her hair damp, as he ran his fingers through it. When he moved down to tug at her breast through her shirt, she cried out, on the verge of an orgasm before he had even touched her anywhere else. She had never felt anything remotely like this before in her entire life, not even with Ben. He lowered his arm down past her waist and that's when she felt his erection through the fabric of his tartan. He pressed himself against her, softly laughing when she whimpered a little.

"Duncan..." she whispered in a breathy voice.

He growled, pulling her top off, seeing she had on nothing underneath. He took one nipple in his mouth, tasting and tugging at it until she dug her nails into his back. He could feel her on the verge, but he intended to draw this out as long as possible. Pulling her into another deep kiss, he wrapped his fingers in her hair. When he pulled back, he smiled wickedly at her and took the other nipple in his mouth, grazing it with his teeth and then sucking as hard as he could until she called his name.

When he pulled away, she was barely able to stand on her own.

He picked her up and lay her across the bed. She was wearing those leather trousers, the ones that made him think of all the things he wanted to do to her when he saw her in them. They contoured to the shape of her backside like skin.

The image of her in those trousers were what had kept him awake last night. He could think of nothing but getting them off her.

He looked at her; her eyes were closed, and her body was begging for his attention. He leaned over and kissed her before moving his lips down past her belly button to the laces on those trousers. He took one of her hands in his and squeezed.

When she looked down, he was using his teeth to pull the laces free. She placed her free hand on the back of his head and pulled him in tighter.

When they were loosened enough to get them off, he tugged them down.

She raised herself up to help him.

He threw them to the side, looking at her completely naked body.

Her breathing was more irregular now, her heart beating fast; as if it might come out of her chest.

Duncan stripped off his own shirt, it was soaked with sweat.

Maggie looked up at him. Without his shirt...*damn*.

He gave her a wicked grin as he ran his finger up the inside of her thigh.

Maggie groaned, sure she was going to erupt before he even touched her anywhere else. She could hardly breathe. She closed her eyes and felt his tongue moving up the side of her thigh until it reached her *there*. Maggie opened her eyes just as he took her in his mouth.

He moved his tongue, tasting her, exploring her.

Maggie put her hand on the back of his head and guided him to the right spot. She moved against him as he buried his face in her until her passion built and she finally released, calling his name.

He moved up to face her, as much out of breath as she was.

"Duncan..."

He bit her lip and stood to remove his tartan.

Maggie gasped as she saw his size.

Duncan was looking strained. He had held himself back for as long as he could, but he could wait no longer. He kissed Maggie, hard and deep as he entered her.

That one movement put her right back to being on the verge of another orgasm.

He moved slowly first, but picked up speed, ramming into Maggie harder and harder until they both found their release at the same time. He fell to the side of her, pulling her with him. They both lay panting, sweating and satisfied, more than either one had been in their entire lives.

Duncan pulled her into a forceful kiss. He pulled back, looking at her with lust in his eyes while whispering in her ear, "Don't get too comfortable, we are only getting started."

Maggie only nodded, too worn out to ask for 'MORE.' She didn't have to ask. He repeated the performance four times that night. The next morning Maggie was sated, exhausted and sore, unable to move.

She had slept soundly for the first time in a very long time.

15 CHAPTER FIFTEEN

Lady Aurnia looked down at the two glasses on the floor. She picked them up, annoyed that someone had spilled whisky on her rug. "Flora, bring me some rags and hot water."

When Flora came in, they both started to clean up.

"Och...these boys. They have always been so messy."

When they were done, Flora turned to Lady Aurnia, "Would ye like me to keep breakfast warm for the others?"

"What do you mean? Who has not been down for breakfast?"

Flora lowered her eyes. "Duncan has not been down."

Lady Aurnia looked concerned. "That is not like him. I had better go make sure he is not sick." She started toward the door.

Flora cleared her throat. "Mistress Bishop has not been down, either."

Lady Aurnia stopped and looked back at her.

"I went to check on her this morning and her bed had not been slept in."

Lady Aurnia looked confused until she looked over at the floor they just cleaned, and an understanding washed over her. A broad smile spread across her face and she folded her arms, laughing softly. "Flora, ye can set aside a few things, but we may not see either of them until supper, if then."

Logan came into the library. "Mother, where is Duncan? Is the lazy oaf still in bed?"

Lady Aurnia was still smiling. "I believe he is."

"I'll go drag his arse out by his feet."

Lady Aurnia put her hands up to stop him. "Nay, ye will not. Leave him be and do not disturb him the rest of the day."

Logan looked annoyed. "We have work to do."

"So, does he, and his work is very important."

Maggie woke the next morning, wondering if last night had been some sort of a dream. The soreness in her limbs and the firm, muscular body next to hers told her that it had not. She tried to move, but her body resisted. She groaned slightly and tried to shift, waking Duncan.

He looked down at her with concern. "Are ye alright? You sound like ye are in pain."

"I am a little sore this morning, that's all."

Well, that was a lie. She was a lot more than a 'little' sore.

Duncan raised up to look her over. "Och... forgive me, Maggie. I did not mean to hurt ye last night. I should have been gentler with ye," the remorse showed in his in his face.

Maggie laughed, laying across his chest. "Please, don't apologize. I enjoyed last night very much, but I don't think I can handle anymore this morning. I am not sure I can even move to get dressed."

"I'll help ye get dressed after breakfast. I know just what ye need."

He kissed her, then rolled out of bed.

After dressing himself, Duncan went downstairs and returned with a tray of food.

They sat in bed together, ate and afterward, he did indeed help her dress. Maggie was in worse shape than she first realized. Between the battle with the highwaymen, the fight with Angus Riley, and last night, there wasn't a part of her body that didn't hurt.

"Come on," he said taking her by the hand. "There is somewhere I wish to take ye."

They slipped down the back stairs to find that Duncan had ordered the horses saddled. He helped her up, then mounted his own horse, before they rode off.

Onyx took pity on her and kept it to a slight trot.

They rode for less than an hour before Duncan announced, "We are here."

He helped her down, gentleness in every touch, and Maggie looked around in amazement. Before them stood the most beautiful, clear, blue... hot-spring pool. It looked like something straight out of an exclusive spa.

Duncan smiled at her wonderment. He took her hand and led her over. "This is one of our special gifts. It does wonders for aches and pains."

He undressed, then helped Maggie to do the same before leading her into the water.

It felt like a hot tub and Maggie was in pure, unadulterated bliss.

One end had a little ledge on it, and Duncan led Maggie over so she could sit comfortably and still be in the water up to her shoulders. He stood before her, his feet planted firmly on the bottom, putting them face to face. He wrapped his arms around her waist and kissed her sweetly while they soaked.

After a while, Maggie's muscles had started to loosen up and she was able to move around in the water easier.

Duncan took her in his arms. "Are ye feeling better?"

"Yes, surprisingly enough, I am. This place is... something else. Thank you for bringing me here. I will definitely miss it when I have to leave."

Duncan kissed her neck and growled, "No one said ye had to leave, lass."

Maggie took his face in her hands and looked up at him with a sweet, sad smile on her face. "I can't stay here forever, as nice as that would be. My home is in Virginia and I have people there with needs, especially with the war going on."

He took in a deep breath and looked at her with lust in his eyes, a sensual smile on his face. He wrapped his hands in her hair and pulled her face closer to his, whispering, "I have a few needs of my own right at the moment," and he pulled her into a passionate, demanding kiss.

She met his fervency with her own intensity, their mutual 'needs' turning urgent.

He lifted her and she wrapped her legs around his waist. He entered her deeply, completely in one move; she was more than ready for him and he was unable to wait any longer. Maggie leaned back on the rocks and they both laughed, with their intensity peaking and releasing at the same instant.

He pulled her over into a deeper part of the water and wrapped her into a tight embrace, kissing the top of her head, never wanting to let her go.

They stayed in the pool, enjoying each other, until the sun started to make its descent. He helped her out of the water, drying her off, and helping her to dress. They mounted the horses and headed for home, side by side at an unhurried pace, she on Onyx and him on his solid white mare, Gavina.

It was suppertime when they arrived, everyone already at the table. Maggie took a seat, and Duncan sat down next to her. Amidst all the curious looks, Lady Aurnia tried to conceal the zeal on her face.

Logan looked at Duncan. "Where have ye been all day?"

Duncan shrugged, reaching for a piece of bread. "Maggie was not feeling well, so I took her to the springs."

Reade looked back and forth between Duncan and Maggie, a sudden understanding coming to him. He could tell by looking at his brother when he had been with a woman and there was no doubt, he had been with a woman. Judging by the way Maggie was walking, it wasn't hard to figure out which woman.

Oh, I am going to have some fun with this. He moved the food on his plate with his fork, trying to look inconspicuous and oblivious. "So, Maggie, are ye feeling better...after your trip to the springs?"

Maggie looked over at him. "Yes, I am. The springs were amazing. I had no idea you had anything like that here in Scotland."

Reade looked at her, cocking his head to the side. "Aye, they are very nice. They are especially good for soreness...ye know, after a hard day of...riding."

Stealing a quick glance at Duncan, Reade caught the murderous look shot in his direction. He pretended not to.

Evan caught the exchange. He leaned back in his chair, looking between Duncan and Reade and then between Duncan and Maggie, starting to comprehend what was going on. He looked at Reade who gave him a nod, confirming it.

Evan grinned. *Why should Reade have all the fun?*

Lady Aurnia tried to run interference. "Maggie, Quinn and I have been going through the books today. Unfortunately, we have not found anything yet."

Quinn wiped his mouth with the back of his hand. "But we still have a great many to get to. I am sure we will come across something."

Maggie looked at them. "I appreciate all you are doing for me. I am happy to pitch in with going through some of the books if that would help."

Logan spoke up, "I am afraid ye would not be able to. Most of the books are in an ancient language that we have all been taught growing up."

Evan pushed his plate away, resting his folded arms on the table. "Maggie, I was wondering if maybe ye would like to come out with me tomorrow and let me show ye some of the property. There's a very nice little secluded spot down by the loch. We can pack some food, a blanket, a bottle of whisky.... spend some time together and really get to know each other.... just the two of us."

Duncan slammed his glass down on the table so hard that Maggie jumped. She looked over at him to see his eyes narrowed at his brother and his face reddening. He was clearly trying to restrain himself as he stated with a stern look on his face, "Tomorrow is a training day, Brother! Did ye forget?"

Reade smacked Evan's leg under the table. "Oh, I think we can spare Evan for one training day. After all, Maggie is our guest and we would not want to be rude and neglect her by leaving her all by herself, would we?"

Evan stroked his chin, keeping an eye on Duncan. "Reade is right. We wouldn't want Maggie to be bored and alone, while she is here. It really is the only decent thing to do."

Reade took a sip of his drink and leaned back. "We should make sure she is comfortable, as well. The weather is turning chilly and I am afraid she may catch a chill in that cold, drafty room of hers."

Evan nodded, looking at Reade, then at Duncan. "Oh, aye Brother, and I would be more than happy to...warm her cold bed for her....so she doesn't take ill, of course."

Maggie watched the exchange like a tennis match, going back and forth, finally closing her eyes and shaking her head.

The rest of the male family members found the exchange rather amusing, obviously used to the brotherly banter, but Lady Aurnia knew from experience that this would not end well.

Duncan, on the other hand, pushed aside his plate, and planted his elbows on the table, resting his chin in his hands; he stared back at his two taunting brothers with a simmering rage. He sneered at them, knowing they had already figured out that something had happened between him and Maggie. He composed himself and raised his head with a smirk on his face. "Oh, I agree, Brother. I think ye SHOULD warm Maggie's bed tonight."

Maggie looked at him, a vexed look on her face.

He slipped his hand beneath the table, grabbed her leg, and squeezed it. He leaned towards Evan, looking directly in his eyes and said, "Ye should probably take plenty of blankets with ye when ye go to it….so ye balls don't turn blue, shrivel up, and fall off in that very cold, frigid bed that ye will be in all alone. You see, Brother, Maggie will be nice and toasty in my bed tonight and for the foreseeable future. Her things have already been moved into my chambers."

The brothers locked eyes across the table, staring, neither willing to yield, good-naturedly butting heads the way that only brothers do, that went a little too far.

Maggie downed a glass of whisky in one gulp, poured herself another, and downed that one, too, rubbing over her brows with her fingers before she got up and left the room.

Lady Aurnia saw Maggie's reaction. She stood up and very loudly shouted. "CEASE!"

The brothers broke their stare and turned to look at their mother.

She threw her napkin down on the table and leaned over, planting both hands on the table. "I know ye boys are not used to this, but we have a guest in the house. A LADY guest in this house and ye are behaving like animals. Och, your father is rolling in his grave at this very moment. He did not teach ye to treat women like ye owned them and neither did I. It's no wonder that none of ye are married. No woman in her right mind would put up with any of ye. Some days I wonder how I do, and I brought each of ye into this world."

Reade looked up with a sullen look. "Mother, we were just having a little fun."

"Ye know we don't mean anything by it," added Evan.

Lady Aurnia glared at Reade, Evan, and Duncan. "A little fun? That woman came to us for help. She is under my care. I am Lady of the castle and everything ye do is a reflection upon me. Women are not like men. We have feelings and we have our dignity...both of which the three of ye disregarded with Maggie tonight. Ye should be ashamed of yourselves...God knows, I am."

Lady Aurnia stormed out of the room.

They all sat silently looking down at the table.

Duncan sighed. "Mother is right. I am an idiot. I should not have let the two of ye goad me so."

Reade looked around. "Och, we should not have drug Maggie into our foolishness. She is not used to a big family like ours."

Evan snarked at Duncan. "Guess I am not the only one who will be sleeping alone with cold, blue balls tonight."

Duncan reached across the table... and punched him right on the chin.

The brother fell back over the bench on his backside. He sat himself up holding his chin, blood coming from his lip. "What did you do that for?"

Logan looked down at him with a disapproving look. "Oh, ye deserved it and ye know it. Quit yer whining."

Duncan stood. "I need to go find Maggie and apologize."

Quinn shook his head. "Ye might want to give her and mother a little bit to cool down. Heaven help ye if you run into Mother out there alone. There might not be anything left of you to tell Maggie ye are sorry with."

The other brothers all nodded in agreement.

Maggie had gone into the library, grabbed a bottle of whisky, and headed down to the water, planting herself on the sand upon arrival. She looked up at the full moon in the night sky, trying to clear her head. She was not in the mood to talk to Duncan. The 'fun' with his brothers had started innocently enough but took a very different turn at the end.

Duncan had her things moved into his room without her permission and expected her in his bed every night. That crossed a line.

She wasn't even sure how she felt about him, or him about her, after last night. They were both drunk, and as fantastic and mind-blowing as it was, it didn't mean anything. Maggie had no intention of falling in love. The last time she had, it hadn't ended well, and she had accepted, given her unusual circumstances, that love really wasn't in the cards for her.

Maggie took a swig from the bottle and noticed a light coming down the path. "Go away Duncan, I have not had enough to drink to deal with you just yet."

But another voice replied, "How about me? Mind if I join ye?"

Maggie turned.

Lady Aurnia was coming towards her with a lantern. "Please."

Lady Aurnia sat down next to Maggie. "I used to come down here and hide out when the boys were out of control." She looked out at the water. "I suppose some things never change."

Maggie smiled. "I guess they have always been a handful?"

"Och, ye have no idea. Those five boys would die for each other, but the bickering and fierce rivalries between them make me want to drown them in this loch sometimes." She looked over at Maggie. "Maggie, I am so sorry for the way they behaved this evening. They were out of line and it is unacceptable."

Maggie looked back at her. "It's fine. I am used to a little good-natured fun. That is not what bothered me."

Lady Aurnia seemed to read Maggie's mind. "It was Duncan assuming ye would be in his bed, not asking if ye wanted to be."

Maggie nodded.

"I am afraid, my dear Maggie, ye will find most Highland men presumptuous in that respect, though these boys were not raised that way. Their father wooed me and made sure I knew how much he loved and appreciated me each day we were together. He was a kind, gentle soul. I have never met another like him. I know my boys have some of his traits deep down...very, deep down...somewhere... but they are there, I have no doubt."

"My parents were that way. I think they ruined it for me."

Lady Aurnia looked at her strangely, "How so?"

"They were so in love and one never let the other forget it for a moment. They were the most amazing couple...and the best parents anyone could ever ask for. Their love was extremely rare, I think, and I had the honor of basking in it every day of my life as a child. I know that kind of love is not out there for me."

"Why would ye say something like that Maggie?"

Maggie took another sip. "I am not supposed to be here...in this time. Anything that I do in the past could destroy the future that I know. One little slip-up and I may never even be born. I made the mistake of falling in love with someone when I knew he was destined to live another life. I had to let him go, so history could take its course or risk my country, or me, never coming into existence."

Lady Aurnia got her first good glimpse into what Maggie had been going through. It was not a life she envied. "So, you have given up on love? On a family?"

Taking in a deep breath, Maggie nodded. "It's not worth the risk of changing things. If I fall in love and marry someone meant to marry someone else, entire generations of a family may not come into existence. So many little things that add up to the big picture. And as far as a family..." Maggie slumped, "I was... with child...by the man I fell in love with. I had decided that I could be happy with loving and raising that child alone. It would have been enough, but the fates saw fit to take that from me."

Lady Aurnia took pity on Maggie, patting the other woman's leg. "Oh Maggie, I am so sorry.
No parent should ever have to suffer such a loss."

Maggie whispered, "The way my parents lost me." She shrugged, "I have accepted my fate, made the best of it even, but my parents...my parents will never have any idea what happened to me. I was just there one day and gone the next, with no explanation, no closure. They will never know if I am even dead or alive. I am their only child, the center of their world. It must be excruciatingly painful for them...the way it is for me." Maggie paused. "So, I have made the people that I care for on my estate in Virginia and, my dearest friend, Gabe, my family and I... take a little... 'comfort'...when and where I can find it. I have learned to make do, it's simpler that way."

Lady Aurnia looked at Maggie with compassion and sadness. "Maggie, ye should never have to settle for 'comfort'. Ye are a remarkable woman and ye deserve to find someone who makes ye happy. The fates would not be so cruel as to expect ye to spend your life alone, especially after all that they have taken from ye. Nay, I think the fates are just taking their time to make sure they put the right person by your side."

"Just the same, I don't think I will lay any wagers on that." It was a good time to change the subject. Maggie looked back out over the water. "It is beautiful here. I can't believe my mother never brought me to Scotland as a child. She was from here."

Lady Aurnia looked a little surprised. "Your mother was from Scotland?"

"Yes, but she never really spoke of it other than to say it was where she was from."

"What clan did she belong to?"

"Her last name was Morgan before she married."

Lady Aurnia looked at Maggie, confused. "I know no clans by that name."

"Scotland in the future is different. There are many names that are not attached to clans."

"What of her parents? Maybe I know one of their names."

Maggie shrugged. "I know nothing about them. I never met them, and she never really talked about them. As a matter of fact, the only time she ever mentioned anything was when she gave me the necklace that I wear. She said her father gave it to her and, when I turned 18, she gave it to me. She never took it off and neither have I." Maggie pulled it out of her top.

Lady Aurnia held the lantern up to get a better look. "It is a beautiful necklace indeed. Such a... special looking stone."

Maggie tucked it back under her shirt. "My mother treasured it. I was shocked when she took it off to give to me."

Lady Aurnia patted her hand. "She must love ye very much and she was very lucky to have such a lovely daughter as ye, Maggie. I am sure she would be proud of ye." Lady Aurnia looked back toward the house, annoyance in her voice. "*I* would have been very lucky to have had a daughter like ye. Maybe an extra woman around the house would have made my boys...less like boys." She stood to go. "I will leave ye to your thoughts, Maggie."

She left the lantern beside Maggie and before she started up the hill, she looked back. "Maggie, I know ye have reason to be angry with Duncan...I am not happy with him myself, at the moment, but he *is* a good man and he has a good heart. Please, don't judge him too harshly." And she was gone.

Duncan was coming into the hall when his mother came inside. He had searched the house for Maggie to no avail. "Mother, do ye know where Maggie is?"

She folded her arms. "Aye...I do." She didn't move, fixing her gaze on his face.

He rolled his eyes. "Will ye tell me where she is?"

"Do not roll yer eyes at me, son. Ye would not have those eyes if it weren't for me."

Duncan closed the aforementioned eyes. "Forgive me, Mother. Now, will ye please tell me where she is?"

She started towards the library. "Aye, I will...after we have a wee talk."

Following his mother into the library—she closed the door behind him and moved to pour herself a drink—Duncan leaned over the back of one of the leather chairs looking into the fireplace, raking his hands through his hair.

His mother came to sit in the other chair. "I am very disappointed in ye, Son. Ye know how your brothers are and how they like to try to get ye stirred up. Ye are very good at ignoring them normally; yet tonight, ye let them get the best of ye. Why is that?"

He shook his head and said quietly, "Mother, I have no idea. I can take their ribbing when it is about me, but when they drug Maggie into it...something in me... could not let it go."

Lady Aurnia looked at her oldest son. He was genuinely upset, something she rarely, if ever, saw since he came of age. Duncan was always the level-headed one, never the one to lose his composure, yet she had seen it a couple of times the past few days.

It seemed that Maggie's presence was the cause.

"You care for her a great deal, don't ye son? Even though it has only been a few days since ye met her."

Duncan came around and collapsed in the chair sighing. "Aye, I suppose I do."

Lady Aurnia knew that look. It was one of a man resigned to his fate. She leaned forward and touched his knee. "Then, ye must do better. If ye truly care for Maggie, ye will need to prove it to her...and that will not be easy. Mind and body, Maggie is the strongest woman

I have ever known. She is remarkable. But that girl's heart is a whole other story."

Duncan turned to his mother. "What do ye mean?"

She leaned in closer. "Maggie has had to endure more loss in her life than any one person should. She has convinced herself that she does not need, nor deserve, to be loved. She has built a wall around her heart that will not be easy to take down. If ye truly care for her, ye will have to convince her that she wants and needs ye like she needs the very air that she breathes."

"And, how do I do that?"

Lady Aurnia leaned back in the chair. "I do not know. Let your heart lead ye...and not your other body parts."

He shook his head, laughing, and stood to leave.

"She is down by the water."

Duncan leaned in and kissed his mother's cheek. "Thank ye, Mother."

She watched him go. *I really hope he doesn't muck this up.*

Duncan stood back, watching Maggie for a few minutes before starting down the path. She lay on her back, with her fingers interlocked behind her head, looking up at the stars. There was a bright full moon; its illumination and the lantern beside her gave her a warm, magical glow. She was stunning.

Maggie didn't need to see him, she *felt* him. She could *see* him in her mind just standing there, watching her. He had been standing at the top of the path for a good ten minutes before he finally came down to stand next to her.

"Mind if I sit?"

Maggie shrugged. "It's your beach...I am just visiting."

Duncan sat down beside her. "I owe ye a very deep and profound apology. What happened at the supper table...was shameful and a disgrace. I should never have let it go as far as it did."

She did not say anything.

He could feel...was it anger? No! Not anger...*irritation* rolling off of her. A sudden thought popped into his head.

That is not what I am upset about.

He took in a deep breath. "And I am also sorry for having your things moved into my room without asking ye. I should not have been so presumptuous. I will have all of your things moved back into your room tonight."

Maggie looked over at him. "Thank you...and I accept your apology."

Letting out the breath he had been holding, he relaxed, just a bit. He noticed she was looking up at the stars. "It is a beautiful night." He stretched out beside her and lay the same way she did.

"It certainly is. I cannot get enough of looking at the stars. In the future, the cities and towns are so bright from all the lights, that it is difficult to see even a few, but here, you can see them all, and it takes my breath away every time."

Duncan pointed out different constellations and told the ancient Scottish stories for each one while Maggie told him the modern-day versions of them. They lay there talking and laughing for hours.

After a while, Duncan noticed Maggie shiver. "Ye are cold. We should go in and warm up by the fire."

"I just want to stay a little longer."

He sighed. "Well, I cannot let ye freeze." Scooting over closer to her, Duncan slipped his arm behind her and pulled her close to his chest.

A little jolt of electricity shot between them.

Maggie looked at him. "Did you feel that?"

"Aye, I did. That was...unusual."

She laid her arm across his chest.

God, the man is a walking furnace.

Maggie settled into the crook of his arm, feeling very comfortable and warm. She snuggled in, feeling drowsy, and fell asleep in just a few minutes.

Duncan looked down. Maggie was out. The poor thing had a long day and she didn't get much sleep last night. She was so sweet looking that he didn't want to disturb her. He managed to pick her up, without waking her, and carried her into the house. In the middle of taking her to his room, he thought better of it, pushed open the door of her room, and laid her on the bed. When he went to cover her up, she reached for him and mumbled in her sleep, "Don't go."

His mother's words came back to him.

"Ye will have to convince her that she wants and needs ye like she needs the very air that she breathes."

This was going to be harder than he thought. He looked down at her, desperately wanting to crawl into that bed to be with her, just to lay beside her and be near her.

Instead, he pulled the covers up over her and kissed her gently on the forehead. "Good night, sweet Maggie."

He went back to his room for a lonely and restless night.

The next morning, Maggie woke up slowly. Before she opened her eyes, she reached over to feel for him. "Duncan?" She opened her eyes and looked around. She was alone in her own bed, in her own room. Maggie looked around the room to see that all her things were back, including her sword. Maggie hopped out of bed and went to it. On top of her sword lay a rose. She picked it up and smelled it. It was from Duncan, she instinctively knew. She closed her eyes and breathed in. His smell from the beach last night was still on her, clinging to her clothes. For a moment, she couldn't think straight.

What was it about this man?

She shook her head, saying to herself, "Shake it off, Maggie, you cannot allow yourself to fall for him."

After dressing, she and went downstairs to find it empty. She stuck her head in the kitchen to grab some bread. Mrs. Manus was there, and she asked about the children.

The cook told Maggie that Duncan had personally seen to the children, moving them to personal quarters inside the castle; their mother had disappeared.

When Maggie went back into the hall, she remembered that it was a training day. Lady Aurnia would be in the hidden library, so she decided to take a walk outside to watch. There were several pairs of men squared off and sword fighting one on one. Duncan strode between the groups, watching and offering instructions on how to improve.

Maybe this isn't such a good idea after all.

Duncan was stripped to his waist again, his hair braided back in a long plait, showing off his chiseled facial features even more. The man had the body of a god.

Maggie sucked in her breath, finding it hard to breathe, her heart racing and she started to feel very flush. She felt an urgency that *needed* to be satisfied. She didn't have much time here...maybe she should enjoy it, and him... while she could.

Duncan caught sight of her and smiled. He came over to her. "Good morning. Did ye sleep well?"

"I... uh...did. Thank you for the rose and for returning my sword."

"The sword is yours. It always has been."

That 'need' was growing by leaps and bounds.

Duncan noticed her flush and irregular breathing. He looked at her, suddenly concerned. "Maggie, are ye having one of your panic attacks?"

"Oh, I am having some kind of 'attack'."

Turning back to the training, Duncan motioned to Logan to continue. He placed his hand on her back and led her up to her room, closing the door behind them, his very touch almost pushing Maggie over the edge.

What the hell is going on? Why am I like this suddenly?

He looked at her. "What can I do?"

Maggie sashayed to the bed. "You can come over here and take care of this sudden urgency that I have."

He moved closer to her and she pulled him into a deep kiss. The kiss was greedy, but he pulled back.

She looked at him, perplexed.

He closed his eyes, trying to compose himself; it proved to be extremely...hard. "Nay Maggie, I will not do this."

"Huh?"

He took her by the arms, looking into her eyes. "I will not be presumptuous again."

Maggie waved her hands in front of her body. "You are not being presumptuous. I am here, freely offering, pleading actually...I really, really want you to come over here and take care of my 'needs'...and I can see that you are in 'need' as well."

Duncan looked down. There was no denying that! He wanted nothing else than to throw her down on that bed and spend the entire day making love to her. He had spent the entire night thinking of doing nothing but that and being that close to her was making it so much worse. It took all his strength just to pull back from her kiss, but he had made a decision. He wanted Maggie...all of Maggie...mind, body, and soul...and he would not rest until he had what he wanted. He felt as if his very life depended on it.

He swallowed hard. "Maggie, I don't want there to be just... 'this' between us. I want something... 'more'."

"What do you mean by 'more', Duncan?"

Duncan took her hands. "I want ye, and not just in my bed. I want the two of us to be together. Maggie, I have only known ye a few days, but I feel this unexplained desire and need to be by your side...always. I cannot explain it, but I know it as I have never known anything before in my life."

Maggie pulled away and leaned against the bedpost, saying in a low voice, "I do not have the luxury of giving anyone 'more'."

He closed his eyes. A voice from somewhere deep inside him spoke.

This woman is meant for ye, Duncan MacGregor. Ye just must help her see it.

He took her hand, kissed her forehead, smirked, and leaned close to her ear to whisper, "Then, I will be unable to satisfy your… 'needs'…until ye can see fit to satisfy mine."

He brushed his lips against her cheek, as he did that first night, and turned to stride to the door. He looked back, smiling a devilish grin at leaving Maggie frustrated by the bed. Turning the doorknob, he still watched her.

Maggie leaned back on the bed, seductively, bit her lip and said with a diabolical smile, "Guess I will have to satisfy myself then. Too bad you are not invited to stay and... watch."

Duncan stroked his chin, took in a deep breath, and went out the door. Shutting it, he stepped forward, leaned over the stair rail, and closed his eyes while pushing his hair back. *Now, I have that image in my head. Maggie may not be the only one that has to take matters into their own hands.*

It was going to be a long day. He smiled back at the door and walked away.

Maggie threw herself face down on the bed. She rolled over to look up at the ceiling. Duncan had decided that he wanted to play hardball? Well, two could play that game.

16 CHAPTER SIXTEEN

Back outside with the men, Duncan tried to focus
on what they were doing, when he saw her come around
the corner. She was looking around, taking in the scene.
When she saw him, she slowly smiled.

God help me; she is up to something. He pretended to
ignore her, correcting one of the men in front of him on
his stance, but keeping a wary eye on Maggie.

Maggie glanced around until her eyes fell upon what
she was looking for. She sidled her way over to the water
buckets set out for the men. She could feel Duncan
watching her, even though he was doing his best to
pretend that he wasn't.

It occurred to Maggie, that she seemed to be catching a
great many vibes off him. She had always had a certain
sense of the people around her, even being able to
anticipate moves before people made them...one of the

reasons she was so good with the sword. But with Duncan, it was different. It was almost as if she could feel what he was thinking every time they were anywhere near each other. It was kind of like a... connection.

Speaking of making a type of 'connection'.

Duncan made his way back up the line of men to where Maggie stood by the water buckets.

Maggie cut her eyes over to him, chewing on her lip.

He leaned with his elbow against the fence and looked at her through narrowed eyes in a mockingly serious way. "Is there something I can help ye with Maggie?"

She looked up. "A great many things, actually, but you don't seem to be interested in 'helping' me, do you?"

Raising an eyebrow, he leaned over, whispering, "I would be more than happy to 'help' you. I just want something in a return."

Maggie gave him a hard look, then licked her lips. "I am so hot and very thirsty, Duncan. May I have some water...please?"

He stepped back and waved his hand. "Oh, be my guest. You know how to... 'help yourself', don't you?"

Reaching over, Maggie took the ladle, keeping his gaze trapped the entire time. She lifted the ladle to her mouth, and, as it reached her lips, before she went to sip, she turned it over, intentionally pouring it back and forth down the front of her shirt...her very thin, light-colored shirt that had nothing underneath it. The wet shirt making her breasts noticeable to anyone with eyes. She may as well have been shirtless. "Oops. Look what I did. I am SO clumsy."

Damn it, Maggie. Duncan had just gotten himself under control from their earlier encounter...and now he was right back where he started. She was playing dirty. He could play dirty, too. He gave her a feigned sympathetic look.

"Och, Maggie, ye still look...very hot. Allow me to help ye with that." He smiled, stalked close to her....
picked up the bucket and dumped it over the top of her head.

Maggie sucked in her breath and let out a little squeal, stunned as much by the cold water as she was by his nerve. It really wasn't that hot outside and the water was freezing.

He set the bucket down and leaned over to whisper, "Did that help cool ye down, Maggie? I wouldn't want you to overheat." He turned, laughing, and walked away.

"Oh, Duncan?"

He stopped, looking straight ahead so he didn't have to see Maggie.

Everyone in the courtyard had stopped to observe the show, his brothers watching with happy smiles on their faces. A little too happy...they were looking at Maggie...completely soaked in her very thin clothes, clothes that clung to every curve on her upper half, snug leather trousers on the bottom half.

Damn it.

He called back without turning. "Yes, Maggie?"

"I think you are looking a little too hot yourself. Let me help *you* with that."

Afraid that she may have stripped down to nothing judging by the wide eyes and anxious grins on his brother's faces, he turned to answer...

...and was met by a bucket of cold water right in his face.

Maggie dropped the bucket and strode past him to the house, chuckling the whole way.

Duncan stood there, solid as stone, only moving to wipe the water from his face with one hand. His brothers cackled with laughter behind him. The rest of the men just stared, waiting for him to explode. He turned and started towards the house. "Logan, take over!"

This was war….and it wasn't going to be pretty.

Maggie was still laughing by the time she got to the house. The look on Duncan's face had been priceless. She wrung the water out of her hair before going inside. Her clothes were still dripping, but she made her way to the library where a small fire burned. The door slammed behind her. *Oh...he must be angry.*

She poured herself a drink and moved to the front of the fireplace, enjoying the warmth, to wait for him.

He came in the room, pulling the tie from his hair, and shaking it loose, looking like a wet St. Bernard shaking himself after a bath. When he stopped, his hair was wild, untamed, looking like a rock star god, and his dripping wet tartan clung to every rippling muscle that he had.

Shit! He is twice as hot-looking like that.

He spotted her and immediately moved to her with a sly smile on his face, wrapping one arm around her waist, and roughly pulling her close to him.

Angry sex! Yes!!!

He leaned close to her face; Maggie closed her eyes and waited for the welcome, brutal assault on her lips.

He took his other arm and reached around behind her….to pull a blanket from the back of the chair and wrap it around her, encasing her body in it, like a parent wrapping a child in a towel who just got out of the tub. He pulled it tightly closed in the front, frowning and scolding her. "Ye should not walk around soaking wet. Ye may catch a very bad chest cold."

He turned his back to her, grinning when he knew she couldn't see, and went to get another blanket from the other side of the room to dry himself off.

Maggie looked over at him, scowling with a look of annoyance.

Lady Aurnia came around the corner into the room. "Oh Maggie, I was just coming to look for you…. why are ye soaking wet?"

Duncan cleared his throat.

His mother looked over at him. "Duncan? Why...oh never mind...I don't want to know. I need to talk to both of ye, anyway. Duncan, close the door and come over here."

Duncan did as his mother commanded.

Lady Aurnia took one seat by the fireplace while Maggie took the other. Duncan came to stand behind Maggie's chair.

"Maggie, I found out something about your bottle."

"You know what it is?"

The older woman nodded. "I do indeed. I found a reference in one of the books. When the Fae first went underground, they still maintained contact with people they had grown fond of. They would often send little gifts or notes to those people in a type of...vessel. In order for these vessels to get to the correct person, they would be engraved with a certain set of symbols on the outside. Let's say, for instance, I wished to send a package to your home in Virginia. I would put yer name and where ye live on the outside and hire a messenger to deliver it. The messenger would only be able to give it to ye, the person's name who was on the package, the one it was intended for. These vessels work the same, only in a magical way. That bottle had yer name on it and yer location on it. No one else would have been able to even find it. It WAS meant for ye and ye alone. Ye did not just stumble upon it by accident."

Maggie rubbed her forehead. "And the note inside was intended for me?"

"It was not a note, Maggie. It was a spell."

Maggie blinked hard. "A spell? They really exist?"

Lady Aurnia leaned forward. "Aye, they do. They are rare indeed and they only come straight from the Fae themselves. Ye said ye read it aloud. When ye did, those words that ye spoke brought ye back to this time. But Maggie, if ye were not meant to do it, ye would have never received it, to begin with. Ye are here because ye are supposed to be. And if indeed ye do something to change the future, it is because it needs to be changed, for whatever reason that we cannot see. Something that ye do makes a major shift in this world's future." She paused for a moment. "We have also found vague references to a few others who were sent back in time long, long ago and while no details were given, it was clearly stated that they were always sent for the betterment of mankind in some way."

Maggie looked into the fire. "No pressure there! Why me? I have no connection to these Fae. I had never even stepped foot in Scotland before a few days ago."

Lady Aurnia looked down, as if she wanted to say something, but was unsure if she should.

"What is it, Mother? What are ye not saying?" asked Duncan.

She looked at Maggie, tilting her head. "YE have no connection to Scotland, but ye know someone who does?"

"You mean, my mother."

Duncan looked down. "Yer mother was Scottish?"

Maggie nodded. "But, she never even spoke of it."

Lady Aurnia touched Maggie's knee. "Which begs the question…. why would she never tell you anything about it? About her family, her roots? I know not one Scot who is not proud of their heritage and is happy to share that information with anyone willing to listen."

"So, what am I to do? How do I know what the…thing is that I need to do…to make this all-important…shift?" Maggie threw up her hands in exasperation. She opened her mouth to say something, only to close it again. She didn't even know how to express the question, much less figure out the answer.

Duncan could feel her distress and placed his hands on her shoulders for comfort, kneading fingers into tightening muscles.

Lady Aurnia looked at her with compassion. "I do not have that answer, but if I were to venture a guess, I would say that ye should just live yer life as ye see fit. Ye never intended to end up in Scotland, yet here ye are anyway. Whatever ye are meant to do will find a way to put itself in front of ye…and if the Fae have this much faith in ye, I have no doubt that ye will make the right choice, whatever it may be."

The woman patted her knee. "I still have some more books I wish to go through. Will ye be alright?"

Maggie didn't answer.

Duncan looked at his mother and said in a low voice, "I will look after her."

Lady Aurnia left the room.

Maggie stared at the floor trying to absorb everything she had just heard. She was here to change something, to help mankind, but she had no idea what...or how.... or when.... or anything. One of her headaches start to come on.

I need a drink!

Duncan handed her a glass.

She never even felt him take his hands off her or knew that he had crossed the room and returned to her side. She looked at the glass and back at him strangely.

"What?" he asked. "Why are ye looking at me that way? Ye wanted a drink!"

She looked at him, puzzled. "How did you know that I wanted a drink?"

He shrugged. "I just knew." It was his turn to give her a puzzled look. "Didn't ye ask for one?"

Maggie shook her head slowly and looked back at the glass.

That was strange!

"Strange indeed!" Duncan said aloud.

Maggie downed the drink, looking at Duncan peculiarly the whole time. It occurred to her that she was still wrapped in the blanket and soaking wet.

Duncan looked at her. "Ye should go change. Ye are freezing."

Maggie stood and pointed her finger at him. "Stop doing that!"

"Doing what?"

She shook her head. "Never mind. I am going to find some dry clothes."

A few minutes later, Maggie was in her room and had changed into a dry shirt, one of many that she had, and was hanging her trousers on the back of a chair to dry. She sat on the floor in front of the fireplace with her knees up to her chest, leaning against the footboard of the bed, all the new information from the library rolling through her head. So many more questions than answers.

Then there was Duncan. Her physical need for him was becoming... overwhelming, to say the least, but he wanted from her what she was not able to give. Even if she were to allow herself to fall for him, she would have to leave, and it wasn't like they could hop on a plane to see each other on weekends. It would never work out long-term, but she would like to enjoy some time with him while she was here. Maggie had grown extremely fond of him, and not just in a sexual way...she legitimately enjoyed being around him. He was funny, smart, and an all-around good man.

They seemed to have some sort of unexplainable connection for some reason, and she could not explain why.

Duncan went to his room and changed out of his wet tartan, the image of Maggie in that damnable wet shirt still fresh in his mind. He had almost given in and taken her in the library, only being able to suppress his urge by covering her up with the blanket.

It was a good thing, too, because his mother would have walked right in on them, and that would have been awkward. He was glad for the fact, however, that he was there when his mother relayed the information that she had. Duncan could see how it troubled Maggie, and he feared that she might have fallen into one of her attacks...and not like the one from this morning, another image still rolling around in his head.

Denying her, and himself, was proving more difficult than he had ever imagined, but if he could convince her of what he already knew, it would all be worth it.

He needed to get rid of some pent-up aggression, and he could do that by rejoining the men and partaking in a little swordplay. Perhaps it would make him too weary to think about her.

Maggie got up and went to the window. She folded her arms and watched the men training in the courtyard; Duncan had rejoined them. He was sword fighting with one of the other men, and he was very good at it, fighting with an intensity that was almost frightening.

She watched him put the second man on the ground in a short amount of time.

He stepped to the side, breathing hard, getting ready for his third round. He looked directly up at her as if he knew she was watching. He smirked up at her.

Maggie wanted him to feel some of the frustration she was experiencing, so she waved at him, smiled a huge smile, blew him a kiss...and lifted her shirt top to expose her completely bare breasts to him, pressing them against the glass for added emphasis.

Duncan's jaw and sword simultaneously dropped.

She closed the drapes and turned around, very pleased with herself.

Mission accomplished.

Maggie's trousers were still wet by suppertime, so she decided to wear the gown that Lady Aurnia had loaned her the first night. Duncan was at the bottom of the staircase waiting when she came down.

He looked at her with a pleasant look of amazement on his face. "Maggie, ye look very lovely tonight."

"Thank you, Duncan." She let him lead her towards the dining room.

She leaned in close and whispered, "Did you enjoy the show from my bedroom window?"

He looked straight ahead. "Oh aye, I did. Ye are not playing fair, Maggie. Just remember that when the tables are turned."

She looked at him suspiciously, wondering what he meant by that.

He seated Maggie to the left of his mother, who was at the head of the table and he sat to the right, directly across from Maggie, so he could keep an eye on her.

The rest of the MacGregor brothers joined them, happily making small talk about training day.

Lady Aurnia looked over at Maggie while they were eating. "Maggie, what is written on that bracelet that ye wear?"

Maggie looked down, "Oh, it's a verse by Shakespeare. 'The course of true love never did run smooth.' It is from a Midsummer Night's Dream...ironically."

"It's beautiful. Wherever did ye get it?"

"Oh, it was a gift from a dear friend."

Lady Aurnia smiled. "Is that your friend...Gabe, was it?"

Maggie looked uncomfortably over at Duncan who was watching her.

"No, it was from my friend, John. It was a departing gift when my ship left Philadelphia."

Duncan narrowed his eyes and tilted his head. "Ye seem to have many male friends."

Looking down, Maggie smiled inwardly, knowing that it bothered Duncan. "Do I? I suppose I do." Looking back up, a realization hit her, causing her to rub her forehead with one hand while grimacing. "The ship! I completely forgot about the ship!"

Everyone turned to look at her.

Lady Aurnia looked concerned. "What did ye forget?"

"That my ship will be back in Edinburgh for me in a few days. I completely lost track of time."

Duncan sat back. "It's your ship, surely it will wait for ye."

Maggie shook her head, anxious. "That is not the problem. The problem is that there is going to be a former British colonel on that ship, and he is going to be furious when he steps off, especially if I am not there waiting when they pull into dock. If he is unable to locate me, he will take Scotland apart piece by piece until he does."

Duncan leaned forward, extremely concerned. "What man and why will he be so angry?"

"My friend, Gabe. I came to Scotland to retrieve his nephew who was in some trouble, and I did...I just didn't return with him. I didn't tell him I was staying on in Scotland alone to pursue the map."

Logan spoke, "Why didn't your friend come to get his nephew?"

Maggie looked around the table, "He couldn't. He has a newborn at home."

Lady Aurnia looked confused. "Why didn't his wife stay with the bairn?"

Maggie explained the situation with the baby and how Gabe had become a father rather unexpectedly. "As much as I hate it, I will have to leave in a few short days."

Duncan paled, like he had been punched in the stomach.

Lady Aurnia saw the anguish on his face...it was almost as bad as what was on Maggie's.

After supper, Maggie went looking for Duncan. He had slipped away quietly while she was talking to his mother. Maggie couldn't believe she had been so caught up with her little game with him, that she had completely forgotten about the ship. She searched the whole house to no avail.

Now, she stood in the foyer, trying to figure out where he had gone.

Where is he?

Something inside her answered: *Down by the water.*

Maggie shook her head. *What the hell?* Where had that answer just come from?

She took a lantern and started down the path. Sure enough, there was another light on the beach. She walked down to the shore, wrapping her arms around her to ward off the chill coming from the water. Someone had built a small fire and a tartan lay spread out beside it...Duncan's tartan.

Maggie looked around the shoreline but did not see him. Just as she was getting ready to go back inside, she noticed movement out of the corner of her eye, in the water. She looked closer.

The moonlight and the glow from the stars illuminated the top of the water, causing it to give off a ghostly, almost unearthly glow. Maggie blinked and looked again because she could scarcely believe her eyes. Duncan was coming out of the water toward her, his gaze focused directly on her, a determined, lustful look on his face. He appeared wild and untamable, like something out of a strange, mystifying dream...the kind of dream that you desperately struggled to retain with the dawning of the new day. A creature that could be either an angel or a demon, depending on his mood and current desire. He raked his loose hair back with his hands and he made his way to her, the light playing off his finely chiseled features, making him look ancient, a forgotten god from the days of old, coming to reclaim his place in the universe. A rush of heat radiated through Maggie's entire body when she saw that he was completely naked...and standing ready for *her.*

Game over. Drop the mic.

Maggie's brain was completely void of anything except the man in front of her. There was no room for anything else in her mind or body, but him. She was too astonished to say anything.

He took one hand and cupped her face, his mere touch bringing her to the edge.

Well, fuck me!

He leaned in, smiling wickedly at her. "Well, if ye insist." He grabbed her around the waist and pulled her into a powerful, raw, unadulterated kiss, one that set every nerve in Maggie's body afire, sucking the very air that she breathed from her body.

Maggie knew at that moment that he had...WON.

She would agree to anything and everything to have this man in her life and in her bed, even if it meant selling her very soul to the devil himself. Maggie's past fell away; it no longer mattered. There were no others before him and there would be none after him. A deep awareness penetrated her very being.

This man was brought into this world for her.

The future did not matter…it would take care of itself. As long as he was by her side, all would be well.

He pulled back from the kiss and looked into her eyes. "I have a price," he whispered.

Let the devil have his due.

"Name it," she answered, her eyes still closed.

"Become my wife."

Maggie opened her eyes to gaze into his, not seeing any future worth living that did not include him.

"Yes."

Duncan's smile was victory itself, and he pulled her into another breathtaking kiss then gingerly lay her down on his tartan. He lifted her gown and shift off in one move. He took his time, claiming every part of her body, leaving nothing untouched, until she flipped the scene and returned the favor.

They worked in synch, finding their own rhythm, their own timing, one refusing to climax without the other. They were one in every way that mattered, the moon and stars being the only witnesses to their newly formed union. They made love for hours before the fire went out. Duncan then carried her inside to his bed, where they made love until dawn. The next day, they slept and loved until suppertime.

Maggie lay stroking his chest. "I am starving."

Duncan looked down, chuckling. "Ye should be if I am doing anything right." He kissed her and slipped out of bed. "Let's gets dressed and go share our news, while we regain our strength."

Maggie looked at him lovingly. "Duncan, you know we have some obstacles to overcome."

He narrowed his eyes at her and folded his arms. "Ye are not backing out of this marriage. I will not allow it."

"No...and I don't want to. But I have my responsibilities in Virginia, and you have yours here. We will have to make some decisions."

He leaned down and kissed her, tucking her hair behind her ear. "We will figure things out. Dinna fash lass, all will be well." He rubbed her backside all the way down. "Now, get dressed. Ye have a wedding to plan."

When he turned to fasten his tartan, Maggie noticed something. "What's that on your lower back?"

"Hmmm? Oh, it's the mark that all the members of the family that protect the Fae secrets carry. It is done with ink during a ceremony when we come of age. It is a proof of loyalty to the family and the cause." He sat on the bed to give her a better look.

"It's a tattoo."

"Is that what ye call it?"

"Actually, we call it something else, but that's another story entirely."

The mark was an ivy circle that consisted of ancient Celtic symbols forming a tree with a sword, like hers, as the trunk. The unusual thing was the color itself...a warm dark gold with flecks of something else. Maggie touched it, feeling a little jolt when she did.

"Did you feel that?'

Duncan looked around at her, confused. "Aye, I did."

Maggie sat up. "Has that ever happened before?"

He shook his head. "Nay, but I am not in the habit of letting women touch it. However, *ye* can touch it whenever ye like," he added, grinning.

"What else can I touch?" she asked as she rubbed his thigh.

He kissed her. "Anything ye like."

They dressed and went downstairs for supper.

Everyone stopped talking to give them curious looks when they entered the room.

Reade looked them over. "And where have ye been, Brother? Ducking out of work again."

Evan piped up, nudging Reade. "The rest of us don't get to spend all day in bed."

Maggie sat down and Duncan took the chair beside her.

Duncan reached for a piece of bread, taking a bite and chewing as he looked at his brothers. "Actually..." Duncan swallowed and turned to his mother, "we were celebrating. Maggie has agreed to marry me."

Lady Aurnia's face lit up. "Truly?" She jumped up, her expression ecstatic, and skipped to stand between the two of them, hugging them both. "Ye do not know how happy that makes me."

Logan smiled. "Congratulations, Brother, and we cannot thank ye enough. Ye just took some of the pressure off the rest of us to take a bride."

Lady Aurnia shot him a disapproving look. "Hardly."

Reade elbowed Evan. "Look! Mother is already counting the grandchildren in her head."

Everyone laughed and congratulated them.

Lady Aurnia returned to her seat. "How soon would ye like to have the ceremony?"

Maggie looked around. "I don't know. We have a few things we need to settle first."

The lady looked concerned. "Like what, Dear?"

Maggie looked at Duncan. "Well, there is the matter of Duncan's home here and my home in Virginia. They are not exactly a day's trip apart and I cannot be away much longer."

Duncan frowned; those at the table went silent.

"Surely ye will stay here, will ye not?" asked Quinn. "We have the matter of the collection here and that comes first."

"As the oldest son, Duncan is Laird here. He is next in line to Mother," added Logan.

Duncan took Maggie's hand, kissing it. "We will make it work."

Maggie wasn't so sure.

Lady Aurnia gave Maggie a reassuring look. "Duncan is right. Ye will figure it out. Nothing needs to be decided at the supper table this evening. Tonight, we will just be happy with the new addition to our family."

After supper, the whole family retired to the library for celebratory drinks. Duncan was cornered by his brothers, who gave him a hard time, while Maggie and Lady Aurnia took the chairs next to the fireplace.

"Maggie, I cannot tell ye how delighted I am about ye and Duncan, Ye are just what he needs, and he will be a good husband to ye."

Maggie smiled. "I know."

"Have ye given any thought to the details of the wedding, when ye will marry...or your gown? Of course, we will have our 'own' ceremony."

Maggie shook her head. "I have not given thought to anything. This is all very sudden. We have so many things that we have not discussed yet." She cocked her head, "What do you mean by 'our own ceremony'?"

"Well, as ye well know, our family is not like most. There is a ceremony in the Fae text that binds a couple together and makes ye part of the family as a protector of the collection. It's one of the reasons my boys have not taken wives...they can only bring in someone that will know the importance of what we do and keep our secrets."

Maggie nodded. "Does that involve taking the mark that Duncan has on his back?"

"Well, that would be your choice. It is typically only given to those born into the family, but I think we could make an exception in your case, if ye wish."

She let out a deep breath. "Any idea why I would have felt something when I touched it?"

Lady Aurnia raised a brow and leaned closer. "What did ye feel?"

"It was like a jolt of energy. It was very strange."

"That is strange indeed." Lady Aurnia looked down and away, her frown deepening.

Duncan came over and stood behind Maggie, touching her shoulder. "Are ye ready to head up to bed Maggie?"

"Yes."

They bid everyone good night and, as soon as they were in Duncan's room, Maggie sat down on the bed, taking in a deep, shaky breath.

Duncan closed the door and came to sit beside her, slipped his arm around her waist and kissed her neck. "What's wrong, Maggie?"

"I am just feeling a little anxious about all the wedding talk...and the gown...and the date. Then there is my ship coming into dock and, apparently, there is some kind of Fae ceremony.... there are just too many things we need to figure out. It's all so...complicated."

He pulled her in close, gently turning her face to his. "Did anyone ever tell ye that ye worry too much?"

Maggie bobbed her head matter-of-factly. "Gabe...on a daily basis."

"He is right. Ye are not alone anymore. These little details will work themselves out." He kissed her forehead. but she looked back at him with an upset look.

"Duncan.... where will we live? You are needed here, and I am needed in Virginia. That is not a little detail."

Duncan instinctively knew how to calm her. He took her face into both his hands and pulled her into a slow, deep kiss that cleared Maggie's head, making her forget everything that was bothering her. He pulled back, tucking a strand of hair behind her ear. "And what was it that ye were so worried about again?"

She tried to remember but couldn't. *How did he do that? How did he just make me forget everything that was bothering me?* Maggie shrugged, still half-drunk from his kiss. "I am worried you are going to leave me hanging here and not finish what you started."

Grabbing her, Duncan growled and pulled her onto the bed. "Then, ye have nothing to worry about."

The next morning, when Maggie woke up, she knew he wasn't in the room. She sat up and looked around, noticing all her things were back.

The staff must be getting tired of moving all this stuff back and forth.

Memories of their lovemaking flooded back. He had distracted her from all her questions. He did more than that. Now, she *knew* somewhere deep down that all would be as it should.

Maggie dressed and went downstairs. As she reached the first floor, the entire MacGregor family spilled out of the library, their faces solemn, Duncan and Lady Aurnia being the last ones out.

Maggie looked around. "What's wrong?"

Duncan moved to her side, giving her a good morning kiss. "Nothing, my love. We were just discussing some things and making some...arrangements."

She eyed him with suspicion. "What kind of arrangements?"

A twinkle came to his eye, and he reached to pull her into a deeper kiss.

Maggie pressed her finger to his lips. "Oh no you don't, mister. I am on to your whole…" she waved her hands around in front of him, "'distract my mind with your body' thing that you do. At some point, we have to have some real conversations."

"Maggie…"

The front door flew open. One of the men that stood guard came rushing in, out of breath.

Everyone turned.

"My Laird, there is thick black smoke coming from the outer perimeter of the tenant's village. They may be under attack. The men are saddling your horses."

Almost as one, the MacGregor men moved to gather their weapons.

Duncan turned to Maggie, taking her by the shoulders. "I have to go. Those people are under our protection. Stay here with Mother and remain inside the walls. I will be back as soon as I can."

Maggie looked confused. "What people, Duncan?"

"Mother can explain, but these people, they are our responsibility. We have given them our word."

"I will ride out with you."

He shook his head. "Nay, you will not. If the village is indeed under attack, I need ye to be here, safe. I cannot help anyone if I am worried about ye."

He pulled her into an embrace and whispered in her ear, "Take care of Mother for me. I will instruct the men that stay behind to pull up the gate after we leave. I love ye and I will be back soon."

She grabbed his arm. "Promise me you will be back, and in one piece."

He cupped her face and kissed her. "Nothing will keep me away."

His kiss did not relieve her mind this time.

Maggie and Lady Aurnia watched them ride off from the window.

Lady Aurnia saw how concerned Maggie was.

"Maggie, my boys train for this constantly. Dinna fash...they will be fine."

Maggie turned to her. "Who are these people? I thought everyone was within the walls."

Lady Aurnia moved toward the chairs at the fireplace, motioning for her to come. They both sat down.

"We have needs that cannot be provided for within the walls...crops, cattle, and the such. As much as we have tried to avoid the outside world, we cannot do it completely. We just try to stay as discreet as possible. Many years ago, some of the families within the walls expressed a desire, as the castle community grew, to be further away from so many people, so we built homes for them and protected them in exchange for their helping. They eventually formed a little village, the nearest one to us, and we occasionally go in to buy, sell, and trade things and to hear news from the outside world. It has been useful. We offer them our protection in exchange for not mentioning who we are and exactly where we are. It was easy to go unnoticed when Scotland was younger, but the population has grown far too rapidly in recent years, and there are too many families scattered to the wind after the conflicts that it has endured. I often wonder how much longer we will remain anonymous here."

Maggie looked through the window. "Then where did the people within the walls come from?"

"They are the descendants of the original families that were here when the castle was new. Their lines go back for generations and many remain out of loyalty to their ancestors. People here are aware that we protect something very old and important, they just do not know what. Most of them like the solitude we offer, especially when they hear news from other areas when they go into the village."

"Then who would attack them and why?"

"I do not know," answered Lady Aurnia. "Our people sometimes have occasional rows with people passing through, or with the outlaws that come near our boundaries...like the MacLarens who attacked ye in the woods, but for the most part, we are left alone." She reached over and patted Maggie's hand. "I am sure it is not anything serious."

However, Maggie had a strange feeling that it was.

"Come, Maggie, let's go to the kitchen and find ye some breakfast."

"Thank you, but I am not hungry."

Lady Aurnia stood up. "Why don't I have a hot bath sent up to ye? Flora made some wonderful soap with the herbs from the garden. It might help ease ye some…and maybe later we can talk about some plans for the wedding?"

"That sounds lovely," said Maggie, not wanting to be rude.

Lady Aurnia went to find Flora.

Maggie sat staring into the fire, wishing she was by Duncan's side, instead of sitting there wondering what was happening.

17 CHAPTER SEVENTEEN

Later that afternoon, Maggie was still anxious. She went to find Onyx, thinking that one of his comforting hugs may be in order. Grabbing an apple, she headed out to the stables. When she got there, all the doors were closed, which was unusual during the day. None of the stable hands were in sight. Maggie opened the door just far enough to slip in. If Onyx was stopped up in there, he would not be happy.

The entire stable empty, Onyx nowhere in sight.

Well, at least he wasn't penned in.

Maggie turned to slip back out, wondering where Onyx might be when she noticed something in one of the stalls, the sight holding her gaze after her body had already turned.

Everything after that seemed, in Maggie's mind, to go in slow motion.

Maggie felt a tiny sharp pain in her lower right back side, like she had been stung by a bee. It was a prick at first, then a little burning sensation. She was too absorbed in the picture in the stall to realize what was happening to her.

In the stall was little Christopher Manus, bound and gagged. His eyes were wide with horror and he was trying to tell her something, writhing and banging his tied feet on the stall floor. He was trying to scream out, but the gag prevented it.

Maggie tried to turn to go to him when the irritating pang into a much stronger, more demanding pain, one that made her drop to her knees. Her hand reached around to touch the area, feeling something sticky pooling in her palm and dripping through her fingers. She brought her hand around to see that it was covered in a bright red substance. She looked down at her hand, confused. It took a few seconds to register what it was. Maggie fell to the floor of the stable on her back.

Standing over Maggie was that bastard, Angus Riley, laughing, and he was holding a dirk in his hand...covered in HER blood.

He leaned down, looking at her as she lay bleeding. "Not so big and bad now are ye, ye fecking cunt."

I am so killing this bastard...if I don't bleed to death first.

Duncan, where are you? I need you!

Angus Riley reached over and grabbed Maggie by the arm, dragging her over next to Christopher, leaving a wide trail of blood in their wake.

Maggie was so focused on keeping herself awake that she didn't make a sound.

He went out of the stall and two more men came into the stable to speak with him.

Maggie turned her gaze to Christopher, who was staring at her, his face now streaked with dirty tears.

Maggie licked her lips, managing to whisper, "Christopher, has he hurt you?"

He shook his tiny little head.

"Good. I promised you he wouldn't, and I intend to keep that promise. I just need you to be strong, for me, okay?"

He nodded and his tears slowed.

"Good boy."

Angus Riley came back over to her, squatting down, the two men behind him.

"Where is it, you fecking bitch! Tell me where the treasure is, and I'll leave ye to die in peace."

Maggie looked at him, trying to control her breathing. "What treasure?"

Riley laughed. "Oh, did Duncan MacGregor not tell his whore about the family treasure?" He sat down on the ground next to her, leaning against the stall, pointing his dagger in her direction. "Well, let me fill ye in. Ye see, there have always been little references to a grand treasure being somewhere here in the Scottish Highlands, legends and old wives talk, nothing more...or so I thought. I never paid much attention to it until I met this little bastard's mother in that tavern about a year ago. She had more than her fair share of ale and started rattling off about the 'grand MacGregor clan' and their 'secrets' that everyone kept for them. It didn't take much to figure out what she was talking about. So, I showed up at their door one day, told them my name was Riley and that I needed a job, spinning them a sad tale about how I had no family left in this world. They felt sorry for me and took me right in. I earned their trust to the point they treated me like one of their own, just like I planned. It made me want to wretch every time I had to sit at their table and act like I liked any of them. I only needed another month and I was going to sneak in that house after they all went to bed, find the treasure, and burn that wretched house to the ground…. after I locked all their doors and trapped them, of course. Nothing would have made me happier than to see that whole family burnt to a crisp."

He leaned over her, pointing the knife close to her face. "But then ye had to come along and ruin everything. They trusted me until ye showed up and spoiled it. I had to ride back to the family home and gather all my fellow MacLarens that I could find to come back with me. So, I sent a few men and had them set that village tavern on fire, knowing the whisky inside would create a big black cloud, big enough to get those brothers out of here while the rest of us slipped inside the walls early this morning and waited for them to leave." He whispered, "Ye cost me so much and now I have to share the treasure with these other men instead of keeping it for myself. I didn't even get the chance to have a taste of this little sweet one over there." He eyed Christopher in a way that made Maggie want to vomit. "He is my little unfinished business. I think I will just take him with me and take my time."

I am SO staying alive just to kill this bastard if it is the last thing that I do. Maggie closed her eyes. "That will never happen. You have my word on that."

Angus stood up as two more men came into the stable. He started towards them but turned back to scowl at Maggie. "There is no one here to save ye. All your precious MacGregors are gone and the men they left behind to guard the house don't even know we are here.

We will be long gone before they know what happened...their treasure gone, their home on fire, and their precious womenfolk dead. Make peace with your God now! Ye do not have much time left in this world."

He and the rest of the men stormed out.

Maggie opened her eyes and looked around. They all went out the opposite door that Maggie came in. She gathered her strength and reached down in her boot to pull out one of her hidden daggers. Crawling over to Christopher, she carefully cut his hands free, the action taking all the strength she had. He pulled his gag off and took the knife to cut his feet free.

"Christopher, I need you to do something."

He looked at her, his little eyes opened wide.

"I need you to go out the door that I came in, get into the house, and find Lady Aurnia. You need to warn her. Do not let them see you. Can you do that?"

"I cannot leave ye here, ma'am."

Maggie took his hand. "If you don't leave me, we will all die. I need you to do this...for me."

He looked unsure but nodded in agreement.

"Christopher be careful...and after you find Lady Aurnia, go find one of the guards that your Laird left. I don't know how many MacLarens are here or who to trust, but you must find help. They must get that gate down, so the brothers can get back in. If it stays up, we are all dead."

He nodded, terrified out of his mind, and slipped out the door.

Maggie laid back, trying to focus her mind. *Where the hell is Onyx when I need him?*

The MacGregor brothers and most of their guard were riding hard towards the village, the smoke getting thicker the closer they came. Duncan brought most of the guard with them, leaving a handful of men behind to close the gate and keep watch. He was on Gavina and leading the charge.

He caught a dark movement out of the corner of his eye and turned to see what it was.

It was Onyx.

The great black horse was riding directly horizontal to him on the outside flank of his group, matching, almost exceeding his pace. Onyx was neighing and moving his head as if he were trying to get his attention.

Duncan held up his hand, indicating to the men to stop. When they slowed, Onyx came directly to Duncan, pawing and stomping at the ground, snorting, extremely agitated with SMOKE coming out of his nose. He demanded attention, even using his mouth to take Duncan's horse by the reins, to pull her back in the direction of the house.

"What the hell is wrong with ye beast?" It hit Duncan that the only reason Onyx would be here was if Maggie was in terrible danger. He closed his eyes, focusing on Maggie...and a thought slamming into his mind.

Duncan, I need you.

Duncan's eyes flew open. He turned to his brothers. "There is trouble at home. Evan and Reade, you take half of the men and go to the village. The rest will come with us."

His brothers nodded, and the groups separated.

Duncan rode full gallop, trying to keep up with Onyx, who was well ahead and leading the charge.

I am coming, Maggie.

Maggie heard the men coming back. She slipped the dagger back in her boot. She may not be able to stop them all, but maybe she could rid the world of one that no one would miss. She closed her eyes when a silent, powerful thought blasted into her mind.

I am coming, Maggie.

Maggie blinked and smiled.

Duncan knew something was wrong and was on his way. She just hoped she could hold out until he got there.

Two of the men came in and noticed that Christopher was gone. They were looking for him when Angus came in, fuming. He went straight to Maggie, pulling her up by her shirt.

"Where's the fecking boy?"

Maggie grimaced and then smiled. "The boy? Is he not here? I was having a lovely nap and I didn't notice."

Angus slapped her hard across the face and dropped her with a thump. "Find that boy! He will ruin everything!"

Angus slammed his fist into one of the stables, shouting to himself. He was becoming unhinged.

The other four men came back in, indicating they could not find the boy.

Angus rubbed his chin, trying to figure out the next step. He turned and looked at Maggie. "We take the house now. Get in and block all the entrances to the main part of the house so no one will bother us."

They left, and he came over and grabbed Maggie, throwing her over his shoulder. The blood ran down her back and she was lightheaded.

He threw a horse blanket over her to hide her and carried her into the house. He took her in the library and dropped her onto the couch.

Lady Aurnia was there by the fireplace. "Maggie!"

Angus grabbed Lady Aurnia by the arm, throwing her towards the couch.

"Patch Duncan's whore up. I am not done with her yet." He stomped out of the library.

Maggie yelled after him. "I am getting really tired of being called a whore, you fucking asshole."

Lady Aurnia moved to Maggie, looking for her wound. "Maggie, let me help ye turn a little, so I can get a better look? Did he stab ye?"

Nodding, Maggie rolled as far as she could; the pain was horrific.

Lady Aurnia looked at her strangely, working to get a better look at her wound. She moved to one of the side tables and pulled out some rags to stop the bleeding. "Ye are very lucky Maggie."

"I don't feel very lucky."

The lady stripped some of the fabric from the bottom of her shift for longer pieces. "It seems the leather in these trousers of yours kept the blade from going in too far. There is a good deal of blood, but I do not think there is too much damage."

Maggie let out a breath, whispering as she got close, "Did Christopher get to you?"

Lady Aurnia looked back at the door. "Aye, and I sent him to find Duncan's most trusted man. It was very smart of ye to tell him to get the gate down."

"Duncan is on his way."

Lady Aurnia looked at her, blinking. "How do ye know?"

Maggie chuckled through the pain. "I don't know. I just know that he is on the way. He and I seem to have a strange, unspoken mental connection. If I focus, I can hear in my mind what he is thinking, and I am pretty sure it works the same way for him. I can send him a specific thought and he, somehow...gets it. It's a little unnerving if you think about it too much."

Lady Aurnia's look of amazement turned into a smirk, as she remembered something that she read in one of the Fae books. "That happens when two fortunate souls who are *truly* destined for each other, first meet. They fall in love rather quickly, and their minds seem to become as one. It is also an extremely rare and remarkable gift that will increase greatly over time."

Lady Aurnia finished her bandages and poured Maggie a whisky. "Drink it...for the pain."

Maggie downed it. "Thank you." She whispered, "He is after the collection you know, but he thinks it's a different kind of treasure."

Lady Aurnia nodded, "He will never find it. The chamber is well hidden."

Maggie shook her head, "You don't understand. He wants the 'treasure'...yes...but he intends to burn this place to the ground, with us in it. He is losing his mind, more and more by the minute...and he is a MacLaren."

"A MacLaren...that was in our guard? Good Lord!"

Lady Aurnia and Maggie looked at each other, concerned, as they heard the men breaking furniture and blocking the doors.

Angus returned looking very disturbed and aggravated "Where is the treasure? Tell me and I will kill ye quickly." Lady Aurnia looked up from the glass she was sipping, and calmly said, "There is no treasure. Ye are wasting your time."

He looked at her thoughtfully and made a click with his mouth, snarling. "Very well, ye burn like the she-witch ye are. I will tie ye to that dining room table before I light the pyre beneath ye myself."

The men came back in, one of them speaking for the group. "We have searched the whole house and have found nothing."

Angus shoved him backward. "Ye fecking fools. It will not be in plain sight. It is HIDDEN! Look again before I run ye through myself." He grabbed a glass decanter from the table, drinking down as much whisky as he could before throwing it to the floor, shattering it.

He walked over to Maggie, breathing hard and leering. "Ye cost me the wee one, and as much it will pain me to soil myself with the likes of ye, I will have some satisfaction today."

Grabbing Maggie by the waist, her pulled her roughly up to him, grabbing her intentionally in her wound.

His breath smelled of rotting teeth and his body smelled of disease. Vomit rose in the back of Maggie's throat, horrendous pain filling her, blood dripping through her bandage.

Lady Aurnia tried to pull Maggie free, but Angus backhanded her in the face, sending her to the floor. He dragged Maggie up the stairs to Duncan's room, slamming the door and throwing her down on the bed.

He looked around. "The Laird has a fine room. Did he have ye in this bed? I wonder how he will feel when he knows that a MacLaren has taken ye in the same bed." Angus took off his belt and used it to tie one of Maggie's hands to the bed post. She was in no shape to run, she was barely standing from the blood loss that was pooling at her feet.

"I think I will only bind your one hand so ye can put up a fight. I like it when ye fight." He grabbed Maggie by the face and kissed her.

Maggie took the chance to bite his lip.

He growled when he stepped back and wiped the blood from his mouth. When he saw it, he slapped Maggie across the face. He grabbed her by the hair. "I told ye I like it when ye fight. Look what it does to me."

He rubbed his erection against her thigh.

Maggie looked at him, anger and disgust fomenting under her skin.

"Let's get a better look at ye." He ripped open her shirt exposing one of her breasts and grabbed her roughly with his hand. "I wonder how this will taste?" He leaned in as she tried to push him back.

A banging on the door interrupted him.

"What do ye want?" he bellowed.

"We have one of the MacGregor men."

Angus looked at Maggie and smiled.

He opened the door and the three men brought Duncan in.

"Well, well. The Laird has returned just in time to see me feck his whore in his own bed."

Duncan looked at Maggie, going weak in the knees at the sight. Maggie was barely standing, tied to the bed with a belt, a pool of blood at her feet. Her face was bloodied and bruised. Her top was torn, and she looked like she was in shock.

He had failed to keep her safe.

Angus moved to Maggie's side, taunting Duncan. "Quite a woman ye have here." He grabbed her around the waist, pulling her close to him so that he was behind her, facing Duncan. He licked her neck while watching Duncan's anguished face.

Rage engulfed Duncan. He sailed towards Angus only to be stopped by the three men, who beat him to the ground.

Angus walked over, kneeled, pulling his head up, spitting on him. "Tell me where the treasure is, and I will let ye have a moment with your woman before ye both die. If ye don't tell me, I will make ye listen to her scream in agony the rest of the night."

Distract him, Duncan. I only need a moment.

Duncan looked at Maggie and nodded. He leaned close to Angus and spit in his face.

"You filthy dog. Ye will pay for that." Angus kneed Duncan under the chin as Maggie collapsed against the bedpost.

"All right, ye made the decision. Ye get to watch while I rape your whore until she is dead. It won't be much longer now. The dagger I sunk into her back is doing the work for me."

Angus laughed and turned to Maggie. He went to grab her by the waist to throw her on the bed when Maggie raised up and turned...sinking her sword straight into his belly...until the hilt and tip of the blade were all that was showing...Angus MacLaren's impaled body draining of life.

The madman looked down, confused as blood poured from his mouth and he fell to the floor, dead, his eyes still wide open.

Maggie looked down at him. "I told you I was getting tired of being called a whore."

Duncan seized the moment to rear back and knock the three men holding him back against the wall.

Maggie tossed the dagger that she had in her hand to him; he used it to kill all the men within minutes.

He looked at Maggie, panting, unable to speak. *How?*

Maggie looked over at him. "I had the dagger in my boot. I used it to cut the belt loose while you distracted him. The dumbass was stupid enough to bring me right to my sword. It was beside the bed and he never saw it."

The adrenaline started to wear off, and Maggie felt woozy from the blood loss, her body crumpling.

Duncan rushed to her side, catching her, scooping her up, and carrying her downstairs.

Logan was in the foyer, surveying the bodies and house damage. He and Quinn had just finished off four of the MacLaren men that were downstairs. Quinn had found their mother and was helping her out into the hall.

"Mother! Maggie needs ye." Duncan's call gained everyone's attention.

They all rushed to the dining room table where Duncan laid Maggie out on the table.

"Help me, boys, roll her over gently," ordered Lady Aurnia.

The wound was much worse than earlier.

"Quinn, get the house staff back in here. I need hot water and bandages. He reopened the wound and she is bleeding badly."

Duncan looked helplessly at his mother. "Will she survive?"

Lady Aurnia looked at Duncan. "If I have anything to say about it, she will. I am too close to getting ye married off and giving me grandchildren to let anything happen to her."

When the scene was cleared, ten MacLaren bodies were stacked on a wagon ready to be taken outside the castle walls. Young Christopher had done as Maggie asked and gotten the gate open just in time for the brothers' return. The front door to the main house was completely blocked when they returned. Onyx had rammed it open, splintering it, the same as he had Maggie's door in Virginia, so Duncan could get inside to her.

Evan, Reade, and the other men had reached the village, helping to put out the fire and keeping it from spreading to the other buildings, before returning home to help with the cleanup.

18 CHAPTER EIGHTEEN

Maggie didn't regain consciousness until late the next afternoon. Duncan's touch, lightly stroking her face, was the first thing she felt. The second thing was the deep, intense pain radiating from her back down her leg. She forced her eyes open and grimaced in pain.

Duncan lay on his side, facing her. Maggie was also on her side, something propping her up from behind, to keep her from rolling onto her wound.

As soon as her eyes opened, Duncan stopped and looked at her, greatly disturbed by her suffering. "Maggie," he whispered, "don't try to move. Your wound has stopped bleeding, but ye must be careful not to reopen it."

Maggie reached up and gently touched the cuts and bruises on his face. "Are you alright?"

Duncan took her hand and kissed it. "It is nothing, my love. Ye are the one I am worried about."

Memories from the day before flooded back. "Duncan, your mother...and Christopher?"

"They are both fine, Maggie. Young Christopher turned out to be quite the brave little soul. We would have never been able to get back inside the walls without him and

Mother is fine. She is the one who tended to your injuries." He smiled sadly. "She has had plenty of practice with me and my brothers. She knew just what to do."

"What about Onyx? Have you seen him? The heathen disappeared when I really needed him."

"I wouldn't say that. He was the one that came and alerted me to trouble at the house. And, he was the one that busted down our front door, so we could get into the house. I will never complain about that beast again."

Maggie relaxed a little. She looked around; they were in the bedroom she first stayed in. "Why am I not in your bed?"

Duncan looked at her with anguish in his features. "Ye did not need to wake up in there and be reminded of what he did...of what happened."

He intertwined his fingers with hers and closed his eyes. "Maggie, I am sorry that I did not get to ye in time. I will never forgive myself for what happened to ye and if ye can never forgive me, I understand." He swallowed hard. "I will release ye from our engagement if ye cannot bear to look at me for failing to protect ye or I will still be very happy to marry ye. I will promise that I will never bother ye in the marriage bed if it pains ye too much." His voice cracked. "No woman should ever have to endure what ye have. I failed to keep safe the one thing that meant the most to me and I will live with that guilt for the rest of my life."

Maggie looked at him strangely. "Duncan, what are you talking about? Why would you say something like that? Are you trying to back out of our marriage?"

"No! NO!" His answer was swift and absolute. "I want to marry ye more than I want the next breath that I breathe. Ye must believe that! I just don't want to cause ye any additional...pain."

Maggie narrowed her eyes, "Duncan, my stab wound will heal. Although, it would be nice if that particular part of my body could catch a break. Being stabbed in the same place I was shot is more than a little annoying to say the least."

Duncan looked at her with even more concern.

"The point is, this wasn't your fault. Trouble tends to find me rather easily, but I will be fine. Why would you not want to come to my bed?"

Duncan lowered his head, "Because of what that filth did to ye. Women who have been... raped..."

Maggie stopped him. "I wasn't raped. What made you think that?"

Duncan looked up, shocked and confused before relief flooded into his eyes. "He didn't? Weren't ye? But, the blood ye were covered in... standing in?"

"The blood was from my stab wound that had been bleeding for a while. Just when it was close to stopping, he reopened it. No, Duncan, I would have used my boot dagger sooner if it had gotten to that point. I was just hoping for a chance to reach my sword first, so I could make certain that bastard left this world before he could hurt anyone else. I would never have let him touch me that way."

Duncan leaned over and kissed her, a few tears of joy streaming down his face. He rested his forehead on hers. "Well then, I take it all back. I will be marrying ye and I will be bothering ye every night in our bed."

He kissed her again. "Maggie?"

"Yes, Duncan?"

"Ye want to tell me about being shot?"

Maggie looked at him hard, touching his face. She had been putting off telling him about the child that she lost, but now seemed like as good a time as any.

"Duncan. There is something I need to tell you. It may not be easy to hear, but there is information that you need to know. It is part of my past and I want to live in the present with you...and only you...if you still want me after you hear what I have to say."

He looked at her gravely and simply nodded.

She told him about her relationship with Ben, the deal she had made for Gabe's life, how Gabe gave up his career for her, and finally about losing the baby.

"Duncan, I know you want children, that you need them to carry on the family line, but I am not a young woman. The one time I became pregnant, I was not able to carry the baby to term. I may not be able to give you a child. I understand if you need to find someone that you know can. That is a decision that only you can make."

Duncan had not said a word the entire time, absorbing every detail. When she was done, he sighed and finally spoke. "Maggie, ye are the love of my life, I have absolutely no doubt in that. If we are not meant to have children, then so be it. I will be happy to spend every day of the rest of my life having ye all to myself." He kissed her forehead and whispered, his voice cracking, "I am very sorry for the loss of your child."

Maggie nodded, tears slipping down the side of her face.

He wiped her tears. "This friend of yours, Gabe...he must truly be a good man that loves ye to do all that he has done for ye."

Maggie's eyes flew open. "Damn it! Gabe! I must get to Edinburgh. He will be here soon."

Duncan shook his head. "Nay, Maggie! Ye are going nowhere. Your wound needs to heal and ye will not be able to travel anytime soon." He thought a moment, "But if ye can write him a note explaining, I can have one of my brothers meet him and bring him back."

Maggie hated to admit it, but he was right. The ship would be here in a few short days and it was a two-day trip back to town. There was no way she could make the trip herself. "He may not believe the note. We made the trip to London on a forgery that someone sent, we still have no idea from whom."

She looked toward the window. "I can, however, send Onyx. That would let him know with all certainty that the note came from me."

Duncan agreed. "That is a wonderful idea...if ye think he will go, that is."

"If you carry me down so I can speak with him, he will."

Duncan grinned at her. "Well, I will not have to carry ye far. We have not replaced the front door yet. He can come right in for supper."

Later that evening, after Duncan wrote out the letter Maggie dictated, he carefully carried her downstairs to meet Onyx, who was waiting in the foyer. Maggie talked while Duncan held her. Onyx nuzzled her neck very lightly as not to hurt her.

"Onyx, I need you to go with Quinn and bring Gabe back."

He shook his head and planted his feet, indicating he didn't want to leave.

She reached up and rubbed his nose. "Onyx, this is very important, and I need you to do this."

He snorted his annoyance.

Maggie was going to have to pull out the big
guns. "Onyx, if you love me, you will do this...for me."

The big black horse cut her a look, snorted, and finally
nodded his acceptance.

"Good boy! And one more thing...be nice to Gabe. No
biting and no headbutting...be on your best behavior."

Maggie could have sworn he rolled his eyes as if to say
'fine.' She rubbed his mane. "Thank you, my friend...and
thank you for getting Duncan to me yesterday."

He nodded his happiness and headed out the door.

The rest of the family had been watching, thoroughly
amused by the whole exchange.

Quinn walked over as he went out the door. "Maggie,
am I safe with him or should I sleep with one eye open?"

"You will be fine Quinn. You may want to take another
horse for Gabe, though. Gabe and Onyx have a love-hate
relationship...I just never know which one on what day."

Maggie laid her head against Duncan's
chest, completely drained, too tired to even speak.

So tired. Please, take me back to bed.

Yes, my love.

19 CHAPTER NINETEEN

Maggie spent the next two days napping and talking with Duncan. She was healing, it was just very slow going. Quinn mixed up some of his special drinks before he left that helped her sleep through the pain at night. Duncan did not want to leave her side and only agreed to do so for a short time because Maggie could no longer stand the smell of him. He had not even left her side to bathe since the battle and the room was putrid. The sheets needed changing anyway, so Duncan sat her gingerly on the couch in the library, kissed her head, and left.

Lady Aurnia came to sit with her while the staff cleaned up and aired things out. "How's your pain, Maggie?"

Maggie shifted herself slightly. "It is still there."

Lady Aurnia got up and poured her a glass of whisky. "This will help."

She took it gratefully.

"Maggie, have you given any thought to your wedding gown?"

"I have actually," Maggie responded, "and I wanted to talk to you about it. In my time, wedding gowns are a huge deal that little girls dream of from the time they are old enough to know what they are. They are also very different from the gowns of this time. Would it be terrible of me to want something more like that for mine? I mean, the ceremony will be here, and the family already knows that I am not from this time." Maggie looked down. "It would be nice to be...a little selfish...for my wedding day."

Lady Aurnia patted her hand. "Of course, it would not be terrible. The time ye were born in is a big part of who ye are. It only makes sense that ye would want to bring some of it to the ceremony and ye are right...no one will make any judgment here, that I promise you. What can I do to help?"

Maggie spent the next little while drawing out an image and explaining it to Lady Aurnia.

"I will say, that is a little different, but I like it and I think it will beautiful. I actually have a big bolt of off-white silk I had been saving and I think it would be perfect."

"Really?" Maggie asked hopefully. "You don't think it will be too much?"

Lady Aurnia looked down at the drawing, smiling, "Nay...I think it will be wonderful because once Duncan sees ye in this. I am fairly sure I will have grandchildren in no time."

The night before Gabe and Quinn were to return, Maggie felt much better. Her wound was still healing, but she could move around better and the bruises on her face were starting to fade. With a little help from Duncan, she was able to make it downstairs for supper.

Lady Aurnia looked at Maggie. "Now that ye are feeling better, have ye and Duncan picked a day for the wedding?"

Maggie looked at Duncan, "No. We still haven't settled the matter on where we will live."

Lady Aurnia gave her and Duncan a confused look. "I thought it was already decided."

"I haven't had a chance to tell her, Mother."

Maggie looked back and forth between the two.

"Tell me what?"

The entire table went silent; Duncan took Maggie's hand and spoke.

"The morning that everything happened, we had a family meeting. I have decided to pass my title as Laird on to Logan, so that I can go to Virginia with ye."

Maggie was stunned. "Duncan, we need to talk about this. I can't ask you to give up your title...and your entire life...for me."

Chuckling, Duncan took her face in his hand. "Maggie, ye do not have to ask, I am freely doing this. I am giving up nothing compared to what I am gaining. Besides, the people on your estate have no one else, the people here have my mother and my brothers."

Lady Aurnia cut her eyes around the table. "The rest of my boys have also given their words to put in more effort at finding suitable wives."

The rest of the MacGregor brothers all dropped their heads and focused on their plates.

Duncan looked down and chuckled again. "Yes...well. Once things in your country have settled down after the war, we will visit when we can."

Maggie smiled sweetly at him, touching his face. She couldn't believe all that he was willing to give up just to be with her. Any doubt that she had about this marriage was now completely and utterly gone.

Lady Aurnia pushed her plate away. "This is as good as time as any to bring this up. I have been giving a great deal of thought to something since the MacLarens broke into our home and I wish to discuss it with all of ye.

Everyone stopped to focus on Lady Aurnia as she continued.

"It seems that we have not done as good a job of keeping the collection safe as we thought. It is painfully obvious that word has seeped out that we protect something of great importance here. I am afraid that we have not seen the last of people searching for 'treasure'." She looked down and simply stated, "I think we need to take drastic measures to protect, at least part of, the collection."

Duncan looked at his mother, his eyes wide. "What do ye mean, Mother?"

Lady Aurnia looked at Maggie. "The collection contains many things, but the most important of that, are the books. There is information in them, that if in the wrong hands, could cause a great amount of damage. It is imperative that the books are protected above all else. Maggie, our country is old, but your country is new. It has not been established long enough for so many rumors to form. Ye said ye have a great many hiding places on your property and that outside people were afraid of the land...that would help to keep strangers away. Would ye be able to hide something like this?"

Everyone turned to look at each other, all speaking at once, the din rising exponentially.

Lady Aurnia held up her hand to silence them. She looked around at her sons. "Ye all know the importance of keeping the books safe. No one would ever look for them in Virginia. We can keep the other part of the collection here, but the books...they must be safe above *all* else." She turned back to Maggie.

Focusing on her thoughts, Maggie nodded. "Well, I do already have safe places in the house. I have no idea how much space the books take up, but the people that I have are loyal to me, I could add additional space if it were needed without the worry of word getting out."

Logan looked at his mother. "Are ye sure this is the best idea? Taking them out of Scotland?"

Lady Aurnia looked around. "I do not wish to, but I think it would be best."

Evan shrugged. "Mother may have a point. If this week has taught us anything, it is that we are not as well fortified as we thought."

Reade looked at Duncan. "What do ye think?"

Duncan took in a deep breath and looked around. "It *is* something to consider. The decision would have to be Maggie's, though."

Lady Aurnia spoke to Maggie. "Of course, it would! It is a great deal to ask of anyone and an enormous responsibility...but ye would have Duncan there. He knows the collection and what to do with it. If something were to happen again, it would be better to only lose half of it as opposed to all of it."

Maggie looked at Duncan. "If you think it is best, I don't see why not."

"Moving it would be the hardest part," stated Logan.

"No! It wouldn't!" Reade looked around the table. "Maggie has a personal ship. No one would question books."

Maggie nodded. "We were planning on taking back a shipment of books from Gabe's nephew's store anyway. We could slip them in easily, without question, and the ship can be sailed right up to my personal dock not far from the house. There is one thing that you must consider though."

They all looked at her.

"Gabe would have to be told everything. I cannot hide something like this from him and I would need his help. He already knows everything about me, but your secret is not mine to tell. That is a decision *you* will have to make."

Everyone fell silent until Lady Aurnia broke the silence. "Maggie, ye trust this man that much?"

"I trust Gabe with my life. I have never seen him go back on his word to anyone."

"Well then, I think we all have something to think about and discuss," said Lady Aurnia.

Later that night, Maggie and Duncan were lying in each other's arms.

"We need to set a day for our wedding, Maggie."

"How will that work, Duncan...with the regular ceremony and the Fae ceremony?"

"We have a small chapel with a priest here that can take care of the legal and religious formalities, and later, that evening, we will have an intimate, candlelit ceremony, in the chamber for the Fae ceremony."

"There is a chapel here?"

"Oh aye. It is not very big, but it is very nice. I can show ye tomorrow."

Maggie ran her finger over his chest. "I have been thinking and I have decided that I want to take the MacGregor mark when we are married. Your mother said that I could if I chose to."

"Are ye sure?"

"I am...and I want you to do it if you can."

"I would be honored to do that for ye, Maggie."

Duncan pulled her into a kiss.

She moved in closer, deepening the kiss, running her hand down the length of his chest and lower down to his thigh.

Duncan caught her hand and pulled it back up to his chest. "Nay Maggie," he growled. "I would love nothing more than to have ye right now, but ye are not well enough for that." He kissed her on the nose and smiled. "I want ye fully healed for our wedding night."

Maggie wrinkled her nose at him, pouting. "But, Duncan, I have spent the past few days in this bed doing nothing but thinking about you...and all the fun we could be having. I am bored and in 'need' of attention."

Duncan laughed. "Your 'needs' tend to get me in trouble, my dear Maggie."

"Duncan, please don't make me beg. I can play dirty and turn on the tears if I have to." Maggie gave her best puppy dog eyes.

But Duncan shook his head, half amused and half feeling sorry for her. "I will *not* reopen your wounds by doing 'that'...but there may be something I can do to.... 'relieve your suffering'."

He laughed, and she squealed as he raised the blanket, pulled it over them and slid down the length of the bed until his tongue reached its intended destination.

"Oh! Duncan, you are too good to me!" she said, eyes closed as she received her 'relief'.

20 CHAPTER TWENTY

The next day, Duncan escorted Maggie to the chapel that was very near the house. Maggie's face beamed when she saw it.

The entire church was made of the same stone as the house. It was very simple and primitive, but that was the beauty of it. It looked as ancient as the house, giving it a magical and mythical feel.

"Duncan, this is beautiful. I love it!"

"I thought ye might. It was built when the house was." He helped her to one of the pew seats. "So, my dear Maggie, can ye see yourself becoming my wife here?"

Maggie nodded and leaned against his chest. "I think I can."

Duncan carefully slipped his arms around her, kissing the side of her head. "Ye are very quiet today, Maggie. What's bothering ye?"

"I guess I am just a little nervous about Gabe's arrival. He will probably still be upset with me for not coming back to London with Wyatt, and I feel bad that I am keeping him away from Kat even longer."

Maggie turned to him, trying to figure out how to best word what she wanted to say. "Duncan, Gabe and I will probably need some time alone to work things out. Please, don't take it the wrong way. Gabe and I are just...extremely close and we spend a great deal of time together. There is nothing we don't know about each other."

She took his hand. "There is going to be an adjustment period for all of us and I will need both of you to be...understanding during that time. It is imperative that we find a way to make it work. I NEED both of you in my life."

Duncan warily rubbed his chin, then sighed. "As long as ye are not sharing his bed, I do not see any issue."

Maggie grimaced.

Duncan narrowed his eyes at her. "Maggie?"

"Have we ever slept in the same bed? Yes, many times. I will not lie about that. Sometimes we fall asleep talking. Have we had had physical relations? NEVER! Never have and never will. You have my word on that."

Duncan was genuinely confused, and suspicious. "Maggie, I am not sure I understand. How is it that ye can be in a man's bed and not...?"

Maggie rolled her eyes to the ceiling. "Let's just say that I am not his type."

"What are ye not telling me?"

She looked him straight in the eye. "There are things that are not mine to share. Believe me when I tell you that you have nothing to worry about." She took his face in both of her hands, kissing him, slowly and gently.

"I love you, Duncan. You will be my husband. That place is for you and you alone."

He pulled her back into the kiss when Maggie slipped her hand down the front of his body while she smirked.

Duncan chuckled "Maggie! Stop it! We are in a church. We are not wed yet and ye are not well."

Maggie blinked and tilted her head. "Are you going to make me wait until our wedding night, Duncan?"

He teased. "I might."

She raised her eyebrows. "You wouldn't."

He grabbed her by the waist, growling while he kissed her. "Oh aye, I would. If that is what it takes to get ye to pick a date. Ye can have your way with me all ye like after that."

Maggie was so exhausted by the time they returned to the house from the walk, she could barely stand. Duncan swept her up and carried upstairs. She curled on her side as soon as he lay her down. He covered her up and kissed her before heading downstairs.

The rest of the family was gathered in the library. Duncan poured a drink and moved to the fireplace.

"What is the decision?" he asked.

Logan moved next to his brother. "We are all in agreement that it would be safer to send the books with ye. That just leaves ye and Quinn to have yer say. We all need to be together on this Brother, most especially ye."

Duncan stared into the fire. "I am unsure about trusting this friend of Maggie's. We know nothing about him, and he *is* an English soldier."

"*Former* English soldier," his mother corrected, "and if Maggie trusts him as much as she does, I think we should too. Ye know her instincts are far sharper than most."

The front door opened. Quinn and Gabe appeared at the library door. Quinn was quick to make introductions.

"Forgive me for being rude, but I need to see Maggie," Gabe said impatiently.

Duncan set down his drink. "Of course. She is resting, but I will take ye to her."

When Duncan reached the foyer, he turned to Gabe. "Maggie is recovering. She does not need to be upset and, as her husband to be, I will not allow it."

Duncan had instructed Quinn to not give Gabe any details, just to tell him that Maggie was hurt and unable to travel, under the care of the MacGregor household.

Gabe narrowed his eyes, concerned anger forming in his face. "It is best if you take me to her now."

Duncan nodded. "We can talk later."

Maggie woke up to the sound of someone's voice softly repeating her name and smoothing back her hair. She opened her eyes and smiled. Gabe was sitting on the bed next to her.

"Gabe!"

"Hello, sweetheart."

Maggie sat up, grimacing.

Gabe looked her over, seeing the pain in her face. "Where are you hurt? What happened?"

"My back right side. I caught a little knife in the back."

Gabe paled. "A 'little' knife? Let me see it."

Maggie groaned but rolled over. Thankfully, they were alone. Duncan would have flipped his lid if he saw her hiking up her shift for Gabe to get a good look.

"Damn it, Maggie. It is in the same spot that you were shot."

"You're telling me? That spot still aches every time it rains. And, by the way, it is not like I got stabbed in that same place on purpose."

Gabe helped her roll back over and covered her up before sitting back down beside her. "No! But you did come here on your own on purpose. Maggie, you have no idea how furious I am. You planned that from the beginning. What in the hell were you thinking?"

"I was thinking that I wanted some answers and that I did not want you away from Kat that soon and for so long. Gabe, you are not responsible for my decisions. You have other, more pressing responsibilities now. I am perfectly fine."

"Maggie, you are not fine. You have a hole in your back and your face looks like it hit a brick wall." He leaned closer. "Did these people do this to you?"

"No! Absolutely not! The MacGregor family has been nothing but good to me."

Gabe shook his head. "Then, what is going on here? What happened to you?"

"I will fill you in on the details later, but the short story goes something like this. I discovered a child molester, picked a fight, embarrassed him, he came back with ten men, they are all dead now."

Gabe sat there, his face full of disbelief. "Dear God, Maggie."

She leaned towards him. "I had every intention of being at the dock for you. This happened right before I was going to leave. I am so sorry. I am even more sorry that you are away from Kat right now. That was the last thing that I wanted." She sighed. "Now give me news of her. I have missed her so much."

Gabe narrowed his eyes. "Don't think this lets you off the hook."

"I know."

Gabe's face lit up. "Kat is wonderful. She is growing and thriving. She has taken to the wet nurse quite well. My mother and Martin were thrilled with the idea of getting to keep her while I came here. Olivia has taken her over. She is already including her in tea parties."

"And Wyatt made it home fine?"

"Yes! He is extremely grateful that his new found 'Aunt Maggie' came and paid his bill at the tavern so he could come home. He can't say enough good things about you."

Maggie made a face. "Tavern, huh? You would have thought he had time to make up a better story than that."

Gabe gave her a look. "What do you mean?"

"Let's just say your nephew takes after his father. He was holed up in a whorehouse with a huge bill that he could not pay." Maggie filled him in on all the details, including the part about him mistaking her for a whore.

Gabe was laughing so hard tears were coming out of his eyes. "Oh, I wish I had seen that. No wonder he has been on the straight and narrow since he came home."

Maggie laughed. "I threatened to tell his mother and grandmother if I ever caught him again."

When Gabe had regained his composure, he took Maggie by the hand and became serious. "Maggie, that man downstairs said you were to become his wife. Please, tell me he is lying."

Maggie squeezed his hand. "I cannot. We are to be married."

Gabe shook his head. "You have been here for two weeks, and you are engaged? Two weeks ago, you had no hope of ever falling in love and now this? I don't understand."

She shrugged. "I can't explain it. I guess what they say is true...when you meet the right one, you know it."

"Don't you think it is a little fast? What of Virginia? What about the people at home?"

"Duncan has decided to give up his title as Laird and come back with me."

"Are you sure you are not using him to forget about Ben...and the baby?"

Maggie stroked his hand with her fingers. "I am sure. I love Duncan. It makes no sense, I am the first to admit it, but I cannot imagine my life without him now."

"Maggie, I don't know about this."

Maggie leaned over. "How long did you know Jonathan before you knew you loved him?"

Gabe closed his eyes. "The day I met him."

Pressing her forehead to his, she whispered, "And, how soon would you have married him if you could have?"

Tears slipped down his face and hers. "You are not playing fair, Maggie."

She kissed him on the forehead, and she wiped his tears. "I know. I am taking this happiness where I can find it, and I am holding on for dear life. If the future is damned, then so be it. I cannot live without him...and I won't."

He opened his eyes, blowing out a deep breath.

"Gabe. I want you to do something...for me. Spend some time with Duncan and get to know him. He is a good man. You two are the most important men in my life and I need both of you so much. We all need to find a way to make this work."

A soft knock at the door broke the moment.

"Come in."

It was Lady Aurnia. "Forgive the intrusion. Colonel Asheton, I have prepared a room for ye and had a hot bath brought up. I thought since ye have seen that Maggie is well that ye might like to clean up before supper."

He looked straight ahead. "Thank you, Lady Aurnia. I am grateful for your hospitality...and for taking care of Maggie."

He stood and kissed Maggie on the head. "I will see you in a bit."

He left to follow Lady Aurnia.

Duncan came right in, Maggie giving him a scolding look.

"Have you been pacing the hall the whole time?"

"Nay...not all of it. How did it go?"

"Better than I thought."

Duncan sat down on the bed. "Did ye tell him anything about the family?"

"Of course not. That is not my place."

"Maggie, we just to spoke to Quinn. All of the family has agreed to the move and telling Gabe about us, save one, and the decision must be unanimous."

"Who is not sure?"

Duncan looked her directly in the eye. "It is me. I am the only one who has not agreed."

Maggie was puzzled. "I don't understand. What is holding you back?"

Duncan stood up. "I think the move is a good one. Mother is right. Losing half a collection would be better than losing it all. The colonies would be a perfect place. No one would ever look there for any kind of treasure. My concern is...Gabe."

"Duncan, you can trust him as you do me."

He tilted his head. "I have always erred on the side of caution when it comes to what we protect. I know ye trust him, but I do not know him. I cannot entrust such a precious thing to a stranger."

"Then get to know him. The two of you need to do that, anyway. Remember Duncan, you did not trust me when I came here, and we see how that turned out."

He laughed. "Indeed. Although, I highly doubt I will be proposing to him anytime soon."

"Duncan, you do realize that we cannot set a date until this is settled."

"What do ye mean?" he asked.

Maggie sighed. "Because arrangements need to be made. We need to sail back to Virginia soon, and whether we are taking additional cargo will affect those plans. You and your family will need time to decide what stays, what goes, and it will have to be moved in secret, at night. At some point, preferably sooner than later, Gabe and I have to go back to London to get Kat and say our goodbyes."

Duncan folded his arms and looked out the window. "Ye are right. I had not given that any thought."

Maggie moved to him. "This decision needs to be made as soon as possible."

Supper was a strange affair. It seemed more like a job interview for Gabe, the brothers taking turns asking him

questions regarding discretion and loyalty, while
Lady Aurnia did her best to rein them in.

Duncan was quiet, taking every opportunity he could to
study Gabe.

After supper, they moved to the library for drinks,
where the talk turned much lighter. Gabe and
Lady Aurnia happily chatted away about raising children
when the subject of his new role as a father was brought
up, the two of them getting along very well.

Gabe had turned on the charm, something he would
often do without even realizing, and he was rapidly
winning over the family...all but one.

It was getting late, so Lady Aurnia rose to excuse
herself.

Maggie looked between Gabe and Duncan trying to
figure out how to get them alone to talk. "Duncan, I am
going to walk up with your mother. I need to
discuss...wedding details with her. You take your time."

She stood and kissed him. *Talk to him.*

Duncan nodded in reluctant acknowledgment of her
silent message. "I will be up soon."

Maggie went to Gabe as he stood. He kissed her on the
cheek. "Sleep well, Maggie."

"Good night Gabe. I will see you in the morning."

Lady Aurnia shot looks at the other MacGregor
brothers, who each excused themselves, leaving Duncan
and Gabe alone.

Maggie and Lady Aurnia exchanged concerned looks as
they ascended the stairs.

The next morning, Maggie woke up alone. She lay in
bed, thinking the worst. To a certain extent, Duncan was
jealous of Gabe and the close bond they shared. She

could feel it every time she mentioned Gabe's name, no matter how much she reassured Duncan.

Then, there was Gabe. Gabe's first priority was always to keep her safe, no matter what. He was skeptical of Maggie's love for Duncan, and understandably so. Even though it felt as if they had known each other much longer, it *had* only been two weeks. Normal people would have been crazy to marry in such a short amount of time, but then again, nothing was normal about her life, so why should this be?

Duncan and Gabe both had strong personalities and they were both fiercely protective of her. They were bound to butt heads and not get along.

A headache was coming on. Maggie dressed and headed out into the hall to find out exactly how bad it was.

Well, might as well see if they killed each other last night.

Quinn was coming down the hall as Maggie opened the door.

"Good morning Maggie."

"Oh, good morning Quinn." She stopped him. "Quinn, I want to thank you for going to get Gabe for me."

He smiled. "Ye don't have to thank me, Maggie. I volunteer to leave the stronghold every chance I get, especially to Edinburgh. Besides, Gabe and I got along surprisingly well. He is a very likable man."

"Yes, he is. I just wish your brother felt the same way."

"Och, Maggie, Duncan is so caught up in ye that he cannot think straight, not with his brain anyway. I wouldn't worry, he will come around."

"I hope so Quinn. Say, did Onyx behave?"

Quinn laughed. "For the most part. He does like to argue though, doesn't he? The first thing Gabe did after

239

reading your letter was to berate Onyx for not keeping ye safe. They spent a quarter of an hour quarreling after that."

"Yes, that sounds about right."

Quinn held out his arm. "May I escort ye downstairs, Maggie?"

"Please. I need to go see exactly how bad things got last night."

The house was very quiet.

"Quinn, where is everyone?"

"It's training day."

Maggie walked into the library, looking around. *No blood. That's encouraging. Still...Duncan never came to bed last night. And that was not a good sign.*

The sound of swords hitting broke her concentration. She looked through the window to see what was happening. A large crowd had gathered to watch the show. Duncan must be taking out his frustration on one of his brothers again.

Maggie went outside and slipped through the crowd, her heart dropping when she saw what was going on.

Duncan was taking out his frustrations all right...on Gabe.

Damn it.

Maggie glared at Duncan. *Why are you doing this...to me?*

Duncan instantly lowered his sword and held up his hand to Gabe to stop. He could feel the sadness and anger pouring out of Maggie. His eyes found her and watched her turn to go inside the house.

"What's wrong?" Gabe asked while trying to catch his breath.

"It's Maggie. She's upset." Duncan tossed his sword to Evan, who was standing nearby, and marched towards the house.

"My God, man! Can ye get through *one* training day?" Logan called to him as he departed.

Gabe moved to Evan, handing him the sword he was using, before following after.

Maggie was in the library when Duncan came in.

"Maggie? What is troubling ye?"

Maggie turned. "I asked you to talk to him, not to try and beat him to death with your sword. I know you don't like the relationship that Gabe and I have, but it is part of me and if you want me, you must accept it. I will not allow him to leave my life."

Duncan gave her a strange look.

Gabe appeared at the door. "Mags? What's the matter?"

Maggie sat down, rubbing her temples. "I need the two of you to get along, that's the matter."

Gabe was puzzled. He turned to Duncan. "Any idea what she is talking about?"

Duncan shrugged. "I have no idea. I was hoping ye did."

Maggie looked at them both. "Why are you two trying to kill each other there?"

Gabe sighed. "Mags, we weren't trying to kill each other."

"You weren't?"

Duncan folded his arms, giving her a disapproving look. "Nay! We were not. Ye told me that Gabe was the best swordsman in the colonies and that's why ye got him to train ye. I just wanted to see how good he was." He turned to Gabe. "Ye are excellent, by the way."

Gabe tilted his head in acknowledgment. "Thank you. You are, as well. I would like you to teach me that little maneuver you caught me on though. That was impressive."

"Oh yes, I'd be happy to. It's all in the way ye plant yer left foot. Ye have to turn slightly, like this," he said, demonstrating.

"Oh, like this?" Gabe asked, imitating the move.

Maggie shook her head and threw up hands. 'What kind of bizarro world did I wake up in this morning? Last night, you didn't say two words to each other. I go to bed and when I wake up, you are...sharing sword secrets? What did I miss?" She stroked her forehead.

Duncan sat down beside her, rubbing her leg. "Granted, we were a little...hesitant about each other. But I did as ye asked and talked to Gabe. We ended up talking until dawn. Ye were right. He is a good man."

Gabe came and sat on the other side of her. "We actually got on very well. I wasn't comfortable about the two of you becoming engaged so quickly, but after hearing what he had to say and warning him that I would kill him if he ever hurt you, I feel really good about things."

"Oh aye. I now have a better understanding of the relationship that ye two share and I am not bothered by it all. Gabe knows that if he ever tries to touch ye in a non-brotherly fashion that I will slit his throat while he sleeps."

Maggie looked back and forth between them. "Just like that? Everything is good?"

Gabe and Duncan both nodded in agreement.

Gabe took her hand. "Maggie, Duncan and I have one thing in common that matters above all else. We both love you and want you to be happy and safe."

"Aye, and we will do whatever it takes to make that happen."

Maggie leaned back. "Really?" She asked, tearing up a little.

"Aye."

"Yes, Maggie." Gabe blinked, "And Maggie, do not start crying. You know that I hate it when you cry, even happy tears."

"Och," added Duncan, "that's the worst, isn't it?"

Gabe nodded back.

"Okay," Maggie laughed, "No tears. The two of you have given me the best wedding present that I could ever ask for. Thank you."

Gabe squeezed her hand. "Speaking of the wedding, when is the big day?"

Maggie looked at Duncan who looked back at her.

"Aye, about that. There is something that my family and I need to discuss with ye tonight, Gabe. After that, hopefully, we can pick one."

After supper, they all sat in the library. Maggie next to Gabe, holding his hand as Lady Aurnia told Gabe the exact same story she told Maggie. Maggie filled in the holes with the bottle, the book, and the sword.

Gabe was stunned. "I am not sure I believe all of this Fae stuff." He looked to Maggie for guidance.

"Don't look at me. What do I know? I'm just a girl from the year 2018."

"Oh, that's right. I keep forgetting." Gabe bantered back, his tone dry.

"Gabe, I had a hard time believing all of this, too, but, in all honesty, it is as good an answer as any. It's more information than we had two weeks ago, and it makes sense when you lay it all out."

Gabe downed his glass. "I suppose you are right."

Maggie took in a deep breath. "There's more, Gabe. The family needs our help."

Duncan explained about the break-in, the need for splitting the collection, and the plan.

Gabe looked at Maggie, thinking about how close he came to losing her...again. He closed his eyes and held onto her hand for dear life. "And you are onboard completely with this plan, Maggie?"

"I am, Gabe. They are family now and you know I will do anything for family."

Gabe sighed. "Of that, I am painfully aware." He shook his head and rolled his eyes. "If you are part of it, then so am I. That goes without saying."

"If it makes you feel any better, you will have Duncan to help you keep me out of trouble," Maggie said encouragingly.

"I am not sure that two of us are enough," Duncan added sarcastically.

"So, how about we make it three."

Everyone turned to look at Quinn.

"Quinn?" Lady Aurnia asked alarmingly, "What are ye talking about?"

Quinn stepped forward, nervous, "Well, Mother, it only makes sense that if half of the collection is going, that half of us should go as well. Duncan will need help moving them and two MacGregors will be better than one. I have always wanted to travel...ye know that, Mother. I would like to go if it is alright with Maggie and Duncan...and Gabe."

Lady Aurnia went to Quinn and hugged him. "I do not wish to lose ye, Quinn."

"You won't, Mother. I will come back to visit. I just feel like my place is with them and the books right now."

Lady Aurnia touched his face, a certain understanding passing between them. She always knew Quinn was not like her other sons and that his path would lead him away from Scotland. The vision she had when she carried him resurfaced in her mind, reminding her that this needed to happen for her son to be happy.

"I will miss ye terribly, but ye are your own man and I will not try to stop ye."

Maggie looked around at the group. "It is not my decision, but my home will always be open to all of you and at any time."

Duncan looked at his little brother. "Are ye sure, Quinn? I would love to have ye there, but ye must be certain. Virginia is not Scotland...it will be different."

Logan, Reade, and Evan stood, all quiet, while Gabe looked over at Quinn.

"Duncan is right, Quinn. You need to be clear that this is what you want," Gabe said to him softly.

Quinn slowly nodded. "I am."

Lady Aurnia looked around at the group. "All right then...it is settled. The book collection sails with the four of ye to Virginia. We will need several days to sort and pack everything."

"Gabe and I need time to get Kat, the shipment of books from Henry, and to say our goodbyes. We can do that while you prepare for the move. We can sail there, take care of everything, and be back in two weeks."

Duncan squeezed Maggie's hand. "What about the wedding?"

"Your gown is not finished yet, Maggie. It should be completed by the time ye return from London, though," said Lady Aurnia, "and I can have everything waiting for the ceremony at that time."

"Very well. Gabe and I will go, and Duncan and I will wed as soon as we get back. It will give me a chance to pick up a few things."

Duncan looked concerned. "I think ye should rest another couple of days before ye go Maggie. It is a two-day ride and ye are still very weak. Ye do not need to reopen that wound."

Gabe agreed. "Duncan is right. You haven't even regained your color yet. Really, Mags, I can go alone."

"I will be fine, Gabe. I need to say goodbye to your family."

Gabe smiled. "All right, but we wait a few days and you *will* rest during that time."

Maggie was propped up on some pillows, Duncan standing at the foot of the bed, while they prepared for sleep.

"Maggie, I am going with ye to London."

"That isn't necessary, Duncan. You have a great deal to do here."

He walked around to the side of the bed and took her into a kiss. "I do not want to be away from ye."

Maggie ran her hand over his chest. "I know. But you need to spend some time with your family, especially your mother. I don't know when we will get back to

Scotland and she is losing two of her boys. All of you need to be together as much as you can, while you can.

Duncan growled. "Aye, ye are right. I just don't want to let ye out of my sight for that long. Ye have no idea how much it is torturing me not to take ye right now."

Maggie rolled her eyes. "Oh, I think I might have an inkling. You are not the only one suffering."

He kissed her forehead. "Ye just make sure ye are completely recovered for our wedding night." Duncan undressed and slipped in beside her, wrapping his arms around her, kissing her back.

"Duncan?"

"Hmm?"

"What about the mark? When will you do that?"

He laid his chin on her shoulder. "We can do it anytime. It does need to be done in the chamber though. When would ye like to?"

She rolled to her back, wincing a little. "Where exactly does it go? I mean...how far from my wound would it be?"

"It will go down further and in the center. It will be away from it. Why?"

"I was just wondering if I needed to worry about infection and how much pain I would be in. I mean, I am already in pain, so a little more won't be an issue."

Duncan propped up on his elbow. "Nay, there is no pain and there is no concern for infection."

"What do you mean?"

He slipped his hand over her waist. "The symbols prevent it. The ink itself goes in black, but as the symbols form, they turn a bright golden color, that will eventually fade over time. There is some magic in the formation that prevents pain and any complications. If the truth be told, it is quite relaxing."

"So, we can do it before Gabe and I leave? I mean, it is one less thing to do, and I will be resting, so there is no problem there."

"Aye, we could. It *is* done on a padded altar, so you would be comfortable."

Maggie smiled at him. "So, let's do it tomorrow."

"If ye wish. Since ye will be a caretaker, it is about time I showed ye the collection anyway."

He pulled her tight to him. "Get some rest tonight Maggie. Tomorrow is a big day."

21 CHAPTER TWENTY-ONE

The next afternoon, Duncan led Maggie to the library, closing the door behind them. Gabe, Quinn, and Lady Aurnia were waiting there. The family had decided that Gabe deserved to see what he was protecting as well.

"Ready?" Duncan asked.

"As I will ever be."

Lady Aurnia moved to the fireplace, to the part of it with the ornate carvings. There were five tiny crescent moons within the carving. Much to Maggie's surprise, Lady Aurnia pulled these out a little way and turned each of them to a unique position, much like a tumbler lock.

Maggie couldn't believe she had never noticed them before. The moons were so inconspicuous that no one ever would. Maggie and Gabe looked at each other, grinning.

"Okay, that is pretty good and much better than my secret room entrance."

When Lady Aurnia turned the final crescent, one of the bookcases behind them popped open slightly. Once it opened, the lady of the castle turned the moons back to their original place and pushed them all back in.

The bookcase was a door to a passageway that led down a narrow set of stone steps, illuminated by lit torches on the walls.

Duncan helped Maggie, keeping a tight hold on her to keep her steady. Eventually, the narrow steps opened to a much wider staircase that led to...nothing. At the bottom was a natural chamber that appeared much like a cave, completely blocked by a wall of fallen rock. It looked as if there had been a cave in and it was a complete dead end. Maggie looked at Duncan, puzzled. He kissed her hand and smiled.

He moved to the bottom stone step, and much to Maggie's surprise, he slid the stone off the bottom step. It was on some sort of track and the step was hollow and empty—or so it seemed. After closer inspection, Maggie noticed there were three little indentions in the bottom. Duncan went to three corners of the chamber, picking up three different stones, no two shapes the same, that he placed in the indentions.

"They have to be the exact same weight, or it doesn't work," he said, placing the last stone.

Ingenious.

A stone wall to the left of the staircase cracked open. Placing the stones back in the corners, he came back to Maggie. He pushed the door open and led Maggie out onto a circular stone balcony, one of two, with a rail that Maggie used to lean on. What she saw, was the strangest and most wondrous thing that she had ever seen in her life.

Straight ahead was a grand fireplace, a large fire burning to heat the room. Logan, Reade, and Evan were standing in front of the fireplace, smiling up at them.

Gabe came to her side, he was as taken as her, no words for what they beheld.

Duncan came up behind her, wrapping his arms around her waist, and resting his chin on her shoulder. "Welcome to the collection."

The grand staircase fanned out at the bottom, and Duncan led her down. The room was much like the castle library, but on a much grander scale. It was very warm and inviting, gold spun tapestries hanging from the walls depicting different aspects of Fae life. Beautiful golden rugs lay on the floors, obviously not worked by human hands. To the left were three walls of books in a 'U' shape, all ancient and leather-bound, much like the one she had received. A golden table and chairs were in the center of the library section.

Maggie wandered around. The fireplace itself was stunning. It was etched with more scenes of Fae life, but the edges of the scenes were brushed in gold to give off a soft glowing hue. If you looked long enough, the scene almost seemed to come to life. Hanging over the fireplace was a large golden circle of ancient symbols including a sword, matching perfectly with the mark on Duncan's back. Several comfortable chairs made a semicircle shape around the hearth, upholstered in leather with gold fabric accents.

Moving to the right of the staircase, Maggie examined the wall containing a collection of gold weapons, everything from spears, to shields, exquisitely forged swords, and even a few archery pieces. Several sets of gold armor were also on display. The wall directly across contained the MacGregor swords like Maggie's. There were twenty in all, a place for each one and the MacGregor shield above them.

On the furthest wall hung portraits and artwork, more scenes from the past with images of people from long ago. Golden statues, small and large, were scattered throughout the entire chamber.

Gabe came to stand beside Maggie, Duncan already by her side.

"What do ye think?" asked Duncan.

"I don't know what to say," said Gabe, his eyes wide with excitement.

Quinn joined him. "It is pretty amazing, isn't it?"

Gabe just nodded.

"Maggie, ye are very quiet," said Duncan, snaking a comforting arm around her.

"What do you say to all of this grandeur? I had no idea."

A shield on the wall next to Maggie caught her eye. She moved closer to get a better look. Its pattern consisted of flowers, children, and tiny symbols, all mingled and connected in a circle. The detail work was magnificent. Something about it greatly appealed to her.

"Duncan? What do you know of this?" Maggie could not seem to move her gaze.

"Ah...That shield belongs to Danu, the goddess of nature and fertility. She is the bringer of good harvest, wisdom, and renewal."

Maggie was completely captivated by it, feeling as if she were in some sort of an unbreakable trance.

Duncan laughed, amused by her reaction. "Come, let me show ye the best part.

He took Maggie by the waist, pulling her to another chamber off the library.

Maggie shook her head, releasing herself from the spell.

That was weird.

"This is where our ceremony will be held."

The main wall of the altar room was covered with rectangular gold plates depicting more Fae scenes, mostly ones showing their love of mankind and Scotland. The biggest plate in the middle depicted the mark, a MacGregor crest in the middle. A large, gold altar table was at the front, a thick, leather-bound book splayed open upon it. Different sizes and shapes of candles filled the table and the floor, producing the effect of a scene out of a dream.

"Duncan, this will be beautiful."

He kissed her. "Aye, it will be."

Another smaller, more private room was off to the side, concealed by a closed door; it was a miniature version of the main one. Here was the padded altar table, set in the middle, that Maggie would receive the mark on. Another table was covered with a folded cloth, an opened book, and the inking materials. The walls of that room were covered with ancient symbols, like the ones on the bottle and the book. The entire room was lit by at least a hundred burning candles.

Maggie closed her eyes and took in a deep breath, absorbing the smell of wax and old books, making her feel a part of something ancient and ritualistic. It felt right.

Lady Aurnia appeared at the door, smiling. "Are ye ready, Maggie?"

"I am."

Entering, moving to her side, Lady Aurnia kissed her cheek. "We will leave you two alone. Welcome to the family, Maggie."

Lady Aurnia left, closing the door behind her, leaving them completely alone.

Duncan smiled. "Ye will need to disrobe completely and lay face down. I will cover ye from the waist down."

He kissed Maggie and helped her to undress.

"It's not fair I am the only one naked here you know," she teased.

"Don't remind me." He moaned. "I still have work to concentrate on. Mother will kill me if I get this wrong."

He helped her get comfortable on the table. When she was settled, he covered her from the waist down with a soft gold-hued fabric, the likes of which Maggie had never seen. It made her feel warm and loved, like she was wrapped in her lover's embrace. She took in a deep breath, watching Duncan begin his work. Maggie felt a little light headed and spacey; he was enthralled by his all-important task, not even breaking his concentration to speak. Every now and then he would stop to move to the other side of the table to work, always pausing to kiss her on the head. Soon Maggie was so relaxed that she drifted off to sleep.

She was awakened by the touch of his fingers pushing her hair back from her face, and his whisper in her ear.

"I am done, my love. I just need to say the incantation over it."

Maggie smiled a sleepy smile.

Duncan picked up the book, laid his hand over his work, and spoke a few words in an ancient tongue. Maggie's back tingled and became warm. At his final word, an electrical jolt ripped throughout

Maggie's entire body, as if she had been struck by lightning, causing her to push herself up quickly, panting and out of breath. She'd felt it from the top of her head to the tip of her toes; every nerve in her body sparking.

Duncan held his hand back, looking at it then at Maggie, a horrified look on his face, as he looked into her eyes, unmoving.

"Duncan? What happened? What's wrong?"

Duncan shook his head. "I... don't know. I felt a shock of some sort when I said the last word." His eyes were still fixed on Maggie's. "Maggie, your eyes…"

"What about them?" Maggie asked.

He cupped her face in his hands. "Yer eyes, they now have flecks of gold in them."

Maggie sat in a chair at the fireplace, Duncan beside her, holding her hand while everyone else gathered around.

"Tell me again what ye felt, Maggie," Lady Aurnia said.

"It felt like I had been hit by lightning. A stronger version of what I felt when I first touched Duncan's mark on his back."

Duncan looked at his mother. "The mark took and turned as it always has until I said the incantation."

Lady Aurnia gave her best reassuring look. "It is normal to feel a little burst when the incantation is spoken. It is the power of the Fae magic entering your body. Maybe ye just got an extra dose because ye are not part of the bloodline."

Lady Aurnia wasn't even buying her own story.

Gabe moved next to Maggie. "How do you feel?"

Maggie shrugged. "I feel fine now. It was just that initial jolt when the words were said."

Lady Aurnia shot Duncan a look. "Maybe ye and Gabe should take her upstairs. When we are packing the books; it will be a good time to check them for some answers. In the meantime, Maggie, go rest. Ye leave soon and ye need to be ready for the trip."

Upstairs, Maggie drank the whisky that Duncan poured for her while looking in the mirror. The flecks of gold seemed to move and float in Maggie's eyes, like the flakes of gold in a bottle of Swiss schnapps when it was shaken.

Duncan stood behind her, the expression on his face troubled.

Maggie shrugged and went to sit down next to Gabe. "At least it looks cool."

Gabe reached and gently turned her face to his, squinting to get a better look. "It is the strangest thing that I have ever seen."

She wrinkled her nose at him, pointing to her face. "THIS is the strangest thing you have ever seen?"

"It is certainly at the very top of the list."

Duncan paced the floor with his arms folded.

Maggie watched him. "Duncan, please sit down. You are making me nervous."

He moved to stand at her side, placing his hand on her shoulder. "I am sorry Maggie. I am just concerned about ye."

She reached up and took his hand. "I am fine. I feel remarkably well, actually."

He moved around to the front of her and kneeled to look at her eyes again. "It seems to be fading."

Maggie wrapped her arms around his neck. "I am sure it is as your mother said. Besides, when has anything gone as it should with me? I am not exactly your average person, am I?"

Gabe offered Duncan a sympathetic look. "Maggie has a point, Duncan. Nothing normal surrounds her."

Duncan asked Gabe to stay with Maggie while he went to speak with his mother.

After he left, Maggie turned to Gabe. "Let's go get some fresh air."

They took a couple of blankets and headed down to the water with a fresh bottle of whisky.

"This place is marvelous, Maggie. Look at the view from here."

"It really is. I will miss it." She leaned her head over on his shoulder and he wrapped his arm around her.

"Are you sure you want to leave?"

"You know I have no choice, Gabe. This trip has been wonderful, but I have to return to reality soon enough." She looked down at the sand and said softly, "Are you sure you want to leave London?"

He pulled back and looked down at her. "What do you mean?"

"Gabe, you and your family are getting along so well, and you have Kat now. I would understand if you wanted to stay with them. I'd miss you more than I would my right arm...but I would understand."

"Mags, I still feel the same as I did before we came here. My home is no longer in London. My home is where you are." He kissed her head. "Although, now that you are coming back with a husband, I can't exactly call you my fiancé anymore."

Maggie chuckled. "Oh, my dear Gabe, you have no idea how much more complicated your life has just become."

He gave her a questioning look.

"Gabe! The only thing sexier to a woman than a single, handsome man such as yourself, is a single, handsome man with a baby. It sets their nether regions all aflutter to see a man trying to raise a little one all by himself. They will be lining up at your door with food and offers to help in 'any way they can.' Prepare yourself for the onslaught of corseted bosoms, my friend."

Gabe grimaced. "You are joking!"

Maggie laughed. "I am not!"

"Really? Women do that?"

Maggie nodded.

"Oh, good God! I don't suppose we could start a rumor when we return that I was gravely injured in that department, can we?"

"We could...but that might keep you from finding someone you actually *want* to be with."

Gabe frowned, accompanying it with a smirk full of sarcasm. He leaned over, "So, can I see this new artwork that you have taken on?"

"Sure!" Maggie raised her shirt and he got a good look.

"That is amazing. And Quinn said the ink went in black and then turns this gold color? Unbelievable."

"You should get it done too."

Gabe tilted his head. "I thought it was only the family."

"Well, you will be a protector, too, and they do make exceptions. I don't see why you couldn't, but the family would have to decide. Who knows? Maybe you will get cool gold floaty eyes, too."

"I think I am good." He took one of the blankets and wrapped it around her. "So, Mags, we haven't had much time to talk. Tell me about you and Duncan and this whirlwind courtship."

Maggie gave him all the details from the beginning, including the little games they had been playing along the way."

Gabe took a swig from the bottle, laughing. "I am sorry I missed it."

Taking the bottle, Maggie took a long drink before she told him about the beach proposal.

Gabe looked out at the water. "Damn! Now, that was a proposal."

The memory of that night flashed in Maggie's mind. "Yes, it was!"

"And then there is the other little thing that we have going on." She told Gabe about how they were able to communicate silently with their minds.

"Now, that's a bit unusual."

Maggie rolled her eyes. "Just a bit? You think?"

Gabe leaned back, propping himself up on his elbows. "Are you sure that is what it is? Maybe you are reading each other's body language and it just seems like you are hearing each other's thoughts."

"Well, let's test that theory. I am going to send him the silent message that I need him." Maggie's smile was near feral.

Gabe leaned forward grinning. "All right! Let's see."

Maggie closed her eyes. *Duncan, I need you. I am by the water.*

Within minutes he was coming down the path at a rapid speed. "Maggie, what's wrong?"

Maggie looked at Gabe, smirking. "I didn't mean to frighten you. I just missed you, my love."

Duncan's frown broke into a broad smile and sat next to her.

She leaned over and kissed him as he pulled her in close.

"I should be with ye anyway. Ye will be gone for two weeks and I want to spend every minute I can with ye."

Gabe went to get up. "That's my cue to leave. I will see you two at supper."

He left the lovers alone, wrapped up in the blanket, and looking out over the water.

22 CHAPTER TWENTY-TWO

Less than a week later, Maggie and Gabe were opening the front door of Gabe's mother's house. Georgie was in the parlor holding Kat. As soon as he saw them, his face lit up.

"There's my girl." He took Kat in his arms and hugged her tightly. "I have missed you so much."

"Well, hello to you too, Son," Georgie teased. "And Maggie! Welcome back. Where have you been?" They hugged.

"Hello, Georgie."

Maggie gingerly sat down as she told her the story that she and Gabe had made up about her being thrown from her horse and being injured during a short shopping excursion to Edinburgh.

"Oh, my goodness, my dear," said Georgie, full of concern. "I am glad you are alright."

Maggie motioned to Gabe. "Bring me the cute baby cheeks." She took Kat into her lap. "Look how she has grown!"

Georgie smiled. "She has missed the two of you."

Gabe looked from Maggie to his mother. "Mother... Maggie, Kat, and I are going to be leaving in a few days."

Georgie looked down. "So soon?"

"I am afraid so," said Maggie. "As much as we would like to stay, we have to be getting back."

"Well, I will hate to see you go, but I am glad that the two of you came."

Gabe leaned down and kissed his mother. "So am I, Mother."

Georgie went about the business of planning a series of family suppers before they were to leave, just as Cora came in to take Kat to nurse.

"Cora, we will be leaving in a few days."

She seemed thrilled with the news as she took Kat to take up to the nursery.

"Gabe, we need to have a chat with her about discretion."

"I will take care of it, Maggie."

She gave him a grave look. "Double her pay in exchange for her silence."

Gabe nodded. He leaned over and whispered, "I will handle all of this. You worry about healing and your wedding."

Maggie leaned on his shoulder. "That reminds me. I need to ask you something."

"Anything."

"Will you give me away?"

He hesitated before answering.

"No!"

Maggie raised up. "No?"

He took her hand. "I will NEVER give you away."
He grinned. "But, I will be honored to walk you down the aisle."

Later that night, there was a soft knock at Maggie's door.

"Come in, Gabe."

"Not Gabe, but I would still like to come in."

It was Martin.

"Of course, come in."

Maggie was in bed, so he pulled up a chair.

"What can I do for you, Martin?"

"I wanted to check you over from the accident to make sure you are healing, I noticed you favoring your right side a great deal."

"I am well, Martin, really."

He sighed. "Maggie, you have done so much for us, please let me do this little thing for you."

Maggie closed her eyes. "I have a slight confession to make. I wasn't thrown from a horse Martin... I was stabbed in the back."

Martin looked alarmed. "Did this happen when you were helping Wyatt at the whorehouse because he did not mention it?"

"He told you? I told that little idiot to make up a good story."

Chuckling, Martin nodded. "He told everyone else a good story, but he pulled me to the side later and made me swear not to tell anyone else before he told me the real one. He said that you sent him to get checked over by me." He laughed. "It was a good thing you did. Between your threat and my diagnosis, I don't think he will be visiting any more of them any time soon."

Maggie laughed. "Oh good."

"The point is Maggie, I can be discreet. Please let me take a look...for my own peace of mind."

Maggie nodded. She was already in bed, so she leaned over, using the sheet to cover the mark before she lifted her shift.

Martin peeled back the bandages. "How deep did it go in?"

"About four inches. The leather I was wearing absorbed some of it."

Martin felt around. "Maggie, were you injured before in the same area?"

"I am afraid so. I was hit by stray gunfire in Philadelphia. An army surgeon dug it out."

There was a knock at the door. "Coming in, Mags."

Gabe froze when he saw Maggie on the bed and Martin over her.

Martin turned. "Come in and close the door."

"Maggie?"

"Martin is checking my wound."

"Did something happen?" Gabe asked, his voice tentative.

"I told him about the stabbing, Gabe, mainly because it has not been healing the way it should."

Gabe moved to the bed, anger in his voice. "Why didn't you tell me?"

Maggie looked back at him, weariness on her face. "Because, you have had your hands full and you did not need to worry about me any more than you already have been. If I am being perfectly honest, I have not felt completely well since Philadelphia."

"There is a reason it has not been getting better. How long ago were you shot?" Martin asked.

"It has been almost a year, but she recovered from that," Gabe said. "Or so I thought."

Martin winced. "Fragments from the gunfire were missed. Maggie, you probably did recuperate at the time and the pieces left in just weren't any place that would bother you. Your body simply healed around them, but when you were stabbed, the fragments shifted and now there are in the open wound preventing it from getting any better. It will not heal until they come out. I am amazed that infection has not set up in it already."

"Well, let's get them out."

Martin shrugged. "Georgie is out with some of the ladies tonight. I can get my bag and do it now. It shouldn't take long, and I do have some Laudanum that will take the edge off."

"The sooner the better," said Maggie.

Gabe stood with his arms folded looking worried.

Martin administered the medicine and Maggie drifted off. When she woke the next morning, she was still lying face down, Gabe beside her in a chair, dozing.

Maggie pushed herself up slightly to test the pain. There was some, but it wasn't bad at all. Nowhere near what she expected.

A soft knock at the door woke Gabe; it was Martin.

"Good morning. I wanted to check on you while Georgie was still asleep."

Gabe wiped the sleep from his eyes and stood.

"How are you feeling, Maggie?" asked Martin, pulling back her bandages.

"Remarkably well actually."

Martin and Gabe exchanged a strange look.

Maggie rolled her eyes, preparing for the worst. "What is it now?"

Gabe grinned. "Good news for a change. It looks fine."

Martin pressed around on her back. "Better than that, it's pretty darn amazing. The redness is all gone and the incision that I had to make is barely noticeable. I have never seen one look so...healthy the next day. How odd." He replaced the bandages.

"Help me sit up?" asked Maggie.

Martin and Gabe both moved to lend a hand.

Maggie barely felt any pain when she did. "I am shocked that it doesn't hurt more."

"It's no wonder that you feel better," said Gabe, handing her a bowl. "This is what came out of you."

Maggie looked down. There were three pieces of bullet fragments. She picked up a piece and looked closer. "What is this? Lead?"

Martin nodded. "Sometimes, when the bullet hits, it breaks off into little pieces. If there is a great deal of it, and it is in deep enough, it would have been very easy for the surgeon to miss, which explains why you have not felt yourself."

"Lead poisoning," Maggie said aloud without thinking.

Martin and Gabe gave her strange looks.

Maggie saw the question in their eyes, "Oh...there are some physicians that think lead, if it gets in the body, can act as a slow poison, making you very sick over time."

Martin looked thoughtful. "I suppose that is a possibility if you think about it. Maggie, you have the most interesting physician friends. I would still like you to teach me that...CPR before you leave."

Gabe flinched.

"I will Martin, I promise. Thank you."

The doctor started towards the door. "I will check on you later. Get some rest." He turned towards Gabe, "Both of you."

Maggie rested the whole of the day and tagged along for Kat's morning walk on the following one.

"Are you sure you are up for this?" Gabe tried to stare her down.

"Gabe, I feel like a new woman. The pain is almost completely gone. I had no idea that was why I had been feeling so bad the past few months."

"I don't understand either, Maggie. There are plenty of soldiers walking around with fragments like that and they never experience any trouble from them. Why you?"

Maggie cut him a look. "Why me anything, Gabe? Let's face it. My life has never been, nor will it ever be...normal."

They spent the next few days preparing for their departure. Gabe, Henry, and Wyatt loaded the ship with books, while Maggie looked after Kat, even taking her on her first shopping trip. Gabe spent some much-needed time with his mother and brothers. The day before they left, Maggie and Gabe took Kat out to visit her parent's graves one last time.

They said their goodbyes and sailed for Edinburgh.

After the ship docked, they purchased horses, along with a small wagon to make it easier to travel with Kat, and slowly made their way to the MacGregor stronghold.

Soon, they had reached the forest that contained the fog. Maggie was able to lead them through with no issues, the mark having given her the ability to see clearly in the mist. As soon as they were on the other side, Maggie sent Duncan a silent message.

We have arrived.

Duncan and Quinn rode out to meet them. Duncan dismounted as soon as he was close to Maggie, she doing the same, ignoring the fact that they were not alone as they embraced and kissed.

Quinn shook his head, then cocked it in the direction of the castle. "They may be a while. Let's ride on."

Quinn escorted Gabe, Kat, and Cora to the house, and they were all seated in the library by the time Maggie and Duncan arrived. Lady Aurnia had already scooped Kat up and was having the time of her life with her, using every opportunity to point out to her sons that it was about time there was a baby back in that house. Cora looked a little overwhelmed by the trip, so Lady Aurnia had Flora show her up to her room so the rest of them could speak freely.

Lady Aurnia was walking with Kat, bouncing her around. "Maggie, how are you feeling?"

"Tremendously better." She explained about the fragments that Martin had discovered in her back and how much better she felt after they were removed.

"That reminds me," Gabe said, digging into his coat pocket, pulling out a small fabric pouch. "I kept them for you, Maggie, as a little memento."

Duncan took the pouch and opened it, examining the pieces closely. "They are lead."

Lady Aurnia stepped closer to look. "Lead ye say? And ye say ye healed completely after they were removed?"

Maggie nodded. "The next day, I felt better than I had in months."

A subtle look passed between Duncan and his mother.

Duncan turned to Maggie smiling, "Your eyes are almost completely back to normal. There are still a few tiny bits of gold left, but they are not as noticeable."

"I rather liked the gold-eye look," Maggie teased, kissing him.

"So ye two, when are we having this wedding?" asked Lady Aurnia.

Duncan pulled Maggie closer. "As soon as possible."

"How about tomorrow? If everything is ready, that is?" Maggie asked, gazing into Duncan's eyes.

Lady Aurnia laughed. "That can be arranged. Duncan, ye will stay in another room tonight."

He narrowed his eyes at his mother. "What do ye mean?"

His mother handed the baby back to Gabe. "Maggie needs to get a good night's sleep tonight and she will not if ye are there."

Maggie tried to conceal her giggle. "Your mother is right. I will be too tired to say my vows."

Duncan looked disgusted, "Och...fine!" He turned to Maggie and growled, "Rest well tonight, my love, because, after tomorrow, ye will never have a full night's sleep again."

Supper was a lively affair. All the MacGregor brothers had fallen in love with little Kat, taking turns passing her around the table. Quinn seemed to be the most enamored with her and she seemed happiest with him out of all the brothers.

Lady Aurnia was delighted to see all of them this way, her heart filled with joy at the sight of her family.

Gabe fit right in, now an honorary MacGregor.

When Kat became fussy, Cora excused herself, and took the baby upstairs to nurse. Everyone made a big deal about her departure until the two had disappeared from the room, Reade and Evan making fools of themselves solely for her entertainment.

"Quite a young lady ye have there, Gabe." Lady Aurnia said, amused and pleased by her son's reactions.

Gabe beamed. "She is the reason I was put in this world. I have only had her a few short weeks and I cannot imagine my life without her."

Lady Aurnia looked around the table, a sad droop at the corner of her mouth. "Enjoy her now. She will be grown in the blink of an eye."

Soon, the talk turned to that of the wedding.

"Maggie, your gown turned out beautifully. I must say I am rather fond of the wedding gown style of the future."

Duncan and Gabe both raised eyebrows while looking at Maggie at the same time.

"What?" she asked looking back and forth between them. "I wanted something resembling a gown from my own time. Forgive me."

Gabe chuckled. "I am almost afraid to see it after some of the things you have told me about 'propriety' in 2018."

"There is nothing wrong with a girl wanting a little tradition on her wedding day, especially when it comes to the gown. I only plan on doing this once."

Duncan kissed her hand. "Then ye shall have whatever ye want."

Later that evening, they were all in the library celebrating and enjoying themselves when Duncan pulled

Maggie to the side. "I have something to show ye before the ceremony."

He reached in a pocket and pulled out two rings. "I forged them myself."

Maggie looked at the rings. They were gold, with the same design of flowers and tiny Celtic symbols on the shield from downstairs.

"Ye were so taken with the shield, I thought you might like the design on yer ring."

"Duncan, I don't know what to say. It is the most beautiful thing I have ever seen."

He pulled her close for a sweet, deep kiss. "I cannot wait to be your husband tomorrow."

The rest of the brothers surrounded him.

"Alright, enough of that, Brother. Ye are unmarried for one more night and tonight ye belong to us," said Reade.

Logan grabbed him by the shoulder. "Leave the poor woman be. She will be sick of ye soon enough."

"Don't worry, Maggie, we won't let him get so drunk that he cannot stand for the ceremony tomorrow," Quinn assured her.

"Or for the wedding night," chuckled Evan.

Quinn looked at Gabe. "Ye are coming with us. Ye are part of the family now."

Duncan sighed, still holding Maggie.

"Oh, go on Duncan, you will survive one more night without me."

He pulled her into another deep kiss. "Until tomorrow then. I love ye, Maggie."

"I love you too, Duncan."

They pulled him out of the library and out of the house.

The next morning, Maggie was up early. She went downstairs to find Lady Aurnia having breakfast with Kat and Cora.

"Good morning, Maggie."

"Good morning." She took Kat from Cora, so the nurse could finish her breakfast.

"Where is everyone?" asked Maggie.

Lady Aurnia rolled her eyes, "Sleeping off last night would be my guess. The liquor cabinet was completely empty this morning."

Maggie laughed. "Cora, have you seen Gabe yet?"

"No, ma'am. He has usually taken Kat from the nursery by now, but he did not this morning."

"He rarely drinks to excess, but when he does, he feels it the next day. I will go check on him and Duncan."

"Nay, Maggie, I will check on my son. It is bad luck for the two of ye to see each other before the wedding. Besides, ye should relax. I will have a bath sent up for ye and be up later to help ye get ready. Flora is at your disposal today."

"Thank you." She looked at Kat, nuzzling her nose into the baby's soft hair. "Let's go wake your father, shall we?" She turned to Cora. "Take your time and enjoy your breakfast."

Maggie and Kat slipped into Gabe's room. He was lying face down, snoring loudly, still in his clothes and boots, with his shirt askew. Maggie walked around to where his head was and pushed his hair back. "Wake up, Gabe. You are missing breakfast. I think Mrs. Manus fried up some nice greasy bacon just for you."

"Go away," he moaned.

"Gabe, someone is here to say, 'good morning'."

He cracked open one eye and pushed himself up. Sitting, he reached out for Kat, giving her a kiss on the head. "Good morning, princess. I am sorry I missed our morning story time. I will tell you two at bedtime tonight."

Maggie sat down. "You are such a good father. Kat is so lucky to have you."

"No, I am the lucky one to have her. I never thought I would get the chance to be a father again and I am going to appreciate every moment of it, even more so when my head is not exploding with pain."

He blinked and winced. "By the way...I am convinced those brothers and Scottish whisky have been sent straight up from Hell itself."

Maggie chuckled, "Couldn't keep up with their drinking last night?"

"I tried, but they drank me under the table...literally...I woke up at one point under a table."

Cora knocked on the door and came in to take Kat to her room to nurse. The baby was starting to fuss, so the timing was fortuitous; the nursemaid knew Kat's schedule.

Maggie watched them leave, a bit of wistfulness in her gaze. "What did you boys do last night?"

Gabe shook his head. "Honestly, I don't remember most of it. We started out drinking down by the water, we went to the library, and ended up in the chamber at some point... I think."

He reached over to the side table to get a glass of water, his shirt lifting slightly, as Maggie caught a glimpse of something. She pulled his shirt up further.

"That's not all you did," she giggled.

Gabe looked at her strangely. "What are you talking about?"

"Go look in the mirror."

Eyeing her with suspicion, like she was playing some sort of prank, he stumbled over to the dresser, pulling up his shirt. "Son of a... are you kidding me?"

The MacGregor mark was on his back.

Maggie could not contain her laughter. "They did you say you were one of them now. I guess they made it official."

Gabe came back over to the bed, pointing to his face. "Are my eyes gold, too?"

Maggie leaned over to look, laughing so hard that her eyes were teary. "Red....yes. Gold...no. You are good."

"Bloody Hell." Gabe fell back down on the bed.

Maggie patted him on the chest, and she propped up on one elbow next to him. "I will send Quinn up to see if he can get you something for that hangover. He is very good with the medicinal cocktails."

"I am not sure there is enough medicine in Scotland for this."

"I have to go get ready, Gabe."

Gabe sighed. "I will get myself together and join you soon. Mags?"

She turned.

"I love you. I am very happy for you and Duncan."

Maggie smiled. "I love you too, Gabe...and welcome to the family," she chuckled as she went out the door.

She had finished her bath and was sitting on the bed when there was a knock at the door.

"Maggie, I have your gown."

An hour later, Maggie was standing in front of a full-length mirror looking at herself.

Lady Aurnia had outdone herself on the dress. It was a simple A-line, with long sleeves and lace across the top, very proper for a church wedding, but the back was completely cut out, fabric starting just below the mark, displaying the symbol perfectly. The train was about four feet long. Maggie had picked up some material for a veil in London, enough to make it as long as the train itself. Flora and Lady Aurnia had put Maggie's hair up, placing little tiny flowers in it before attaching the veil to the back.

Lady Aurnia stood back. "Oh Maggie! Ye look magnificent and that gown is perfect for you."

"Really? You did such an amazing job on it. I cannot thank you enough."

Taking her hands, Lady Aurnia squeezed; she couldn't hug Maggie without ruining something. "It was my pleasure and I am over the moon to have ye as my daughter."

Someone knocked at the door.

"Maggie, it's Gabe. May I come in?"

"Yes."

Gabe opened the door and stopped. "Maggie!" He closed the door and came to stand in front of her.

"Well, what do you think?"

Gabe's face lit up with a smile. "You are...breathtaking." He leaned in and kissed her on the cheek.

Lady Aurnia and Flora started towards the door. "We have some details to see to. We will come to get you when it is time."

When they were gone, Gabe turned back to
Maggie. "Let me get a good look at you." He walked
around to see her from all sides. "Maggie! I think your
gown is missing a piece in the back."

Maggie laughed. "Modern girl, remember?"

"I am not sure Duncan will be thrilled about his brothers
seeing that much of you."

Maggie waved her hand. "He'll survive. You look like
you are feeling better."

He took a seat and crossed his legs. "You were right
about Quinn. He has amazing cures for a hangover. He
said something about having to mix an extra big batch for
the family this morning."

"No doubt," laughed Maggie.

Gabe looked her over again. "You really are a vision.
Duncan is a lucky man. Are you nervous?"

"Would it be horrible if I said I was?" Maggie replied
with a wince.

"Not at all. It would be perfectly normal."

Maggie sucked in a breath. "I was fine until I put the
gown on, and then it hit me. I will be married by the end
of the day. Gabe, promise me something?"

"Depends," he said sarcastically.

"Promise me that we will always be as we are. Come
spouses, come children, come hell or high water, promise
me that our relationship will never change."

He stood and took her into a careful hug. "That is a
promise I will not hesitate to make. You have my word."

When Maggie pulled back, she started patting
his coat. "Give it."

He shook his head and pulled out not one, but
two flasks, holding them up and shaking them. "I took
your advice and started packing an extra one."

Maggie laughed and took a big drink, thought about it, and then took another.

"Easy there, my dear, you still have to walk down the aisle."

She handed him back the flask. "I wonder if Quinn has anything in his arsenal for nerves."

"He is a wonder...with the herbs, I mean."

"So, who did it?"

"Did what?" Gabe asked.

"The mark. Who did the work? Do you even remember?"

"Oh, I am pretty sure it was Quinn. Bits and pieces are starting to come back. I vaguely remember the discussion with the brothers as a group and I am fairly certain that it involved a wager that I lost. That'll teach me to drink with them. At least I don't remember it hurting."

"Oh no, it didn't. It was the most relaxing thing I have experienced in my life. When people get tattoos in my time, some of them are screaming like babies. I actually drifted off to sleep."

Gabe shrugged. "It's alright. If truth be known, the MacGregor family has made me feel like one of their own. It is their mark and I am proud to wear it...and it is out of sight."

Lady Aurnia knocked on the door. "Maggie, it is time. My boys are already at the chapel."

Gabe helped her adjust her gown and held out his arm. "Ready?"

"Ready!"

Outside her door, Lady Aurnia handed her a bouquet of wildflowers, winked, and led the way.

Gabe leaned over. "Last chance if you want to make a run for it."

Maggie grinned. "I think I will take my chances. Besides, if I don't get him into bed soon, I may very well explode."

Gabe couldn't contain his laughter and it caused Maggie to break into peals of her own.

"The funniest thing is that you think I am joking."

When they were ready to leave the house to walk outside to the chapel, Lady Aurnia stopped them. "Maggie, I have to tell ye something so ye are not startled." Maggie was alarmed. "What is it?"

Lady Aurnia held up her hand. "Nothing bad, just something ye need to know. Duncan has been arguing with Onyx all morning. Onyx planted himself outside the chapel and refused to let anyone in, not wanting to be left out of the ceremony. Since he is too big to fit in the chapel, Duncan compromised and opened one of the windows for him to be able to be a part of it. He is waiting outside of the chapel for ye to arrive before he takes his place."

Maggie laughed, amused and touched all at the same time.

Gabe stood with his mouth open, listening to Lady Aurnia, trying hard to form words from his mouth. "Please...explain to me.... how...that whole conversation occurred.... I would be...fascinated to know."

Maggie squeezed Gabe's hand. "Oh! I forgot to tell you. Onyx isn't really a horse."

Turning to Maggie, Gabe moved his ear closer as if he couldn't hear. "Come again? I know he doesn't act like a horse, but to say he isn't a horse..."

Quinn walked up to the conversation. "Gabe, I will explain it to you later. Maggie, your groom is getting very anxious. He said something about breaking in the door and dragging ye to the chapel if ye didn't hurry."

"Well, let's not keep him waiting."

Onyx met Maggie outside the church. She hugged him, told him how much she loved him, and assured him that their relationship would never change.

He seemed satisfied and trotted off to take his place.

Flora helped Maggie to get her gown righted, and the doors to the chapel were opened. Maggie's gaze went straight to Duncan. Dressed in Scottish formal attire, his hair plaited back, family tartan on full display, he was the most handsome man Maggie had ever laid eyes on, and she could not wait to be his wife.

I love you, Duncan.

When Duncan saw Maggie, his breath left his body, his heart skipped a beat, and he felt his knees may give way. Every cliché written in love poems and stories fell upon him at once. She was the most stunning creature he had ever seen, and she was about to be all his.

I love ye, Maggie.

Maggie didn't remember the trip down the aisle, or the people gathered to watch. All she saw was Duncan. When she and Gabe reached him, Gabe gave her arm to Duncan, but only after he kissed her cheek and told her how much he loved her.

When Duncan came to stand beside her, he saw the back of the gown.

He shot her an astonished look and a silent message. *Maggie! The back of your gown!*

She smirked and fired a response back. *Don't like it?*

Duncan grinned. *I didn't say that.*

They exchanged vows and rings before being pronounced husband and wife. Duncan took her into a kiss that lasted well longer than it should. They left the chapel to go to the house for a family supper, the bride and groom unable to keep their hands off each other.

After supper, and after everyone but the immediate family had left the house, they gathered for the Fae ceremony. The altar room was lit with a hundred candles and adorned with fresh flowers.

Lady Aurnia covered them both with a translucent veil-like material covered in ancient symbols. She read from the book, with words that Maggie did not understand, and when she was done, Maggie and Duncan read words from the same book to each other. When all of that was done, everyone left the room to give Maggie and Duncan a few minutes alone.

When they emerged, it was getting close to dusk.

"Maggie, we should leave for our wedding night."

"Leave? Where are we going?"

He kissed her. "I have something special planned."

Duncan mounted his horse and Gabe helped her up to ride side-saddle in front of her husband. Everyone bid them farewell and they were off.

An hour later, they arrived at the hot springs. Duncan had a luxurious tent set up. It was tall, medieval-like, but the inside was beyond recognition. A bed had been made up in the middle, carpets lined the ground, tapestries lined the walls. Pillows and blankets were everywhere. A table had been brought in and stocked with food and wine, lanterns illuminating the inside.

But the springs were the most amazing. Hundreds of lit candles sent their flames up, along the rock edges and in the crevices, making the entire area look like something out of a woman's wildest dream.

"Oh, Duncan, you did all of this for me? It is the most wondrous thing I have ever seen. I could not have imagined anything more perfect than this."

He took her in his arms, "Maggie, I would do anything for ye."

Kissing her, he carried her into the tent. They took their time, undressing and loving each other. They spent the entire night making love without end, entangled in each other arms and hearts for all of eternity.

The next morning, they bathed in the warm waters, enjoying each other in them and went back into the tent for the rest of the day and night. The following morning, they dressed—reluctantly and slowly—and rode back to the house, blissfully happy in their new marriage.

23 CHAPTER TWENTY-THREE

When Maggie and Duncan returned to the house, Gabe and Quinn were stripped to the waist enjoying some playful sword practice outside. They stopped and walked up to greet them.

"I trust you two enjoyed your wedding night," Gabe said, wiping his face.

"Very much so," Maggie said, patting him on the chest. "Quinn teaching you a few things?"

Gabe turned back to Quinn. "Yes...he is, as a matter of fact."

"Ye two are just in time for the midday meal." Quinn motioned for one of the stable hands to take Duncan's horse.

Duncan wrapped his arms around Maggie from behind. "Why do ye think we came back? We are starving."

The four made their way to the house, laughing and joking.

Lady Aurnia watched them from the window, smiling, thinking how much she would miss them when they were gone. She met them at the door. "Welcome back."

"Hello, Mother." Duncan kissed her cheek.

Maggie and Duncan devoured their meal as everyone happily chatted around the table. Afterward, the newlyweds stole away to their bedroom upstairs until the next morning.

Duncan kissed Maggie and moved to get out of bed. "Where are you going?"

"Training Day," he said, dressing. "I have to officially pass command of the men to Logan."

Maggie sat up and sadly said, "I guess it is getting close to the time for us to leave."

He moved back to the bed. "Ye sound like ye do not want to leave."

Maggie took his hand. "I will miss it here, I have to admit, but I know better than anyone that we must go."

Duncan leaned over, kissing her. "Aye, Scotland will always be special...and here. We can return to visit whenever we like."

Two weeks later, everything was loaded on a wagon and on its way to the ship.

Lady Aurnia, who had grown quite fond of Gabe, gifted him with one of the ceremonial swords and two of their stunning white mares, one for him and a young mare for

Kat for when she was older, declaring him officially part of the family.

Gabe was so taken aback, that he was speechless.

Duncan and Quinn brought their horses and ceremonial swords, as well. All the brothers accompanied them, traveling at night for secrecy, taking turns sleeping and guarding the wagon during the day.

Once they reached Edinburgh, the ship was loaded to the brim and ready for departure. Everyone said their final goodbyes, with promises to reunite soon.

Maggie hugged Duncan tightly as the ship pulled away; she felt the sadness he was determined to never let her see.

The days at sea were long and arduous, especially with a newborn onboard.

Maggie and Duncan spent a great deal of time in their room still being newlyweds, but they had dinner and supper with Gabe, Quinn, Cora, and Kat each day.

One night, Maggie was having trouble sleeping. Duncan was fast asleep, so she slipped out of bed and dressed, heading to Gabe's room to see if he was still awake. They had not had much time to catch up since the wedding, and she missed him immensely.

Just as she was about to knock, she heard something. Maggie stopped and listened, ear pressed hard to the door. The sounds were unmistakable. Gabe had company...and they were not talking. Maggie's hand flew to her mouth.

Who could it be?

Maggie's question was answered when the other person spoke a few words in the throes of passion, the voice unmistakable.

It was Quinn.

Maggie crept away silently, heading above deck for some fresh air.

Oh my God!

She was flabbergasted. She had no idea that those two were an item. It must have happened right under her nose...and Gabe had not said the first word, given no indication that they were seeing each other. Oh, he was going to pay for keeping her out of the loop on this one. She went back downstairs and undressed to climb back into bed.

Duncan opened his eyes, catching her slipping back the covers. "Where were ye?" he asked.

"Oh, just getting some fresh air. Go back to sleep, my love."

He pulled her close and growled, "I am wide awake now."

She laughed and he slipped under the covers, pulling her with him. This man was insatiable.

The next morning at breakfast, Maggie picked at her food, looking between Gabe and Quinn. They showed no evidence of anything going on.

"Sleep well, Gabe?" Maggie asked.

"Yes, very well actually."

"Uh huh," Maggie said, twirling a piece of hair, biting her lip. "I am worried about you being uncomfortable in that room. I know there's something about that particular bed that is very...HARD...to deal with."

Gabe shook his head. "It's fine."

Maggie shifted, still eyeing Gabe. "Still, I think I will have it replaced when we get home. I wouldn't want your backside to get sore from such uncomfortable quarters. I passed by there last night and heard the bed creaking all the way out in the hall. It almost sounded like it was GROANING.... from the waves POUNDING...into the... STERN of the boat, no doubt."

Gabe put his fork down, placed his arms on the table and narrowed his eyes at her.

"Something on your mind, Maggie?" he asked.

Maggie continued to stare at Gabe but spoke to Duncan. "Gabe and I haven't had any quality time together since the wedding. Why don't you and Quinn take Kat up for some fresh air and give Cora a break, so he and I can catch up?"

Duncan looked between the two of them. *What's going on Maggie?*

Everything is fine my love. Just give us a few minutes alone to chat.

"Certainly." Duncan kissed the top of her head and took Kat from Cora.

Cora excused herself as Quinn looked back nervously at Gabe and he followed Duncan.

When they were gone, Maggie stood, closed the pocket doors, then spun around. "Spill it, Gabe! How long have you and Quinn been together?"

"Does Duncan know?" he asked in a low, grave tone, staring down at the table.

"Has his head exploded? Of course, he doesn't know." Maggie sat down, reached across the table, and took Gabe's hand in hers. "Why didn't you tell me?" she asked softly.

He squeezed her hand. "I wanted to. We just haven't had much time alone since it happened."

"Well, we are alone now, and I want details."

"I don't know where to begin. Quinn and I hit it off when we first met in Edinburgh. Other than being terribly worried about you, that trip was very...nice. Quinn was easy to talk to. After I found out you were alright, we would find ourselves in the same room or out by the stables, just enjoying time together. I had no idea that he favored men. Do you remember the day of your wedding when I told you that I didn't remember much about the night before?"

Maggie nodded.

"Bits and pieces started to come back to me later in the day. I remembered Quinn being the one who gave me the mark, but then the memory of him kissing it when he was done came back. I did not know what to think except that he'd had too much to drink, as had I. After you and Duncan left that night, I went down by the water just to be alone. He followed me and we talked; it became clear that he did not prefer the bed of women. His story was much as mine. His brothers pushed him to be with women, but he never enjoyed it, found it a chore even. He found himself more drawn to men but was afraid if anyone ever found out what it would do to his family. It was one of the reasons he wanted to leave Scotland...he was hoping for a little more freedom to be who he was. We kissed that night and took every chance we could to be alone together after that."

Maggie smiled. "Do you love him?"

Gabe closed his eyes. "Yes, I do. After I gave you grief for falling in love too soon, I turned around and did the exact same thing."

Maggie grinned and winked. "I won't hold it against you. The MacGregor brothers are quite irresistible."

Gabe laughed. "I suppose they are."

"The two of you need to tell Duncan," she said with a sudden, serious look on her face.

"We cannot, Maggie. Not everyone is as understanding as you, and Duncan will not take it well. I am not sure I can ever forgive myself if Quinn were to lose his brother over this."

"Gabe, he is not blind nor stupid. He will eventually figure it out, and he will be more upset if he finds out that it has been kept from him. Besides, I know now and that is dangerous."

"What do you mean?"

"Gabe, you remember this mind thing I told you about, where we can hear each other's thoughts if we focused?"

"Yes."

"Since the ceremonies, it has grown tremendously. We can pick up each other's thoughts without even focusing hard. I am afraid he may find out accidentally through me."

Gabe stroked his chin, concerned. "It is really that strong?"

Maggie nodded. "You and Quinn need to have a conversation and soon. I will do whatever I can to help."

"Thanks, Mags."

"Gabe. You look very happy and I could not be more thrilled for you."

"Mags, there is one more thing you should know..."

The pocket doors slid open. Kat was crying, and Quinn was toting her. "I think she is missing ye."

Gabe took her in his arms and spoke softly to her; she quieted instantly.

"I am going to find my husband. Gabe, remember what we talked about."

He nodded.

Maggie found Duncan on the top deck. She came up behind him, pressing herself against him.

He turned around. "Ye are cold. Let me warm ye up."

After supper that night, Maggie answered a knock at the door. It was Gabe and Quinn.

"Duncan, Gabe and I would like to speak to you about something."

Gabe nodded at Maggie who moved next to Duncan, but in front of Gabe.

"What is it, Quinn? Ye look so serious."

"Duncan, let me first say that I love ye. Ye are my family and I hope nothing will ever change that."

Duncan looked puzzled. "Of course not, Brother. We are blood. What is wrong with ye?"

Quinn took in a deep breath and looked to Gabe, then back to Duncan. "Gabe and I are together…as in, a couple. We are in love with each other."

Duncan was too stunned to move; all the color left his face as he looked back and forth between the two men trying to comprehend Quinn's words.

When he was finally able to speak, he narrowed his eyes at Gabe and spat, "How dare ye seduce my brother and have your way with him? And, then ye convince him that it is love? I will kill ye for this."

Duncan started to lunge at Gabe, but Maggie stepped in front of him, placing her hands on his chest to stop him.

"No, you will not! You will not harm Gabe as long as there is breath in my body."

Duncan moved close to her face. "Ye cannot stop me, wife."

Maggie put her hands on her hips. "But, I can make you sleep alone the rest of this trip…and it is a very long trip. Not only that, I will walk around this ship completely naked just to show you what are you missing. It's not like I have to worry about these two over here bothering me. I do absolutely nothing for them in that way."

"You wouldn't!" Duncan folded his arms across his chest.

Maggie folded her arms, too. "You want to test that theory? I went over ten years without sex. You want to see if *you* can?"

Quinn shook his head at the conversation, holding up his hands to interrupt it. "Nay, Brother. Gabe did not seduce me. If anything, it was the other way around."

Duncan jerked his head toward Quinn. "I do not understand."

Quinn lowered his head. "Duncan, I have never wanted to be with a woman. I did when ye and our brothers pushed me into it, but I never took any pleasure in it. I have always preferred the company of men. I was just afraid of what trouble and shame my true nature might bring upon our family name. I am still your baby brother and I look up to ye just as I did when we were children. Disappointing ye is the last thing I ever want to do."

Duncan took in a deep breath, as he ran his fingers through his hair. "Quinn, ye can be hanged for something like this."

Gabe stepped forward. "Not if he learns how to be discreet. In Virginia, no one will know anything about him. He just needs to keep it that way."

"He is right, Duncan," said Maggie.

Duncan suddenly became aware of a painful fact. "Ye knew! My own wife knew about this and did not tell me?"

Duncan was furious.

"I only found out this morning, but I have known about Gabe since the day we met."

Duncan turned to Quinn. "What would Mother say? What would this do to her, Quinn?"

"She knew," Gabe said softly.

"What?"

Gabe took a step toward Quinn. "Lady Aurnia took me aside a few days before we left. She said that she had a vision of Quinn when she carried him."

Quinn turned to Gabe, this information new to him, as well.

"She said that she saw that he would not be like the rest of you and that he was destined to never be content with a woman. He would have to leave Scotland to find happiness and she was amazed that he had not left sooner. She asked me to take care of him. I gave her my word that I would...and I intend to keep it."

Quinn sighed and smiled at him.

"You are telling me that our mother gave her blessing for Quinn to live like this?"

"She did more than that, Brother," said Quinn. "The night before we left...she married us."

It was Maggie's turn to be stunned. "What did you say?" She narrowed her eyes at Gabe, fury in her face as she lunged at him.

Duncan grabbed her by the waist and pulled her back so fast that Maggie's arms were still reaching for Gabe.

"You...got married...without me there? Gabe! How could you? I wouldn't dream of doing that to you."

"Maggie, I am so sorry. Lady Aurnia woke us and took us to the chamber after everyone was in bed.
She knew, and she asked if we would like her to perform the Fae marriage ceremony. We discussed it and decided

that it was what we wanted. I tried to tell you this morning but didn't get the chance. Please, forgive me."

"It was her way of letting me know that she understood and that she loved me anyway," said Quinn. "We are happy, Brother, as happy as ye and Maggie. I do not want there to be any secrets between us, and I hope ye will not hate me for being who I truly am."

Duncan lowered his head. "I could not hate ye, Brother. Never! I do need time to adjust to this and to come to terms with it, but I will never turn ye out or stop loving ye."

Quinn took a step toward Duncan and they embraced.

Maggie rubbed Gabe's arm as she leaned against him, tears starting to flow.

"Damn it, Maggie, no crying," said Gabe.

"Nay! Stop that wife. We have had this discussion," added Duncan, jabbing a finger in her direction.

"Oh, shut up, you two. I am a woman and I am allowed."

Gabe and Quinn left to go back to their room.

But before they were through the door, Maggie stopped them. "Gabe?"

"Yes, Maggie?"

"You might want to triple...no quadruple Cora's pay...and build her a house, you know, in exchange for her discretion. Women like houses, especially their own."

Gabe stepped back and kissed her on the cheek. "Good night, Maggie."

Maggie closed the door and turned to Duncan, who was sitting on the bed his head in his hands. She moved to stand in front of him, taking his head in her hands. She pulled his head up and kissed him. "You okay?"

"Nay, Maggie, I am not."

"What can I do?"

He wrapped his arms around her waist. "Help me understand?"

"Duncan...love is love. It is not up to us to decide in what form or fashion. When you find some happiness in this world, you have to hang on to it for dear life...like I did with you." She reached down, popped open a cabinet by the bed, and took out a bottle. She sat down next to him and pulled out the cork. "And when life gets to be too much, meet my other best friend...rum."

Maggie took a swig and looked at the label. "Oh, how I have missed you, old friend."

She handed the bottle to Duncan who laughed and took a drink. "It's not whisky, but it's not bad."

Maggie grabbed at the bottle. "Well, if you don't like it, then that leaves more for me."

He held it up, out of her reach. "I have something 'more' for you," he teased, pulling her down on the bed. "Ye really went over ten years without a man in your bed?"

Maggie nodded.

"Well, ye have a great deal of catching up to do. Let me give ye a hand with that," he laughed, rolling her under him and making love to her.

They spent a good part of the night talking.

Maggie explained how in her time, this was not unusual. Duncan had many questions that Maggie did her best to answer.

The next morning, the shock had started to wear off. Duncan and Quinn spent several hours on the top deck, talking and working things out. Maggie spent that time pacing in their room, stopping to mentally send a message to Duncan every so often to see how he was managing.

By suppertime, the tension had eased, as it continued to do over the next few days. Eventually, things settled down and started to get back to normal.

A few nights before they were to get home, Maggie had a hard time sleeping. Duncan was completely out, so she dressed to go up on deck and get some fresh air. She leaned over the rail, thinking about all that had transpired the past few months. It was a whirlwind of new loves and more questions. She still had no idea why she was sent back to this time, but she had a feeling there was something important she needed to do, but what was it?

She looked out over the water, at the full moon hanging in the night sky, the stars shining abnormally bright. Looking up, she remembered a nursery rhyme her mother used to say. She repeated the words in her mind, the final few she said aloud: "I wish I may, I wish I might. Have the wish I wish tonight."

The ship grew unconventionally quiet; no creaks, no sounds of water splashing against the hull, nothing...until a voice from behind her spoke.

"Hello, Maggie."

The voice seemed familiar. Maggie had heard it before, but not for a very long time. Not since...

Maggie turned, her face full of disbelief.

Surely, she was dreaming. She had not seen this man since she crossed in time. He still looked as he did all those years ago. The man she met in a tavern in North

Carolina...the man who started her on the path she was on.

Finn.

"Finn?"

"My dear, Maggie. It has been a while."

Maggie's body numbed, the blood draining from her face. "How are you on my ship?"

He smiled and moved closer. "Ye wished for answers. I came to help ye with that."

Maggie looked around. All the men on the top deck were slumped over asleep. "What happened to my crew?"

Finn turned and glanced back at them. "Oh, they are fine. Just resting for a bit. I put...what do ye call it, 'the whammy' on them and everyone else on this ship. They will wake when we are done here. I needed some time alone with ye to chat."

"Who are you, Finn?"

He leaned back against the rail, looking at her thoughtfully. "I am known by many names, but my formal title is...King...of the Fae."

Maggie shook her head. "No! I have to be dreaming."

"I assure ye, my dear, ye are not." He turned to look out over the water, Maggie cautiously moving next to him. "I understand ye are looking for some answers. I can be of assistance in that respect."

"You had something to do with my time jump," Maggie stated.

He shrugged. "Ye were needed here more than ye were in 2018."

Maggie forced herself to breathe. "Why?"

"There were many reasons. Two of which are fast asleep below deck. Ye were needed to save the MacGregor family."

"Save them?"

"Yes, that nasty Angus fellow, the plan he told ye about killing the family. If ye had not been there when ye were, he would have done exactly that a few short weeks into the future. He would have drugged their food, so they would sleep while he set the fire, burning the house to the ground and killing every single member of that family in one night. But, because ye came when ye did, ye changed their future and saved them."

"They would have all been dead? Duncan, Quinn, Lady Aurnia?" Maggie felt sick at the thought of all of them being gone.

"Even young Christopher...and death would have been welcomed by him by the time that filthy piece of trash had gotten done with him. But thanks to ye, the MacGregor line that protects our collection did not end. It will go on to endure just as it was always meant to."

Maggie felt faint.

Finn helped to steady her against the rail. He reached down and picked up something at his feet. He handed her a bottle.

Maggie eyed it suspiciously.

"Oh, drink it, it is not poison."

Maggie took a sip while keeping an eye on him. "Vodka?"

Finn smiled. "Yes, I thought ye might like something from your own time."

Nodding, she took another drink. "Oh, that is good. Thank you." Maggie let out a deep breath. "Okay, King Finn of the Fae, since you are feeling chatty. Why me?

Of all the people in the world, why little ole Maggie
Bishop from Williamsburg, Virginia?"

He laughed. "Oh, my dear, it had to be ye. There was no
one else." He stepped closer, staring at the stone that
hung around Maggie's neck, a deep sadness on his
face. "I still remember the day that I gave that to your
mother."

Maggie's blood ran cold. "My mother? You gave this to
my mother?"

He nodded.

"But, she said that it was given to her by her father."

"It was." He smiled. "Ye remind me so much of her. Ye
have her fire."

Maggie started to feel dizzy and lightheaded.

"Drink!" Finn ordered. "I do not need ye passing out
right now."

Maggie obeyed, listening to him explain.

"Your mother was Danu, the Fae goddess of nature and
motherhood....and my most beloved daughter. She gave
up her immortality to live out her life with your mortal
father. She came to me speaking of her love for this man
that she had met...how she could not live without him,
begging me to turn her. I tried to talk her out of it, but she
would not listen. She was so blinded by the love that she
felt for the man and she was willing to sacrifice
everything to be with him for a few short years. As much
as it pained me, in the end, I did grant her wish because,
as her father, I only wanted to see her happy. I still miss
her every day."

"Why wouldn't she tell me?"

"She did not remember. When she gave up her
immortality, she gave up all her memories of it. I cast a
spell that allowed her to retain the memory of the day I

gave her that necklace. I have missed her more than ye will ever know. Which brings me back to your question. It had to be ye because ye were the only one on Earth with nearly pure Fae blood running through your veins."

Finn stopped and sighed before he continued. "Ye see, Maggie, when Fae walked the land, they would often mingle with humans, have affairs, and produce children. Those children were inherently good. They would go out into the world and do great things for mankind. Hercules, for example, was one of ours, as was King Arthur, and many other names ye would recognize from your history books."

"Jesus Christ!" exclaimed Maggie.

"Oh no! He wasn't one of ours."

Maggie gave him a sideways look.

"Anyway, as we were driven underground, those children were no longer coming into existence and the bloodlines were watered down to next to nothing. What we came to realize, is that mankind needed that infusion of Fae blood. In 2018, the world has gone to hell…you are well aware of that. People are self-absorbed in their cell phones and their Instagram. They ignore their neighbors in need, walk by starving children on the streets, never wanting to be bothered with someone else's problems. Nuclear weapons are available at the push of a button. Pollution contaminates your water and land at an alarming rate, no one seeming to care. The Earth itself is screaming for help and mankind is ignoring it."

He paused.

"We hear it ye know…underground. The Earth cries as a mother who has lost her child. That world is on a crash course straight to its demise and if something is not drastically changed, it will not survive another 100 years.

It needs the infusion of the Fae blood to get it back on course."

Maggie looked confused. "Why don't you just come up and do it...mingle with people again?"

"Our numbers are not what they once were. Most of our kind have chosen to go into an eternal slumber to not have to deal with the problems of the world, waiting for it to blow itself into oblivion. Ye see, dear Maggie, ye were sent back to the exact moment that the Fae blood was extinguished. The MacGregor clan carries the last of it, and if they had died, so would have all hope for the future of this world. Ye were needed to set things back on course."

A realization hit Maggie. "You were the one who sent the letter about Gabe's mother."

He nodded. "Timing was everything. If ye had taken ye another month to find the MacGregors, it would have been too late."

"It was all you. The sword, the book, the map..." Something else hit Maggie. "*You* were the peddler with the sword. I knew you looked familiar, but I could not place you. And Onyx...he recognized you because you sent him. That is why he was playing with you that day."

Finn laughed. "Aye! He and I are old friends. He loved your mother more than anything and when he found out ye needed help, I could not have kept him away."

"And Duncan and I?"

Finn raised his eyebrows as he folded his arms. "Are meant to be. Some of my finest matchmaking if I do say so myself. The two of ye will have that epic love that ye always dreamed of from your childhood fairy tales. After saving the family line, ye, my dear, have earned it."

"Wait a minute. You said reasons...plural. What other reasons?"

Finn smirked and leaned forward. "I cannot tell ye everything, Maggie. What fun would that be? What is that phrase that is so popular in the future...*Spoilers, my dear, spoilers*."

Maggie shook her head. Of course, the answers would not be simple. "But Finn, what if I mess things up really badly? I am on a road trip with no map here," she said softly.

Finn placed his arm around her shoulder. "Just keep doing what ye are doing. The things that are meant to be put in your path will find their way and I have no doubt that ye will make the right decisions. Ye are the granddaughter of the King after all."

He squeezed her shoulder. "And I will be around. I am always keeping an eye on ye."

Maggie rolled her eyes. "Huh! Where were you when I was poisoned, shot, stabbed...need I go on?"

Finn chuckled, "But did ye die?"

Maggie laughed. "That's your answer? Seriously?"

Finn turned her and took her by both shoulders. "I am very proud of ye, Maggie. You are a remarkable woman."

He thought for a moment. "I wish to give ye a little part of your mother to remember her by." He kissed her on the forehead, a little jolt of energy rippling through her body as he did.

"What was that?"

"Ye will find out soon enough. Now, ye and that new husband of yours get all the rest ye can, while ye can." A mischievous look came to his eye. "Ye will be needing it."

He turned to go.

"Finn?"

"Yes, my dear?"

A tear formed in her eye. "Are my mom and dad okay? I mean...I was simply gone one day without a trace and I can only imagine how much pain my disappearance caused them. I just wish they could know that I am good...and happy where I am."

Finn lowered his head. "They have had each other. When I turned your mother, I made sure that, for the years she had remaining, the love between the two of them would be special enough to sustain them through any hardship. But if ye wish, I will find a way to make sure they know ye are well."

Maggie nodded. "Thank you."

"Be well, young Maggie." He smiled and walked to the edge of the ship where a strange thick mist had formed...and he was gone.

The crew members started to wake all at once.

Maggie looked out over the water, trying to process all that Finn had said, her mind on information overload. Yet, she knew somewhere, deep down inside, that what he told her was the truth and that everything was as it should be.

She heard them before she saw them.

Duncan, Gabe, and Quinn were coming towards her at an alarming speed.

She turned, smiling at the three most important men in her life. They were quite an impressive group when they were shoulder to shoulder, intent on the same goal.

"What happened?" Duncan said with a stern look, taking Maggie in his arms, looking her over for injuries.

"Duncan and I felt a shift of some sort," added Quinn.

Maggie looked around at the crew members that had awakened, going back to the nightly rounds. "Let's talk in our room below deck."

Maggie sat down on a chair and told them everything about the visit she'd just had. Duncan stood beside her, his arms folded, silently brooding. The three of them exchanged concerned looks as she relayed all the new information.

"That explains many things," said Quinn.

"Like the bullet fragments," added Duncan.

It was Maggie's turn to look confused. "The bullet?"

Duncan shifted. "Aye. Ye said ye had not felt well since ye were shot. The bullet pieces were lead. Lead is like poison to the Fae. That is why ye healed so quickly after they were removed."

Quinn nodded. "Your human half is probably the only thing that kept them from killing ye."

Gabe sat down, leaning over, his face in his hands. "And what Maggie felt with the mark? The gold eyes?"

Quinn rubbed Gabe's back. "It was the Fae blood reacting with the spell. Our Fae blood has been diluted over the years. We feel little when given the mark, but Maggie has a great deal more in her veins. It makes sense that it would have affected her more."

Duncan felt that Maggie needed to be taken care of. "Quinn, why don't ye and Gabe give me and Maggie some time alone?"

They stood to leave. Gabe kissed her on the cheek. "We are here if you need us."

She smiled up at him as they left.

Duncan closed the door behind them. "How are ye feeling with all of this?"

"I honestly don't know, Duncan. How am I supposed to feel? I have my answers, yes, but where do I go from here? It is apparent that I still have something else to do, but I have no idea what."

He pulled her up into her arms. Looking into her eyes as he held her close. "We will figure it out... together." He kissed her and pushed a strand of loose hair from her face.

"My mother, Duncan..."

"Your mother, Maggie, was a woman that loved ye and your father so much that she gave up her world for ye. Ye cannot fault her for loving someone that strongly and deeply. God knows I do."

He kissed her slowly, taking her breath away and making her forget everything else the way that only he could.

They lay in bed after their lovemaking, wrapped up in each other, their fingers intertwined, looking up.

"Duncan?"

"Hmm?"

"What do you think Finn meant when he said he was giving me a little part of my mother to remember her?"

Duncan kissed her forehead. "That is a very good question."

A few days later, at dusk, Maggie and Gabe were leaned over the rail of the ship as the Virginia coastline came into view.

"It seems like a lifetime since we were here, doesn't it, Mags?"

Maggie laughed. "It has been. It was you and me when we left and now, we are taking home a full house. You have a husband and a daughter, not to mention a new stepfather, a new sister-in-law, and nieces and nephews galore."

Gabe shook his head. "It is definitely not what I expected when we left."

"No, it is not."

He turned to her. "And look at you, who had given up on love."

Maggie winced. "I know, I know. It's funny, but I cannot imagine my life without Duncan. His love is truly a gift to me...and he isn't too bad to look at either."

Gabe laughed, wrapping his arm around her shoulders, and whispered, "The MacGregor brothers were blessed in that area...and other areas, as well."

Maggie slapped his chest. "Too much information, Gabe. We need to make a pact here and now to never discuss our sex lives. I do not need to know *that* much about my brother-in-law."

Gabe agreed. "And, I do not need to know that much about mine. Deal!"

Duncan and Quinn came to join them, bringing little Kat along with them.

Gabe took her in his arms and started pointing at the shoreline.

They were close to the dock on the river, nearest the house when Maggie felt a strange tingle on the back of her neck, a little nagging feeling that something was amiss.

Duncan felt what she was feeling. *What is it?*

"Something is very wrong," said Maggie. She looked towards the house and saw it...a black plume of smoke rolling up from the tree line.

She shouted back to the crew. "Ready the horses!"

Gabe saw the smoke as well. "Oh, dear Lord, it's the house."

Maggie sprinted across the deck, barking orders. "Cora, stay on board with Kat. Captain, stay with the ship. Protect the cargo at all costs. If there are soldiers that head for this boat, sail as far away as you can to safety and do not look back."

"Yes, ma'am. You have my word."

Onyx was on the dock before they were tied off, Maggie on his back, riding hard toward the house, Duncan, Gabe, and Quinn, on their own horses, close on their heels.

Welcome back to Virginia!

TO BE CONTINUED...

EPILOGUE

Ana Bishop was busy in her garden when she heard the doorbell. She opened the door to find a package. It was simply addressed: "Mom and Dad"

"Steven!"

Steven Bishop rushed out to his wife, hearing the alarm in her voice. He looked down at the package and the writing.

"Oh my God!"

Ana's heartbeat quickened. It had been 13 years since their daughter went missing without a clue. The authorities said that she must have been caught in a rip current and swept out to sea as many were off the Outer Banks of North Carolina. They, however, had never given up hope since her body had never been recovered.

Steven looked at his wife and tore open the package.

It was a portrait was of Maggie, in a wedding gown, a Scottish man in formal attire beside her. It was very old, but very well cared for.

Ana looked closer. It was definitely Maggie because she was wearing the necklace she had given her.

They looked at each other in disbelief.

Steven searched the back of it, seeing some writing, that he read aloud. "Laird Duncan MacGregor and Maggie Bishop MacGregor on their wedding day. One of three portraits."

He looked at his wife, "Could it be her?"

Ana nodded slowly, staring at the image before her, knowing in her heart that her daughter was well. "It is! I know it is! Steven...see how happy she looks."

Steven looked at his wife, confused. "If it is Maggie, why hasn't she contacted us to let us know she is alive?"

Ana smiled. "I think she just did."

Ana suddenly felt the urge to go to the front door.

Opening it and looking around, she had the strangest feeling that someone was there. "Hello?"

No answer. A strange fog rolled in. Ana stood there a moment longer before she closed the door and went back to Steven.

Finn smiled.

He would slip in occasionally to watch her work in the garden, just to be near her for a few moments when he was really missing her. He was always astonished at how much she would age between visits, but the love on her face was more apparent as time rolled on.

He whispered to the wind, turned, and stepped into the mist. "Dinna fash my dear daughter, I will watch over our sweet Maggie, as I do ye."

And he was gone.

More

ABOUT THE AUTHOR

Tempie W. Wade is a lifelong resident of Virginia and currently resides in Williamsburg. She has a love of history, old architecture, and travel. The author likes to incorporate historically accurate events with a touch of fantasy, in hopes that the reader will become interested enough to do their own research into the past.

Book Three in The Timely Revolution Series will be coming soon.

Follow the author page of Tempie W. Wade on Facebook for upcoming information or visit www.TempieWade.com.

37818227R00189

Made in the USA
Middletown, DE
05 March 2019